Though born in America … Hayes came to England … from Rutgers University … DC. Intending to continue her studies … in London, she instead married an Englishman and stayed permanently, raising four children and settling in the Devon countryside. She is the author of three previous novels and a volume of poetry, *Between Mornings. Still Life on Sand* is her first novel for Black Swan/Doubleday.

STILL LIFE
ON SAND

Karen Hayes

BLACK SWAN

STILL LIFE ON SAND
A BLACK SWAN BOOK : 0 552 99724 2

This edition published simultaneously with Doubleday,
a division of Transworld Publishers Ltd

PRINTING HISTORY
Black Swan edition published 1997

Set in 10½ on 12½pt Linotype Melior by
Kestrel Data, Exeter, Devon.

Black Swan Books are published by Transworld Publishers Ltd,
61–63 Uxbridge Road, London W5 5SA,
in Australia by Transworld Publishers (Australia) Pty Ltd,
15–25 Helles Avenue, Moorebank, NSW 2170
and in New Zealand by Transworld Publishers (NZ) Ltd,
3 William Pickering Drive, Albany, Auckland.

Reproduced, printed and bound in Great Britain by
Cox & Wyman Ltd, Reading, Berks.

For my mother,
Olga Lachowitch

Acknowledgements

Marion Whybrow's book *St Ives 1883–1993: Portrait of an Art Colony*, provided me with many insights into the artist community, as did Marion herself through her constant support and invaluable help.

Others assisted me in various ways: Wendy and Fred Oliver, Jeremy Boreham, and the many people in St Ives, both artists and fishermen, who opened their studios, their boats, and their homes to me during the short but memorable time I lived there. To all of them, thank you.

Chapter One

The weather is colder today. Crispin sniffs pro-
fessionally; there is a scent of snow in the air. The boats
in the harbour are rocking serenely on the undulating
water, but Crispin knows this is deceptive. He can smell
winds coming with the snow, can feel winter arriving
with the high tide.

'I'd stay close to shore today if I was you, my boy.'

Crispin doesn't need to look up from his boat to know
who's talking to him. 'Right then, Percy?' he calls up to
the man standing on the pier above him.

Percy Prynne nods, pulls his dark woolly hat further
down his high creviced forehead like a storm cloud over
a timeless jagged cliff. Crispin, engrossed in his nets,
misses the expression on the old man's face – pure
longing, mingled with a startled loss. Crispin has seen
it before, though. Everyone who has seen Percy Prynne
stare out at the sea since his retirement has witnessed
that look.

'Not going for cod again, boy?' Percy shouts down to
Crispin, who is in his early thirties but will always be a
boy to Percy, just as he was when he had his first job
on the boat. Percy was skipper then, and because he had
no son he taught Crispin all his own father had taught
him about fishing, about the sea.

'No. No cod. I'm going for bass,' Crispin says.

Percy nods again, satisfied. Crispin can drop the nets for bass in the bay, rather than going out at least a mile, maybe more, for cod. Percy can smell winter too; he senses the wind gathering forces in the dark early morning sky.

'Where's the lad, then?' Percy calls above the cry of a gull flying low over the harbour. 'Overslept mebbe?' His voice is strong with hope. Occasionally when Pete, Crispin's one and only crew, is ill or hung-over, Crispin takes Percy out. This hasn't happened for a long time, for Percy is arthritic, clumsy, short of breath, and more of a hindrance than a help, though Crispin will never let on. He just prays that Pete will soon arrive.

He does, half asleep and dreaming. Pete is eighteen, three years older than Crispin was when he first started working for Percy Prynne; summer holidays to start with, and then full-time when he was sixteen.

'You're late,' Percy mutters. 'You'll miss the tide.'

Pete ignores him. Percy's not his boss; he has nothing to do with the *Fair Celt*, not anymore, not since the old man got too old and wheezy and Crispin bought him out.

The wind freshens as Crispin starts the engine, fighting off nausea as he often does at the first whiff of diesel combined with the swell of the sea. He's used to the seasickness now; it passes. Standing on deck taking deep breaths as far away from the engine as he can manage, he suddenly hears his name called, melodiously, tantalizingly: 'Crispin! Crispin?'

'Bloody siren,' he mutters under his breath, but he can't help grinning. He deliberately remains facing the open sea, so that the voice on the pier has to call again. When at last he slowly turns around he catches the upward roll of Pete's eyes, the stoic amusement in Percy's. This scene, or variations of it, has been played before, much to the delight of the other fishermen.

'Ah, Molly!' Crispin exclaims, as if surprised. 'Catching the first morning light, are we? But where are your paints?'

'Sod the sarcasm, Crispin. You know why I'm here,' Molly snaps, her voice no longer tender nor mellifluous.

Crispin takes another deep breath, hoping he won't be sick before the boat leaves the harbour. Pete has climbed the stone steps to the pier and is untying the ropes, trying to avoid Percy's clumsy attempts to help. Molly, squatting now on the edge of the pier overlooking the boat, shouts over the engine's noise, 'You didn't wake me, Crispin. You just walked out on me without saying goodbye, without leaving a note, without waking me like I asked you to.'

'I'm a working man, Molly. I can't just swan around in bed all day waiting for inspiration to strike. You were out like a light.'

Molly looks ready to leap down the steps and into the boat, so Pete hurriedly finishes untying the rope and jumps down there himself.

'You're still bloody sulking,' Molly screams across the wedge of water now widening between herself and the *Fair Celt*. 'You sulked all last evening and you're still at it.'

Crispin looks with relief at the gap of dark-green water between him and Molly and calls out, with maddening cool, 'What would you do if I worked in an office? Burst in on me there? When will you understand that this is my workplace, and treat it with the respect I'm supposed to give to your studio.'

His voice has become louder and louder as the boat chugs further away. Molly, running along parallel until she is at the end of the pier and can go no further, shouts,

11

'Take care, you bastard, all right? I just heard the shipping forecast and it's not that great . . .'

Her voice trails off as she realizes he can no longer hear her. Standing motionless as she watches the boat steam out of sight, she is hardly aware of Percy shuffling up next to her. 'He's a big lad now,' Percy says, almost grudgingly. 'You don't have to tell him his job, y'know.'

Molly shakes her head impatiently, pulling her old wool coat more securely around her. She is wearing nothing but her cotton night-shirt underneath, and the wind is coming up cold and smelling of damp. 'He can't swim,' she says forlornly.

'Most fishermen can't anyhow. I never learned and I survived more'n sixty years on the sea.'

'He gets seasick too.'

'True, he always did. Cheer up, maid, he knows what he's about. No good worrying like you was his mum.'

Molly hugs Percy impetuously, then goes off down the pier towards the town. She looks like a bedraggled mermaid, he thinks, her wild hair flying deep red and golden in the wind, whipping around her face in a damp tangled mass of fluff as she scurries along in her tattered coat.

Percy puts his hands in the pockets of his own coat now, for the wind is laced with flecks of hail, stinging his face, as he turns away from Molly and looks out towards the sea again. He's relieved Crispin is staying in the bay today, though he hasn't forgotten the times he himself went out ten or eleven miles for conger eel in worse weather than this. I've gone all soft now, he thinks sadly, like an old woman, like his old wife Maggie before she died, wanting only to stop in front of the gas fire with its pretend coal and not come out at all except to do a bit of shopping. A sting of sadness hits him like the hail, sharp and nasty. He wishes he were on the *Fair Celt* with Crispin, putting out the nets, letting the hail

12

pelt his face but not feeling it, oblivious to everything except that exhilaration, that tingly anticipation, that hit you every single time you took the boat out.

An old woman, that's what I've become, Percy thinks bitterly as he turns and plods back down the pier. I've become a soddin' old woman. Wrapped in an uncharacteristic cloak of self-pity, he heads home.

Oona North would have something to say if Percy voiced those thoughts aloud in her vicinity. She's heading for eighty like an anchor heading for the bottom, but she feels much the same as she did at fifty: tangy and sharp, like the taste of the sea. She dislikes it intensely when people tell her how spry she is, how young at heart for an octogenarian. She retorts that old women have had a bad press, that she is not unusual.

Most people who know Oona, and that includes a large proportion of the permanent residents of St Ives (since she has lived here for over fifty years), would disagree with her. She *is* unusual, for reasons other than her frenetic energy and youthful vitality. She dresses entirely in black, having decided long ago that her creative eye for colour should be reserved strictly for her paintings. In the early 1950s, she looked less bohemian than Gothic, with her long black skirts, her turtle-necked sweaters and her chalk-white face, her head entirely shaved because she was working on a series of self-portraits and needed to see clearly the contours of her scalp.

Now her hair is white and thick and long, usually pulled back from her face in an intricate French plait but breaking out dementedly when she is engrossed in her work. The locals are used to glimpses of Oona rushing to the shop for a packet of sugar or a jar of instant coffee, with her sea-foam hair loose and blowing about her face, her eyes vague and preoccupied, and know that

13

she is in the middle of a painting. When she is at work she wears tatty canvas trousers and a torn black smock, but when she has finished a painting her jumpers are silk and cashmere and her skirts are soft linen or corduroy or the finest wool, enhanced with amber jewellery. Oona loves amber, feels a continuity between the ancient pine resin and her ancient self, and besides, the tawny gold colour is the same as her eyes. Oona is not without a normal share of vanity, not even at the approach of eighty, except when she is painting and inhabits another, rarer, world.

Now she is standing at her easel in her studio over-looking Porthmeor Beach, drinking sweet strong black coffee and frowning as she looks at her canvas. It's a huge abstract, the size of which alone would diminish Oona if she weren't such a stately woman, tall and big-boned still. None of this shrinking with age for Oona; if anything, she seems to have grown taller, broader, her amber eyes even larger in her wide heavy face.

'Shit,' she says loudly in a tough belligerent voice. She snarls at the canvas, picks up a brush, and begins painting over all of yesterday's work.

Molly North wanders into her own studio, just off the harbour in Downlong, the old fishermen's part of town with its cobbled streets, its small terraced one-room-wide cottages, many of which are now converted into artists' studios or holiday homes. Molly's studio is at the top of her house, an attic made light and spacious by the addition of a huge window on one side, over-looking the rooftops and the sea and harbour. Molly keeps a kettle and all her herbal tea-bags up here, as it's three flights down some steep stairs to her kitchen.

Sipping a mug of lemon-and-lime tea, Molly, still in her night-shirt and coat, perches on a stool and stares at her work in progress, a large canvas which is, at this moment, very green indeed, being a detailed painting of a Cornish hedgerow she spotted last summer on a ramble with Crispin near the village of Zennor. She had taken a whole roll of film of the hedgerow, much to Crispin's exasperation.

'For God's sake, Molly, I'm not out there on the cliffs with my binoculars, searching for schools of mackerel. We're supposed to be ambling, enjoying the countryside, having a day off from work.'

'This is too good to pass up,' Molly had replied. 'Look at the richness of detail, look at the mixture of dogwood and honeysuckle.'

Crispin had looked, had even patiently gone with her back to the car to get a second roll of film from the glove compartment, but had remained strangely silent.

Like he was last night, Molly thinks with a sigh, trying to concentrate on her painting. She is calling it *The Four Seasons*, and each corner of the canvas will depict just that: the same bit of hedgerow in all its seasonal changes. Unlike many of the St Ives artists, Molly is not an abstract painter; a trained botanist, she loves plants, loves to draw and paint, in rich detail, their intricate leaves and stems and flowers and seeds. Her paintings are beginning to sell. A couple of the better galleries have taken one or two, and she is also starting to attract notice by the ecological message of some of her work: fecund meadows slashed across the middle by arid deserts, sere and dead; wreaths of leaves and greenery with a dry dusty stone in the middle.

It was *The Four Seasons* that precipitated last night's argument with Crispin. Molly had heard a weather forecast (which turned out to be wrong) that there would be frost this morning, and she asked Crispin if he would drive her out to Zennor.

'We don't get frost very often down here,' Molly had said excitedly. 'I want to get photographs of that hedgerow for my winter scene, but we'd have to leave early as I'm sure the frost won't last, not so near the sea.'

'I can't, I'm afraid,' Crispin said, not looking at all regretful. 'The tide's early tomorrow and I'll be off. The bass are running too good to miss.'

Molly smiled patiently. They were at her house, in the snug living-room, a coal fire blazing brightly in front of them. Crispin was sprawled out on the Afghan rug in front of the fireplace, and Molly sat on the deep-brown sofa bed behind him. The lights from sturdy ceramic lamps shone softly around them and on a wooden sculpture of a man and woman, a present from Crispin's mother, Esme. A large abstract hanging over the mantelpiece, sweeping colours of blues and greens and greys and browns, the sea in all its formidable highlights, gleamed in the firelight.

'You can catch the afternoon tide, surely?' Molly asked sweetly. 'You've been working every day for weeks. If you're just going out to set the nets, couldn't you do it later? Or better still, take the whole day off. I will too – after I've got the photos – and we can go into Penzance, or just stop in Zennor, have a pub lunch . . .'

She trailed off when she saw the expression on Crispin's face: set, displeased. 'It was only an idea,' she finished lamely.

Crispin, bellicose now, said, 'It's always the same, isn't it. You think I go out there just for the fun of it. You think it's some kind of hobby, because I wasn't born to the job.'

'Look, I didn't mean—'

'My mother's the same, hoping I'll grow out of it. As if being a fisherman is like wanting to be in the circus, nothing more than a childish whim.'

'Crispin, just calm down, all right? All I said was that it'd be nice to have a day off together.'

Crispin was standing up by now, pacing the floor. His

tall frame was slightly hunched, as if walking against the wind. 'I'd love to have a day out with you, Molly. Just one day, somewhere, sometime, when you weren't sketching or taking photographs, when you didn't see every damn tree or rock or flower as something to paint rather than something unique in its own right.'

'It's my work,' Molly said. It somehow sounded inadequate, but Crispin's outburst had disoriented her. When they met a year or so ago at an exhibition of Esme's sculptures, Crispin had made some flippant remark about not getting involved with artists, and when their relationship began soon afterwards, he had made one or two laughing comments along the same vein. But this was the first time he had voiced any serious resentment.

'Fishing's my work too, you know,' Crispin said brusquely, 'but not my life, Molly. Not my life.' He looked at her almost defiantly, and Molly wondered if he was expecting her to say, 'And painting isn't mine.' Stubbornly, she refused to say anything, and the evening passed in polite but wary conversation.

Molly sighs and abandons looking at her painting, instead going down the attic steps to her bedroom where she changes her night-shirt for a pair of faded jeans, a brown mohair jumper she picked up at the Save the Children shop in town. Then she goes down another flight to the living-room, then down the last set of stairs to the kitchen. This used to be the cellar, where the fishermen used to store their nets, keep their coal, and sometimes keep tanks of freshly caught pilchards before they were pressed. The back door is a stable door and leads to a tiny cobbled alley-way, where Witch, Molly's fat black cat, sits and stares at the house opposite, hoping for a hand-out from the neighbours.

The kitchen is compact and modern, with wooden cupboards built on the stone walls and solid quarry tiles on the floor. Though exceedingly small, a pine table big enough for two nestles in the corner with two wooden chairs. Molly's parents own the cottage; they bought it when property was cheap and renovated it slowly over the years. Molly and her brothers had spent their summers in St Ives, their winters in the industrial town where the family originated. Once a dream of Molly's parents to move to Cornwall permanently, the passing of time and the reluctance to leave old friends had caused the dream to fade, but Molly took it over. Having acquired a degree in biology at the insistence of her parents, she found a job teaching in Truro and moved into the cottage at St Ives, from where she commuted every day to work.

Her teaching career did not last long. Simply, she loathed it. All she wanted to do was paint, and several years ago, having saved a modest sum of money to buy materials, she quit her job, sold her car, and began doing just that. Now she lives in a frugal manner on an income derived from teaching yoga several times a week both in the town and in surrounding villages, from the occasional spurt of supply teaching that comes her way, and from a seasonal job in one of the many cafés that proliferate each summer in the town. She buys her clothes in jumble sales and charity shops, accepts hand-me-downs from her brothers' wives with alacrity, and is eternally grateful to her parents for waiving the rent of her house when she quit her job. Her parents say, tactfully, that she is doing them a favour by keeping the house warm and dry all year round, and all they require is two weeks every summer for their holiday. This arrangement has, so far, been satisfactory. Luckily Molly's brothers have no interest at all in St Ives, but prefer spending their holidays somewhere foreign, to expose the children. Molly supposes this means to submit them to other cultures and languages, but it sounds highly suspect to her, like the ancient Spartans leaving their female infants on hillsides exposed to the elements.

Hearing the cat meow, Molly opens the top half of the kitchen door so that Witch can jump inside. The cat is almost too fat to make it, but pride gives her that extra oomph. She has always come into the house this way, disdaining the cat flap Molly installed years ago.

Witch is covered in white flecks that she shakes off like dandruff when she gets into the kitchen. 'Snow,' Molly says out loud. Abandoning all thoughts of breakfast, she grabs her coat, a red woolly fisherman's hat, her camera, and sets off for the top of town where she will try to hitch-hike to Zennor.

Percy, sitting in the fishermen's lodge, the small wood and concrete shelter on the harbour, warms himself at the rusty coal stove and stares unseeingly at the snow outside the window. Years ago, he often came here with his father and older brother; his father stopping for a smoke and a game of dominoes with the other fishermen before heading home. Nothing has changed; the walls are still crowded with yellowing photographs of ships and storms and men long-ago dead; there are still the same benches lining the wall and the old wireless in the corner where the men listened in serious silence to the shipping news. The only difference is that now the shelter is mostly empty, just the survivors like him and a few others still about. The crowds of men that used to relax here are long dead or dying now, the younger ones not interested any more, prefering the pubs for companionship and the telly for entertainment.

'God's truth, it's getting up bloody rough out there!'

Percy frowns at the man who has just opened the door and looks pointedly at the sign hanging on one of the walls: 'No Swearing Allowed'. Though the sign is ancient and no-one pays any mind to it now, Percy likes putting Sid Hocking in his place sometimes.

Coming in with a blast of cold air is a man of Percy's age, but as short and round as Percy is tall and skeletal. Sid Hocking has rosy red cheeks, a robust grey moustache and sideburns, and looks, Percy thinks, like the rogue he has always been. There is no love lost between the two men, for Percy accuses Sid of years of stealing from his lobster pots, while Sid swears Percy misled him more than once as to the whereabouts of a school of whiting. However, time and weariness have forged a rather precarious amnesty between the two men, and they now greet each other, if not with enthusiasm, at least with cordiality.

'Right then, my bird?' Sid says heartily. 'I'm glad I'm not out there in the sea today; it's that cold it'd freeze the nuts off a brass monkey.' He chuckles with pleasure, warming his hands at the stove.

Unlike Percy, Sid has retired with delight, and each horrific extreme of weather bathes him with a pure innocent joy that he is not out at sea in it. Sid spends his winters down at the Union Inn playing darts with his other aged cronies, and his summers strolling along Smeaton's Pier and the Wharf doing his crusty old sea captain bit, entertaining the tourists with imaginary dramas at sea and on weekends taking them out, for a substantial price, on his boat for mackerel fishing.

'I see your boy's gone out. Keen, eh?'

'Yup, that he is.'

Sid settles himself on the bench next to Percy, oblivious of the other man's frown as he crowds his space. Sid, like Percy, wears a black knitted wool hat and an identical shapeless brown coat. They could be a 'before and after' photograph of a Weight Watcher's success story, apart from their height. Percy's face is gaunt, every bone exposed under tight, drawn skin, while Sid's bones are hidden under roly-poly cheeks, massive white sideburns and that excessive moustache.

'Shame you sold him your boat,' Sid says. 'You could of used it for the summer visitors, making a bob or two taking out the punters for the odd day's fishing.'

Percy is aching today, and the old rheumatics always exhaust him, so for once he doesn't retort that he'd rather the *Fair Celt* were at the bottom of the sea than taking out bloody tourists, bloody emmetts, with their pristine cotton shorts and pure white plimsolls, getting sick all over the boat on the balmiest of days.

Sid, oblivious to Percy's lack of response, slaps him soundly across the shoulders and says, generously, 'Well, I must say, you did right by that lad. Crispin's one bloody fine fisherman, seems to have a nose for where the shoals are.'

Percy feels a silly heady rush of pride to his worn-out heart. He can only nod, for he is suddenly all choked up. Daft old fool, he says to himself.

The two men are silent, Percy thinking of Crispin and the sons he never had; Sid thinking about his two lads, one on a huge beam trawler down at Newlyn, not caring a scrap about his dad's boat in St Ives, and the other working on a farm, as far inland as he can get.

After a few moments Sid grunts and stands up to go, finding Percy's company a bit dreary this morning. 'Time I got home, my cock, breakfast'll be waiting,' he bellows. Sid has a wife waiting at home, as round and as ruddy as he is, and though he wouldn't admit it to anyone in the world, he loves her boundlessly. She calls him Captain Sid, just like the punters do; he likes that, likes to feel treated with a bit of respect. God knows, at his age he deserves it. Like Percy, he retired from fishing late; unlike the other fisherman, he feels he's got a lot of living to catch up on.

'Right then, I'm off. S'truth, 'tis colder than a frog's tit

21

out there.' Sid chuckles heartily, thumping Percy again. He has taken up chuckling in a serious way since he's been taking the tourists out; he seems to think they expect it.

Percy waits for a few more moments, then makes his way up the hill to his council house. His grandfather lived in Downlong, which meant down along the harbour, when the houses there were purely fishermen's cottages and the posh folk lived higher up along the town in Uplong. Percy's family was moved away from Downlong to the council houses on the hill away from the harbour when many of the cottages were condemned, and he finds it ironic that instead of being pulled down many are still there now, all tarted up and used as bed and breakfasts or summer-holiday lets. Percy couldn't afford to live in Downlong now.

The snow is blowing wildly off from the sea as Percy slowly makes his way home. Unlike Sid, he wishes desperately he were out there as he limps up the hill. His hip is giving him great pain; he's on the waiting-list for an operation. As he unlocks his door and goes into the musty lounge he wonders if he will ever go fishing again. It is the first time he has had such a thought, which is so frightening that he has to sit down in the armchair. His heart has started to pound, harshly and abnormally, so that for a long time he is afraid to move, afraid that his old heart will shatter, like sand, into billions of tiny grains blown by the wind from Porthmeor Beach and disappear for ever into the sea.

'You what?' Crispin shouts at Molly later that night, as they stand in her kitchen preparing broccoli and sautéd potatoes to go with the two bass Crispin brought over half an hour ago. The bass, fresh from the sea, are under the grill and smelling succulent. A bottle of Sauvignon Blanc is chilling in the fridge.

22

'I hitch-hiked to Zennor, to get photos of snow on that hedgerow. It's a good thing I did; the snow had melted by midday.'

'I hate you doing that,' Crispin grumbles. 'There are so many nutters about these days.'

'Goodness, Crispin. You sound like your mother,' Molly says gently, kissing him lightly over the broccoli. 'Esme worries about me too.'

'She worries about all of us. About me, my brother, about you, about Dad. I don't know how she finds time to sculpt.'

'It's what keeps her sane,' Molly says knowledgeably. 'It's what keeps her connected, unfragmented.'

Crispin grunts and stirs the potatoes. He hates it when Molly goes into what he calls her creative spiel, carrying on as if all artists have this inner secret that needs explaining to ordinary mortals like himself. It's no wonder his father has long ago retreated into mild sarcasm and passive aggression.

'Well, Esme *should* worry about you,' Crispin says, not wanting to get into artists and their needs. 'Your own parents would go crazy if they knew what you were up to, hitch-hiking all over the place, spending nights alone on Bodmin Moor to catch the sun coming up at just the right angle behind an unusual tree—'

'And you?' Molly cries. 'Do you think I have any peace of mind when you're out there in all weather, all seasons, day and night?' She breaks off abruptly, overwhelmed by her ubiquitous fear for him which permeates her entire being whenever he is out at sea.

He recognizes this and goes to her, holds her gently. 'Now you know how I feel,' he says softly, 'when you do crazy things like hitch-hiking in the middle of the night, or sleeping out alone on lonely moors.'

She nods, and for a moment they cling to each other, silently acknowledging that this must be what love is all

23

about. Neither are very sure they like the sensation, but know they are too far gone now.

'Hell, the fish,' Crispin mutters, reaching for the grill. He is just in time; the skin has turned a deep crisp brown and in another moment would have burned.

'Hmm, looks delicious.' Molly gets out plates and cutlery. 'I love the fish you bring back; I'd have starved months ago on my rations of lentils and peanut butter.'

Crispin feels a strange satisfaction seep through him, as if he has been drinking a fine wine. He smiles widely at Molly and she says, amused, 'You look so smug. Like the hunter returned victoriously.'

He does indeed feel this way. Slowly, savouring the moment, he places a perfectly cooked bass on Molly's plate.

Esme Cochran looks out the window of her workroom, the one looking over the garden wall facing the cobbled street. The snow of the previous day has gone, but it is even colder, with a bitter wind coming from the sea. Esme, staring mindlessly out into the road, sees Oona, white hair blowing trenchantly across her finely wrinkled face, striding up the hill clutching a jar of instant coffee. Esme opens the window and calls out, 'Look at you, you haven't even a coat on, just that thin smock. Come in and warm up for a minute; I'll make a pot of coffee.'

Oona looks her age in the harsh winter light, her face deeply lined, the muscles slack, tired. Esme remembers that the woman will be eighty in a few weeks, and wonders when she will begin to slow down. Oona frowns at Esme; though the two are good friends, Oona's mind is clearly focused on some inner vision. Esme says gently, 'It's me – Esme, remember? Can I entice you back into the world for a minute, warm you up?'

Oona's face lifts in a quick smile, but she shakes her

24

head. 'I've got to get back to work.' Waving cursorily, she heads for her own house further along, walking determinedly into the wind without a backward glance.

Esme closes the window, warms her own cold fingers by the small electric blow heater in her workshop. She envies Oona her single-mindedness, her commitment – even at her age – to being the best artist she can possibly be. Esme herself is distracted with Christmas coming, with presents to buy, food to prepare. She wishes that she, like Oona, could counter the wear and tear of family life with the same resolution and blazing determination. Oona has attained international acclaim with her evocative abstracts, and she has done it not only with talent – of which she has, of course, an abundance – but with hard work and an ability to focus steadily while the hassles, the domesticities of life blur around her.

Esme sighs, walks around to the block of stone which she has scarcely touched, and glares at it. The idea she has for it now seems hackneyed, stale. Lately she has given up the serene mothers and children, the tranquil family groups which stand in city centres, in front of municipal libraries, to sculpt more abstract shapes, to hint at discord, yet with soaring lines and harmonious planes that belie the tension just under the surface.

Her family isn't that impressed with her new work, though her last exhibition was highly praised. Crispin, her oldest son, refuses to be impressed by anything she's done, but Esme knows this is because of his father, Richard. Her youngest son, Hugo, is too addicted to surfing to notice anything much, and while this is the source of grievous annoyance to his father, Esme cannot help but admire his self-absorption.

A spray of salty water hits her face and she looks up to see Hugo, wearing his winter wet suit and carrying his surfboard, shaking his head insouciantly like a frisky puppy, splattering her with the excess moisture from his shoulder-length hair.

'Man, what a surf! Ace.' Hugo plants his surfboard next to Esme's workbench, then strips out of his wet suit, using her hose to wash it down. The large garden shed, which was once supposed to be solely Esme's workroom, has had to accommodate not only Hugo's surfing equipment but Crispin's surplus fishing nets and apparatus. Though the latter has a house of his own now, it has no storage space.

'Many surfers out there?'

'Dozens.' Hugo has changed into jeans and a soft blue fleecy shirt which turn his eyes into exquisite blue saucers. They are Richard's eyes, except that time has made Richard's harder, more wary, while Hugo's are still clear and soft and vulnerable.

Hugo has taken out a hair-dryer from a drawer in Esme's tool cupboard and is blow-drying his hair. 'Shouldn't you wash out the salt first?' Esme asks idly.

'I might be going in again later.' Hugo, finished, tosses his long blond hair carelessly, much as Richard used to impatiently shake his own shoulder-length hair long ago in the Sixties, when he and Esme met and married. Richard's hair is now short but still blond; the few grey hairs amongst them camouflaged in a coarse yellow thicket.

Esme puts down her mallet and chisel and takes off the goggles and mask that prevent the fine stone dust getting into her eyes and nose. She has decided it is hopeless to try to work any longer today. Earlier on Crispin had rushed in, practically thrown a couple of huge bass at her, grabbed some more tiers for his nets, and said he'd just had the best catch for eight or nine years.

'Why, Crispin, that's fantastic! These are beauties,

more than enough for the three of us. Do you want to come over for supper? Bring Molly.'

'She's probably sick of bass by now. I brought her some yesterday; we cooked them together last night.'

'Well, I'll cook tonight if you and Molly would like to come by.'

'Fine by me. Could you give Molly a ring? I'm off to Newlyn with the catch. It'll have to be a late meal; I'm going out on the afternoon tide to set the nets again.'

He kissed her quickly on the cheek and was gone, but her concentration was gone too. She spent the morning pottering in a desultory way until Hugo came in, and now he is gone as well, off to his room to play what he calls house music, which Esme can't differentiate from other types of rave music, but to which Hugo is addicted. Hugo drives Richard crazy, with his music, his surfing, his lack of ambition. Esme can't see a problem: Hugo wants to be the best surfer in the world, and if that's not ambition Esme doesn't know what is.

Esme gives up working for the morning and grabs her wax jacket, deciding to take a long walk before buying a home-made pasty for lunch from the bakery on Fore Street, the cobbled main street just up from the harbour. The high winds have brought intermittent squally showers, but at this moment there is a break in the weather and a clear pink light shines over the water as the sun, for the first time in ages, comes out from behind the black storm clouds.

Esme, enchanted by the sudden glow permeating sea and sky, decides to walk along the cliffs and takes a short cut through some narrow crooked alley-ways to Porth-meor Beach, passing the new Tate St Ives art gallery, white and rounded and smooth as the beach itself which the Tate faces. The gallery is also tinged pink, as is the sky above the sea and the sand itself. Once more she thinks how astounding the light here is, and no wonder so many painters have gravitated to this place in the past hundred years. On days like today she wishes she painted, instead of wrestling with huge blocks of stone, wood and granite, for her sculptures.

The wind has dropped as Esme walks along the coastal path towards the Clodgy, an outcrop of rock going into the sea. Behind her the beach is full of surfers; below her the waves crash crazily, foaming and sizzling on the rocks. She walks a short distance and then stops for a bit on a grassy ledge, watching two seagulls swoop down to the water and then soar back again, graceful and assured. In between flights they rest on a jagged piece of rock halfway up the cliff which seems to have been put there just for the gulls, so perfectly do they perch there, so symmetrically do they land and glide and fly from it.

Suddenly, watching the birds, staring at the rock and the blue-green sea below it, Esme feels the slight pricking in the back of her neck, the sensation that all the tiny hairs there are standing on end. She knows what it is, recognizes the familiar feeling, a mixture of fear and exultation. She is going to sculpt this: the rock, the gulls, the exquisite harmony between the two, and though the vision exhilarates her, she knows the fear too, of not being able to create in stone this awesome thing she sees in her mind, in her internal vision.

Esme turns and runs back the way she came, past the Tate, the beach, down a back lane and towards her house, her workroom, her garden shed where miracles are about to happen. She runs and runs, a lean middle-aged woman with a pleasant domestic face, rough chestnut hair, cut short and flecked with silver, and a wild gleam in her eyes, like a prophet after too many days in the desert.

Richard will kill her, she thinks fleetingly as she turns into her house. But it can't be helped.

She doesn't think of him again. She goes into her workroom and without even taking off her coat she begins to work, holding the rock and the gulls in her mind like an epiphany.

Chapter Two

Richard comes home from work to what appears to be an empty house, one light shining like a beacon from the top-floor window, Hugo's room. It's like the beam from a lighthouse, he thinks, warning me away from the rocks below, which are Esme and her sculptures.

Richard often thinks in images like these, especially on days like today when he's been doing metaphor with his fifth formers. Richard teaches English Literature in Penzance.

The house is not only dark but cold. Richard switches on the gas central heating and goes into the empty kitchen. From the top floor Hugo's rave music pulses repetitively, exacerbating Richard's headache. Rushing upstairs he bursts into Hugo's room, a dark den of surfing posters and band advertisements and the accumulation of nineteen years, and says, irritably, 'Can you turn that rave stuff off? Or at least down about ten volumes.'

'It's house music, man. Not the same thing at all.'

'Whatever, it's still dreadful. God, we had the Beatles, the Stones, and you have—'

'Chill, Dad,' Hugo says pleasantly. 'We've done this scene a thousand times before.'

Richard is about to get annoyed when Hugo adds, 'I didn't know it was so late. Would you like me to get some dinner? There's some left-over chicken and other stuff; I could do a quick curry.'

This sounds good to Richard, as Esme is nowhere in sight and he doesn't feel like doing anything right now but collapsing into an easy chair. The saving grace about Hugo, he thinks, is the pleasure he takes in cooking, preparing tasty and original meals and obviously enjoying it.

'You're on,' Richard says, knowing that the curry will not be an ordinary one but something special. He goes back downstairs, taking off his glasses, rubbing his eyes. Looking out the kitchen window he sees a light on in the shed at the bottom of the garden and walks across the lawn in the shadow of the high stone wall to find Esme.

He doesn't see her at once; she is bent over a piece of alabaster, like an angel over a tombstone, her white dusty smock flapping like wings as she works. Esme doesn't notice him. He watches her for several moments, then, suddenly aware of his presence, she looks up, takes off her goggles. She has an evangelical look on her face that has nothing to do with him. Not for the first time, he feels unnecessary.

'The house was dark. Cold. I wondered where you were,' Richard says, unable to keep the taste of bitterness from his voice.

Esme finally focuses. 'You're early,' she says.

'As a matter of fact I'm late. I had a staff meeting, remember? It's after seven.' He doesn't say that he's hungry, that the kitchen seems bare of food. That would be going too far. Since Esme's sculptures have begun to make money, since she now does it full-time, they share the cooking, the household chores. Richard doesn't mind this; what he minds is having not just a wife but a whole garden of stone wives whose lives he is supposed to share.

31

'Hugo is going to do a curry,' Richard says, keeping his voice neutral.

'And I'll do a salad, as soon as I've finished this little bit,' Esme says with relief and gratitude, pointing her chisel at her sculpture. And then, 'Oh Richard, this is going to be the best thing I've ever done. I can feel it, Richard.'

She looks at him, and the glow on her face is like that lighthouse beam again. It warns him away.

He turns without commenting, without looking at her sculpture, and goes back to the house. For a moment Esme watches him; for a moment the old hurt flicks its sharp pointed fingernails on her soft tired heart and she wonders, as she always does, whether she can go on.

But the pain goes, or at least recedes, and Esme turns once more to her stone. As always, it takes a long time to get back into the work after one of Richard's rebuffs. Slowly she puts on her goggles and mask, and picks up her mallet and chisel. It is definitely getting harder, she thinks sadly. Not her work, for she is now on a creative roll and senses that it will be a long one, but her marriage, which more and more makes her feel as if she were swimming against a fierce, dangerous tide. Shaking her head despairingly, she wonders whether she should go to Richard, follow him up to the house, abandon her work for the evening as she has done so often in the past.

She doesn't do it. All she wants is another half-hour; surely Richard cannot begrudge her that? Looking critically at her unfinished sculpture something stirs back to life inside her, and with great determination, she begins to work.

Molly and Crispin are having a domestic again, on the *Fair Celt* moored in the middle of the harbour. Molly had made Pete row her out in the row-boat when the boy had taken it to the pier, trying to get home as he was aching all over with the flu. Molly insisted Pete drop her over onto the *Fair Celt* first, which he did begrudgingly.

'Molly, will you get off this boat!' Crispin says through clenched teeth, trying to keep his voice low so the other fishermen won't hear.

'I've been waiting all day for you to come in, Crispin Cochran. You'll have to throw me off if you want me off.'

'Can 'er swim?' cries Captain Sid Hocking from over on the pier, chuckling as if his sides were splitting from the fun of it.

'Keep your voice down, Molly,' Crispin hisses.

'Tell 'er, Crisp,' shouts Tom, the skipper of the *Girl Lizzie*, anchored not far from the *Fair Celt*.

Crispin lowers his head and carries on with his work, taking out the fish – a lovely catch of bass again – from his nets and throwing them into big blue plastic crates, ready to go to the fish market in Newlyn. He wishes Pete hadn't taken ill and gone, not only because he could use the help, but also to get Molly off his back. He loves her, but she drives him crazy sometimes.

Molly is itching to take Crispin's brown shaggy hair and pull it out from its roots; she is longing to shake his sturdy shoulders until he turns away from those bloody fish and looks at her, really looks at her. He has an old face and a young mouth and eyes; his skin, brown and leathery, looks older than his years; his smile, quick and endearing, much younger.

Fat chance that that smile is going to be turned on me, Molly thinks. She takes deep breaths like she has always instructed her yoga students to do in moments of crisis; to her surprise it helps, and she feels, if not exactly calm, at least less furious.

'God's truth, my lover, I thought the maid was sure to kill'm just then,' Sid says to Percy who has wandered over to the pier. 'She was flapping around him like a beached eel.'

Crispin is resolutely emptying his nets and trying to pretend Molly isn't there. The day is sweet and fine for winter, the wind calm, the air crisp. The harbour curves and curls, like a cat, from Smeaton's Pier to the lifeboat station, and the sun, dodging in and out of soft grey clouds, reflects on the outgoing tide and tinges everything – the little shops on the Wharf, the boats – with a luminous grey-blue.

'Crispin,' Molly begins again, this time keeping her voice lowered, 'you were unbearably rude at your mother's house last night. First you wouldn't listen to her trying to explain her work, then you walked right out of the house without saying goodbye.'

'I can't bear rows,' Crispin replies meaningfully.

'No-one was rowing. Your father was sulking, but then that's nothing new. So do you.'

'I don't. He doesn't. Just because someone is quiet you say they sulk.' Crispin takes a small cod from the net and tosses it to the big brown seal looking at him from the water. The seal, old and scarred, is always on hand when the fishing boats come in, looking for hand-outs. Sometimes there are others, and they swim playfully from boat to boat, eating the discarded fish, rising out of the water and begging for a juicy titbit. The fishermen feed the seals good-naturedly.

Molly, distracted, watches the seal in the shallow water. It is so pleasant here, especially after the storms of the last few weeks, that she's almost forgotten she is angry at Crispin. Last night when they arrived at the Cochran's house for a late supper of bass, they had found Richard sitting alone in the living-room with the remains of a chicken curry, Hugo back in his room playing his house music, and Esme out in her studio working on a new sculpture.

34

'Where's the bass I brought over?' Crispin asked.

'Bass? I don't know. Hugo cooked a curry which your mother hasn't even eaten yet. She's in her shed.'

Molly had bristled at this, the way Richard said 'shed' in such a derogatory manner. He never called it a workroom or studio.

Crispin opened the fridge and there, in the back, wrapped in foil, were the bass. 'She must have forgotten them,' Richard said.

'Did she also forget that she'd asked Molly and me over for a meal?'

'God, I did! I'm sorry, I'm so sorry.'

They all turned to see Esme at the kitchen door, grubby, sweaty and covered with stone dust. Her eyes, green and young like Crispin's, were apologetic. She gave them a quick smile – again, also like Crispin's in that it took you by surprise, compelled you to smile back – and went on, 'I was working on something, something special, and I had to keep going or I would have lost it. I'm afraid everything else went right out of my head. I'll prepare the fish now, it won't take long.'

'I've already eaten,' Richard said plaintively.

'I'll do the fish,' Molly said. 'You go back to your work, Esme.'

'I'm finished for today. I'm exhausted, my left elbow hurts like hell, and I'm suddenly starved.'

Molly and Esme began preparing the fish, and Crispin found the salad Hugo had made earlier and added some tomatoes to it. 'Nothing for me,' Richard said pointedly.

'You'll have a bit of fish, surely?' Esme asked.

Richard refused. He would have liked some of that bass; it smelled delicious and he hadn't eaten much curry because his head was throbbing and he was too cross with Esme. She had never come up to make the salad, and he had refused to call her when the curry was ready. Hugo, sensing stress, had taken his dinner

35

upstairs to eat, leaving Richard sulking alone in front of the television.

They ate the bass in the kitchen, the three of them ravenous, the fourth hungry too but stubbornly resisting. Richard sat at the table, silent, condemning but stoic, feeling like a man on a hunger-strike making a political statement.

When they had finished eating Molly said, 'Esme, what is it you are working on? You sounded excited by it.'

Esme hesitated. Sometimes she wanted to share her work in progress, other times not. Tonight she would have liked to talk about it, but she didn't know how Richard would react. She looked at her husband and son: Crispin so much like her, tall, sturdy, dark; Richard like Hugo, all that blondness, the fine bones, the large myopic blue eyes. Richard stared at her for a moment and she thought irrelevantly that he had new glasses, tortoiseshell frames; they suited him. She was just beginning to explain to them what she was attempting to do when Richard deliberately turned away from her, picked up the *Radio Times* which was on a shelf by the table, and began leafing through it. Crispin smiled politely and said, 'Should we go into the living-room, Dad, and let these two natter on about art?'

Molly shot him such a scathing look that he was taken aback, but he still went with Richard into the other room, and soon the sounds of *Sportsnight* wafted into the kitchen.

'Never mind them,' Esme said gently, noting the look on Molly's face. 'I'm used to it. It's hard for Richard and Crispin to get serious about my work; maybe they're just too close to it.'

She shrugged lightly, as if it were of no importance, but Molly could see she was upset.

'They should.' Molly was indignant.

36

Esme sighed, put her head in her hands. When she lifted it Molly was shocked to see that there were tears in her eyes. 'Sorry, Molly,' Esme said, straightening her shoulders and rubbing her eyes briskly. 'I'm tired, worked a bit too hard this evening. My back aches like hell. Being a sculptor kills the body, I spend a fortune on physiotherapy.'

Molly made sympathetic noises, but silently she was promising herself to have a word with Crispin. Esme, reading her thoughts, said, 'Don't be cross with Crispin. He's Richard's son, remember, and Richard has always felt there was a war on between my sculpture and the family.'

'That's crazy. It's not a battle, there doesn't have to be a winner, for God's sake.'

'Tell Richard that,' Esme said wryly, finding a tissue in the pocket of her baggy trousers.

Molly was silent, thinking about Crispin going on at her about her work being her life. She had tried to tell him more than once that it was like saying her arm wasn't a part of her body. Her work defined her, made her as much who she was as the shape of her face, the texture of her hair. But it didn't prevent her from wanting other things too: friends, a lasting relationship, a family of her own perhaps, one day.

Esme massaged the back of her neck vigorously, trying to alleviate the stiffness there, and said, 'Crispin's not so bad, you know. When Richard's not around, he'll ask about my work, comment on the sculptures.'

'I should hope so,' Molly said tersely.

'It's enough. Come on, if I don't move, all my muscles will seize up. Let's go down to my workroom, I'll show you what I'm trying to do.'

They went down the garden in silence, both slightly downcast, but when they entered Esme's studio Molly said, 'Oh Esme! It's going to be brilliant!' and for nearly

37

an hour they forgot everything else in their shared enthusiasm.

Remembering last night as she sits on the *Fair Celt* with Crispin, Molly is becoming angry again, recalling how Crispin had sided with his father, turned away from Esme. And then, to top everything off, she had come out of Esme's studio feeling both inspired and contented, only to find Crispin gone.

'God's truth, ain't it handsome? She's at 'm again. Lookee there, you, she's shakin' 'm by the shoulders, like a gull thrashing a fish head.'

Sid Hocking is bellowing at all who will listen, and jumping up and down on the pier with abandon, so excited is he by the spectacle on the *Fair Celt*. Percy Prynne frowns, worried. Molly is a lively maid; Crispin will have his hands full if he marries her.

Molly is holding on to Crispin's shoulders and trying to shake him into turning away from his fish to face her. 'It really was bloody rude of you to just leave me there, you know. Telling your dad to relay the message that if I wanted to, I could go over to your place. As if I would, after that.'

Crispin shakes her off easily – for Molly is a slight small woman – and continues sorting fish. 'You and my mum stayed out in that poxy shed so long I thought you were never coming out. So I left. You could have followed me.'

'Oh right, like some sad besotted female, is that what you want? Anyway you and Richard were engrossed in the telly.'

'Oh come off it, Molly.' Crispin throws a fish far harder than necessary at the seal. 'You and Mum all chummy out there, talking about painting and sculpture; you didn't need me. You're as bad as her; not giving a shit about anything else when you're involved in your work.' He throws another fish, even harder, at the seal, who catches it in its mouth and chomps it up greedily.

'Steady on, mate,' Tom calls out from the *Girl Lizzie*. 'You'll lay out that poor seal.'

'S'truth, now Crisp is getting hot under the collar, though, mind, I can't say as I blames 'm. See 'm throw that fish like 'twas a fast bowler out for the batsman's goolies.'

'Sid, give over,' Percy says. Sid's whole body is shaking with merriment.

'Oh sod you!' Molly cries. 'You just won't understand, you just refuse to understand. It's not your mother to blame, it's your shit of a father who is so fucking jealous of your mother's talent and success that he's totally screwing up their marriage.'

'Cor!' Sid exclaims.

'Oh my,' Percy whispers.

'Are you going to let her get away with that, mate?' Tom grins.

Crispin, pale-white under his leather-brown skin, stands up from his nets and says, in a low angry voice, 'Get out of my boat, Molly. Get out right now.'

Molly tosses her head and the red-gold hair goes flying. 'I can't,' she says. 'Pete's taken the row-boat.'

'Then walk,' Crispin hisses. 'You can fucking walk.'

Molly looks shocked, then realizes, not without embarrassment, that the tide has gone out while she has been sitting there and the harbour is dry. With as much dignity as she can muster, she climbs out of the *Fair Celt* and marches across the wet sand to the stone stairs leading up the harbour wall. To her extreme mortification, Sid Hocking applauds her heartily as she climbs up to the pier.

Molly and Crispin, subdued after this quarrel – the angriest they have yet had – stubbornly avoid each other for more than a week, both waiting for the other to get in touch, apologize.

'Sorry about you and Crisp, like,' says Lizzie, Tom's wife. Lizzie is upside down in the shoulder stand and Molly, her teacher, is hovering above her.

'What?' Molly exclaims. She wonders if she is really cut out for this yoga teaching business; peace and tranquillity is what she doesn't have. 'What did you say?'

'Tom told me, like. All about your fight, see. On the boat.'

'Oh. Lizzie, you should be breathing deeply through your nostrils while in the Sarvangasana position,' Molly says primly. 'You should be concentrating purely on your breathing.'

Lizzie takes a few deep breaths and mutters, 'Is this lot gonna help me slim? Tom says I'm as round and meaty as a pasty since we had the baby.'

'It'll help you slim only if you watch your diet as well.'

'Hush, Molly, please.' A sonorous voice rumbles across the room, coming from an ancient figure dressed in wide flowing black trousers and a loose black lamb's-wool jumper. Ropes of amber beads loop upside down as the figure struggles to lift her hips off the floor into a partial shoulder stand. 'It's difficult enough to do this preposterous position without having to listen to mindless chatter as well.'

Molly rushes up to the woman. 'Grandma, do take it easy. I know you are still fit and young at heart, but you are almost eighty. You don't need to do every posture.'

Oona slowly lowers her legs. 'Then perhaps I'll leave this one,' she says with dignity, closing her eyes serenely. Her long amber tear-drop earrings swing lightly towards the floor.

'Now everyone come down slowly; that's it, easy,

40

gently – oh God, Lizzie, don't come crashing down like that, you frightened me to death.'

'Sorry, miss,' Lizzie says. 'I mean, sorry, Molly.'

Molly puts her class through its paces, keeping a sharp eye out for Oona, who had walked into the top-floor studio belonging to Jordan Culpepper a few weeks ago and said she was joining Molly's yoga class.

'But why?' Molly had cried.

'To become more supple, of course,' Oona replied. 'Why not? I resent the implication that it is of no use to be supple at my age.'

'Well, do be careful,' Molly warned.

'Oh bollocks, child. At my age, what is the point of being careful?' She walked over to the far corner of the room, unrolled a thick white blanket on the plain wooden floor, and sat down carefully on it, her legs partially crossed. 'I did yoga many years ago with Swami Satjamurdja, in Delhi. I wonder how the poor man's stomach is now,' she said enigmatically.

Another fact about her grandmother she never knew before now, Molly thought.

This evening Molly talks her class through an extra-long relaxation session, since it is the last class before Christmas. 'Phew, I thought we'd never get to this bit,' Lizzie puffs, flopping down like a boneless sheep, all pink and fluffy and plump in her soft track suit, her fair hair newly permed and frizzing about her head like lamb's-wool. She closes her eyes and before Molly even begins she is slightly snoring.

'Darling, should I light a few candles?' enquires Jordan Culpepper, walking around his studio. It is vast and luxurious, nothing like the studios of the other artists Molly knows. Jordan lets her use it in return for free yoga lessons, not that he can't afford them. He just can't be bothered to leave the warmth and comfort of his own place to trudge down the hill to the cold and damp church hall where Molly used to conduct her classes. He notices that her numbers have gone up since she changed venues; he's not the only one that found the hall intolerable.

Jordan has been solemnly performing his yoga postures in the opposite corner from old Oona, but now he is flitting about adjusting the lighting, fiddling with the long deep-blue velvet curtains covering the huge picture window which looks out over the sea. 'Should I get some candles?' Jordan asks again.

'There's no point,' Molly says. 'We're all supposed to have our eyes closed for the relaxation.'

Jordan shudders slightly at this insensitivity. 'Whatever you say, darling.' He lies on his cushioned yoga mat and begins to breathe deeply.

When the class is over Oona fixes her sharp eyes, which are uncannily like Molly's, on her granddaughter and says, 'What is this about you and Crispin? What was that girl saying?'

'Nothing, Grandma,' Molly replies warily. 'We had a quarrel, that's all.'

'It's not interfering with your work, I hope?' Oona's eyes sharply take in Molly's jumble-sale track suit, spattered with paint, and a fleck of deep-green acrylic on her forehead which she missed as she hastily washed before class. Her heavy cinnamon hair is pulled tightly off her face with a ragged silk scarf, the golden highlights hidden.

Molly smiles wanly. 'No, Oona.' She calls her grandmother by her Christian name when they are colleagues together, discussing work. Oona was her first painting teacher; during all those long delightful summers in St Ives when she was growing up, Molly sat at her grandmother's feet, crayon or pencil or brush in hand, while her brothers roared in the waves of Porthmeor Beach like sea-lions.

Oona is her father's mother. When she was thirty and came into some money, she left her husband and took her son, Molly's father, with her to St Ives where she began to paint in earnest. Three of her abstracts are in the Tate Gallery now. Her reputation is international.

Oona pats Molly's cheek briskly. 'I'm pleased your work is not suffering,' she says firmly. With a brief wave she is gone. She has not asked what Molly's quarrel with Crispin was about. She does not think it is important.

When everyone has left Molly packs up her mat and bag and, as usual, thanks Jordan politely for the use of his studio. 'Oh, no problem, no problem.' Jordan waves his arm breezily. He is a solid man in his mid-thirties and everything about him is big: his beard, which is black and prickly like a bramble bush in winter; his body, with its massive trunk, and arms and legs like the great branches of an old beech tree; and his head, broad and big and partially bald, with a fringe of dark hair growing prolifically around the edges. The only small things about this man are his paintings, which are delicate tiny miniatures, seascapes in watercolours, which are quite popular with the more up-market tourists and sell like hot cakes. Molly can never figure out why Jordan needs such a large studio for such tiny paintings. The whole top floor of the Victorian guest-house, which his wife Alice still runs as a bed and breakfast, was converted by Jordan and Alice several years ago, for it is high on a hill facing Porthminster Beach and has breathtaking views of the sea.

Alice Culpepper paints too, though the studio is Jordan's and not hers. She used to be quite good at portrait painting until Jordan convinced her it was more lucrative to do pastel drawings of the tourists. When she demurred that it wasn't exactly art, Jordan reminded her of highly regarded artists in the past who had sketched the town's more colourful characters, such as Hymen

Segal whose work still hangs in the Sloop Inn on the harbour.

'Doing a ten-minute sketch of a bored tourist munching a hot dog and dripping tomato sauce all over me is not exactly Hymen Segal, Jordan,' Alice had objected.

'It's a question of earning money, darling, and we all have to help,' Jordan had retorted. 'We only do a three-room bed and breakfast, hardly enough to keep the children and you in the style to which you all are becoming quite accustomed.'

Alice, accustomed to the hard work required to keep their three children and the house in some kind of order, said nothing, primarily because she was so exhausted. Her children were bold, obstreperous, demanding, and so, often, were the visitors who stayed at the guesthouse. At least she didn't have the added effort of thinking, making decisions. Jordan, forceful and confident, ordered her to stick with her sketches, and after a few feeble protests, Alice succumbed, not without some relief. The sketches did after all make money, which seemed to be sorely needed in the household despite Jordan's relative success with his miniatures, and Alice was able to knock them off effortlessly, conserving her energy for the kids, the guests and Jordan. Occasionally ripples of dissatisfaction lapped her like the rising tide as she sketched yet another grotty child, bored mother, or disgruntled father on the beach or harbour, but usually she was too exhausted to let them drown her.

'That was fantastic, Molly darling,' Jordan is saying now as the yoga class disperses. 'So cosmic, spiritual. I could feel the vibes, no kidding.'

'Huh?' Molly says. She is thinking of the long walk down the hill to Downlong and home. The rain has started again and there is an icy wind blowing.

'Your class tonight. I really feel I'm getting attuned to

44

my inner self, you know? The child within. I can feel my chakras in harmony, I kid you not.'

'Good for you, Jordan. Whatever turns you on.'

'I wish you did more meditation, though, darling. That little bit at the end, the relaxation, isn't enough. We could do candle meditation, chanting, prolonged deep breathing, alternate nostril breathing—'

Molly smiles, thinking of Lizzie chanting 'om' and meditating on a candle. 'Steady on, Jordan. The people that come to my classes aren't into that. I think they just want to relax a bit, maybe get fitter or more supple, and that's fine with me.' Molly herself had got into yoga when she was a teacher, needing something to cope with the stress and strain.

Jordan sighs. 'Do you want a coffee before you head home?'

Molly is about to refuse, then decides she'd like to see Alice. They go downstairs into the rambling house where Alice is sitting in the kitchen sewing name-tags onto school jumpers. She is wearing an ankle-length patchwork skirt with a deep-blue cardigan; she is as dainty and petite as her husband Jordan is big and solid. Alice has long hair, straight and yellow and shining which reaches down to her waist; her pretty round face, which is devoid of make-up, looks drawn and listless.

'Who'd have three kids?' she says wearily as Jordan puts the kettle on. 'Look at you, Molly; you've just taught a class after painting all day and you don't look a bit tired. You're smart, Molly. Stay smart – don't tie yourself down; stay free. I wish someone at art school had warned me to do the same.'

Jordan laughs. He never believes Alice when she talks this way, never for a moment thinks that anyone married to him can be anything less than perfectly content. Kissing his wife condescendingly on the top of her head, he says, 'You will joke, darling. Look how well your little sketches are doing. Did you tell Molly how much you earned last season with your pastels?'

Alice, embarrassed, begins to make coffee. Jordan says, 'I've put the kettle on for Molly, remember she doesn't drink coffee. You forgot she is a purist.' He turns to Molly with a charming smile. 'Ah, you are something to emulate, darling. I am too chained to the earth to give up freshly made coffee. Perhaps if we did more spiritual exercises in your classes I'd be able to do it.'

'Don't talk rubbish, Jordan. I just can't tolerate caffeine, that's all. It makes me dizzy and hyper.'

Jordan hands her a mug of peppermint tea and Alice a coffee. He starts to sit down at the table with the two women, but to Molly's relief, one of the children shouts for him from the living-room where they are watching television.

When they are alone Alice says, 'So what's up with you and Crispin?'

'God, you've heard too? What a bloody town.'

'I was at Stevens the fishmonger and Sid Hocking was there, chewing the fat. He was telling everyone in the shop about your row. Is Richard really so jealous of Esme's work? She's a brilliant sculptor. He ought to be proud of her.'

Molly groans. 'Oh shit, me and my big mouth.'

'Never mind, everyone will have forgotten it by now. Anyway it's no big secret; everyone knows everyone else's business around here anyway.'

'I've not seen Crispin since then. Over a week ago.'

'Both of you sulking, eh?'

'What worries me is that Crispin is getting just like his dad.'

'I thought he liked your paintings.'

Molly takes out the peppermint tea-bag, goes to the dustbin and throws it in. She doesn't speak until she has returned to the table. 'That's not really the point. He takes an interest, says all the right things, but his heart's not in it. He tries, but sometimes he can't help letting the resentment creep in.'

'What's there to resent?' Alice asks. 'Jordan's quite proud of my sketches, quite encouraging.' She makes a disparaging face. 'But it can't be because of their artistic merit. They're popular and make us a fair bit of cash. Crispin's not even an artist, so you're not in competition. What's his problem?'

'I don't know, I just don't know. I think it's to do with his parents; he sees how Richard is incapable of handling Esme's success and wonders if he'll be the same.'

Alice gets up and pours herself another coffee. 'Richard should be glad Esme is making some money out of her work, at long last. So many of us hardly ever do. Jordan and I are lucky, I suppose.'

She says this so wistfully that Molly can only nod sympathetically, though it saddens her somewhat for she has seen what Alice has done in the past; the intricate studies in oils, the brilliant revealing portraits. Now she no longer paints for herself but for the visitors, sitting on the Wharf or on West Pier drawing away while people gape, dripping their ice-creams and fizzy drinks all over her.

'I used to think marrying another artist was the answer,' Molly muses. 'I thought there would be mutual support, understanding . . .' She drifts off uncertainly.

Alice makes a face. 'Soul mates, eh? No such thing, sunshine,' she says flippantly. Then she feels guilty. Though for years Jordan has discouraged her elaborate portraits in oils, saying they were not commercial, not what the public wanted, he certainly wants her to carry on with her art, with the pastel sketches. She sometimes feels uneasy that it is the kind of art *he* thinks is best, but if she protests he accuses her of selfishness, and in the end she agrees. Her flimsy drawings are extremely lucrative, and she can toss off quite a few on a good day. She supposes she ought to be thankful that Jordan is so encouraging of them, unlike poor Esme with her wretched husband Richard so jealous of her sculpture.

Molly stands up, puts on her coat. 'I'm beginning to lose my faith in soul mates too,' she says wryly.

Alice offers to drive her home but Molly refuses. It's pointless putting up her umbrella because of the gale blowing from the sea, so she pulls up the hood on her old-fashioned coat and plunges down the hill towards home. Turning a corner she can see the harbour in the distance and the light of a lone fishing boat bobbing furiously in the water. Instead of turning down Virgin Street and going home, she runs down to the Wharf where she can see that the boat is the *Fair Celt*.

Molly doesn't hesitate; despite the rain and the wind, she runs to Smeaton's Pier and gets to within shouting range of Crispin. The tide is full and the waves are so strong they come crashing over the back wall of the pier, and the rain lashes the two lighthouses and the boats with a ferocity that nearly pushes Molly into the water. 'Crispin,' she shouts, her voice shrill and hoarse with fear. 'You're not going out there tonight, do you hear?'

The voice comes across the water like a siren's call, and Crispin can no more resist than those ancient sailors who were drawn to the rocks and to their doom.

'And who's to stop me, Molly, my love?' Crispin shouts, his voice strong with joy.

'I will, if I have to swim out there myself!'

Crispin grins. 'You've talked me into it, love,' he shouts. 'I won't go out, not if you go on to my place and get the fire lit. I'll be there in half an hour. That is, if you still have the key and haven't chucked it into the sea.'

Molly laughs, and the rain and salt water splashes her face and she doesn't know when she's been so happy.

'I'll never let go of that key, Crispin,' she hollers. 'You just try to get it away from me. See you at your house. And if you're longer than a half-hour, I'll be gone!'

She won't be, and they both know it. As Molly turns and runs back down the pier, back along the quay the way she came, Crispin turns to Pete who has been stoically standing by listening to all this. 'Now look here, lad,' he says with a grin. 'If you ever tell her that we had no intention of going out, that we'd come in from the bay only a short time ago after setting out the nets, I'll drown you myself, d'ya hear?'

Pete nods and rolls his eyes. He thinks the world of Crispin; he's a bloody good skipper, a bloody good fisherman, but he's a dead loss where women are concerned, getting involved with that artist female. He ought to leave the arty-farties alone, Pete thinks; they've all got a screw loose. That Molly might be a tasty piece, and nice as they go, but she's as nutty as the rest of them.

As they get into the row-boat and make for the pier, Pete looks forward to the evening ahead with his own girl, who will just be finishing at the fast-food place where she works. She told him the other day that she couldn't draw a straight line, and he nearly shouted with relief. Glancing over at Crispin, Pete feels sorry for him, and as they say good night he uncharacteristically, and much to Crispin's puzzlement, smacks him in a sympathetic manner on the shoulder.

The fire is lit when Crispin arrives, exactly twenty-nine minutes later. His house is right on the sea, one wall of the top floor covered in windows looking out towards the pier and the beacon, with the expanse of sea beyond. Though there is a small sitting-room downstairs and a tiny kitchen one floor below that, this is the room where Crispin spends most of his time. His bed is here, in the corner of the room on a raised wooden platform, enclosed within a carved-oak railing separating it from the rest of the room. From here he can wake up to the sea in the morning; and before he closes his eyes at night, he can see the lights on the pier, the beam of the lighthouse, the stars in the night sky.

Crispin loves the sea. He was born here, grew up here. His parents were amused when he informed them, at the age of six or seven, that he wanted to be a fisherman when he grew up. Ten years later, when he informed them again, they were horrified. He had a fistful of O levels and was expected to go on into the sixth form, and from there to university. Crispin expected his father to be uncomprehending, but he was surprised when his mother was against the idea.

'Why can't you understand?' he had shouted. 'I love the sea, like you love carving things, making things out of wood and stone.'

Esme did see, of course. She understood him perfectly; it was Crispin who did not understand her terror, her fear for him. She had not grown up near the sea; she had come to it when she was an adult, after she had married Richard, after he had found the job in Penzance and they had settled here. Crispin had been born immediately, when Esme was still very young, and she was so unprepared for the demands made by a tiny infant and then a young child, that it wasn't until many years later that she decided she wanted another one.

Esme tried to explain to Crispin her fear of the sea, of that dark swirling mass that sucked the rocks and sands with a ghostly haunting sound and pounded nightly on the harbour walls as if trying to force itself into forbidden places. But Crispin was young and didn't understand fear. He liked the sea for the danger in it, he liked the gamble. He never learned to swim because he couldn't be bothered with the sea when it was flat and glossy like an ice pond; he liked it wild, when you could hardly stand up in it, and he preferred being on top of it, in a boat, riding its waves like a cowboy taming a wild horse.

And so Esme kept quiet and, after that first time, kept her fears to herself. Crispin believes she disapproves of his chosen profession, but this is far from the truth. She is simply terrified of it, of the risk Crispin takes each time his boat steams away from the safety of the harbour. She tries to tell herself rationally that fishing is far safer now than it was fifty or a hundred years ago, that there is a reliable shipping forecast and radar to detect storms before they arrive, that there are radios and communication from sea to shore and a modern lifeboat if a boat manages to get into trouble – but all these thoughts dissolve as mist into the air when she thinks of the sea itself, hungry and demanding.

Crispin opens the door of his house and takes off his dripping yellow oilskins, his rubber boots. Then he climbs the short steep bare wooden stairs to the large room with the sea view. The curtains are not drawn; Molly too likes to watch the lights twinkling like stars out at sea and on the harbour. Besides, there is no need to draw the curtains; no-one can look in except the stars, except the rain still lashing against the panes.

Molly is sitting by the fire. She looks like one of Esme's early bronzes, all pleasing contours and curves with her hair, down now, gleaming like a highly polished mahogany table. She is wearing a long woolly jumper of Crispin's and her legs are bare, her hair almost dry by the flames of the fire.

'I took a hot bath, borrowed a jumper,' she says with a smile. 'I was wet and cold.'

'So am I. It's a nasty night out there.'

'A bath will warm you up. I didn't use all the hot water.'

'That's a change.' He grins, and so does she. The room looks soft, welcoming in the firelight. The floors are bare polished wood with a few throw rugs scattered about; the ceilings are high, the original beams exposed. Crispin knocked the top-floor bedroom and the attic together to make this large unusual room and the result is spectacular. A number of Esme's early wooden sculptures stand on their own or with other pieces that Crispin has collected over the years, and there are paintings everywhere, both abstract and traditional, for Crispin has eclectic tastes. Contrary to what Molly and Esme sometimes think, Crispin *is*, as a matter of fact, quite interested in art. He just feels that it is a disadvantage to have both a mother and a lover who are artists.

'I've missed you,' Molly says serenely. 'I'm sorry I made a scene on your boat.'

'And I'm sorry I was so rude at my parents' house.'

They smile, suddenly light-hearted. Molly stands up and walks over to Crispin as he walks towards her. Her eyes are smoky amber in the firelight and as he touches her he realizes she has nothing on under his jumper.

'Your hands are wet and cold and your hair is dripping all over me,' she protests, but not vehemently.

'I'm going to have a bath,' he says, keeping his hands under her jumper. 'Will you come soap my back?'

'Try and stop me,' she smiles. 'You just try and stop me.'

Together, arms wrapped around each other, they walk slowly out of the room.

Chapter Three

Christmas comes and goes. The winds blow viciously, but as Crispin tells both Molly and Esme they are inland winds, and anyway, he is still after the bass which are in the bay, around the beaches.

'Women never stop worrying about the sea,' Percy tells him one day as they sit in the Union Inn on Fore Street having a pint and a bacon roll for lunch. Percy has been going to the Union for as long as he can remember, and he can still usually find a mate or two standing at the bar whenever he comes in. The pub is narrow and small, and full of smoke and the comforting laughter of strong male voices, and everyone greets you by name when you walk through the door. It's one of the few comforts Percy has left, he sometimes thinks. Maybe the only one.

Percy and Crispin are sitting on the narrow bench that runs the length of the wall. Crispin tries to meet Percy at least once a week here at the Union; he likes the old man, knows too that he has a lot to thank Percy for. Percy gave him his first job on the boat, taught him everything there was to know about fishing, and sold him the *Fair Celt* at a ridiculously low price when he was too old and sick to carry on. Crispin knows he has a debt to pay there, and keeps his eyes open for ways to do it.

'My Maggie went on about something fierce about the sea, every time I took the boat out. Some wives keep their worries quiet, others nag. But they all worry.'

Percy takes a swig of his beer, wipes the bit of foam from his lips with the back of his hand. 'I don't even have a wife,' Crispin grunts, 'and still I get nagged. My mum by the silent tense expression she gets when the wind starts to blow a little, and Molly – well, you know Molly.' He grins, and gets up to buy another pint.

'Everyone knows Molly,' Percy retorts, then concedes with a wry smile, 'but she's all right, that maid. Heart's in the right place.'

Crispin knows this is high praise indeed from Percy, and feels oddly pleased, then mildly irritated at his reaction. He doesn't like feeling like a starry-eyed schoolboy, wanting the approval of those close to him for his best girl. The truth is, Molly has been making him feel like a lovesick adolescent quite often lately. It started just before Christmas, after the blazing argument they had on the *Fair Celt*. Crispin, though furious at first, found himself moping around like a seagull with a broken wing after a few days. He missed her like mad, like crazy. That she missed him too was obvious from their reunion that gusty night when she had come down to the pier and then to his house.

'Home again,' she had said, with such deep contentment and peace that he had propped himself up on his elbow to look at her face.

'Do you mean here in my bed? Or are you coveting my house?' he teased.

'Both.'

It was later that night, and Molly and Crispin were lying in the raised bed looking out over the sea, watching the rain lashing the windows, the lights blinking and winking from the pier, the lifeboat moored in the bay. Crispin, the black mood that had been dragging him

54

down all week finally lifted with Molly back in his arms and his life, wanted to say, 'Then stay, love, stay.' But the words never came, the moment passed.

'Reckon you and she be tying the knot d'reckly.' Percy's voice jerks Crispin back to the present. 'Y'could do worse, my boy. Could do worse.'

Crispin is silent. A burst of raucous laughter from the bar distracts them, and when they glance at each other again Percy seems to have forgotten his question, if it was a question. They begin to talk of other things, and the subject of Molly is not brought up again.

Percy hasn't forgotten. He has noted Crispin's silent evasion, stored it away to be pondered over during the long lonely evening ahead. He worries about Crispin, thinks he should be settled down with a decent wife, a family. A man needs warmth and coziness and companionship to come home to after long hours on the boat, after the echoing silence of the sea.

Percy misses that silence, that quiet so full of the noise of the wind, of the sea, the cry of gulls, that it can hardly be called silence at all, yet it was, somehow. For hours he and Crispin never said a word, putting down lines or nets or pots or bringing up the catch, toiling together in such harmony that talk was unnecessary, there in the company of the tides and the language of the moon and the sun and the stars.

Lunch over, the two men leave the pub and, enjoying a sudden outbreak of winter sun, amble for a bit up Pednolva Walk and then on towards the train station and Porthminster Beach, where they say goodbye. Crispin heads back down to his house; he would like to get a few hours' sleep. He was out before four this morning to drop the nets, and he's feeling tired now. Molly stayed at his place last night; he left her sleeping there, making sure he kissed her gently goodbye as she likes him to do. She always wakes when he does this, even if just for

55

a few seconds. She hates him creeping out of bed without that last word, a final quick touch.

He and Molly have spent at least four or five nights a week together since Christmas, either in her house or in his. 'It's crazy, this,' she had said last night. 'Do you realize we've been together every night this week?'

'Is it too much for you?' Crispin murmured, nuzzling her bare shoulder. 'Are you suggesting we're overdoing it?'

'On the contrary,' Molly said. 'But it does seem silly, two houses, and we only live in one of them, most of the time.'

Crispin didn't need to answer, because his nuzzling and fondling had triggered off the expected response and she turned to him, not wanting to talk any more. Later, tactfully, she did not bring up the subject again; or perhaps, he thinks now, it was just something she tossed out, something that did not require any serious consideration.

Crispin is so engrossed in his thoughts as he wanders down the Warren towards home that he doesn't recognize the tall old woman dressed in black, swaddled in a cashmere scarf wrapped around her neck like an adder. She is looking in the window of an art gallery, the Sandpiper. As Crispin trudges past, tired now after making love to Molly most of the night, out with the nets at four, and then two pints at lunchtime, he hears his name being called.

'Good afternoon, Crispin,' the woman says briskly, her pale face half hidden by the scarf. 'You are looking remarkably bleary-eyed today. No wonder you did not see me.'

Crispin recognizes Oona, Molly's grandmother. Now that he sees her, he notices, as he always does, her formidable aura of self-containment, as if she has learned, during her long life, not to need anyone or anything. As usual, he cannot help wondering if Molly too will one day be as insular. The thought troubles him.

'Oona, hello. Sorry, I was up rather early.'

'It must run in the family, this early rising,' Oona says drolly. 'I called in on your mother before breakfast this morning and found Esme already in her workshop, sculpting like a woman crazed.'

Crispin nods. 'Nothing stops her when she's engrossed in a piece of work.'

Oona looks him in the eye thoughtfully. She would like to say sharply that she has known his mother for more years than he has, knows the tearing of the body and the spirit Esme endured when the family was young, moving from artist to wife and mother, back and forth sometimes a dozen times a day, one to the other, trying to have both. Still staring at Crispin with her lion's eyes, Oona wonders if Esme will ever have the ruthlessness to become as great a sculptor as she is capable of becoming.

Crispin deliberately holds her gaze, thinking, not for the first time, how uncannily like Molly's eyes they are, that strange golden-orange colour. Oona is looking quite splendid today, her abundant white hair neatly plaited, an amber brooch encased in silver pinned to her fine wool black coat. She must be between paintings, Crispin thinks, and inadvertently smiles.

'And what is so funny?' Oona asks, responding to the smile with a slight one of her own. 'Do I amuse you?'

'I was thinking that you are looking at me rather sternly today. Have I been taking too much of your granddaughter's time, keeping her away from her painting?'

Oona looks at him with interest. This young man with the thick, rather dishevelled hair the colour of chestnuts and the candid green eyes has, it seems, been reading her thoughts. 'As a matter of fact,' Oona says, 'I believe

57

you have. Of course it is not your fault; an artist must have great strength of will, discipline. Talent is not enough, naturally.'

'I would think that Molly has plenty of discipline,' Crispin replies. 'Wherever we go she has her sketch pad, or her camera to take photos of something she wants to paint. She's always rushing about looking at winter brambles or hitch-hiking out to the countryside to find snowdrops. I don't know why she doesn't just paint the sea like so many of the others; at least it's here, on all three sides of the town; it's hard to escape it. You artists are always going on about the clarity of the light in St Ives, yet Molly has to go off to the moors or inland to find her inspiration.'

Oona fixes her amber stare on him again. She has never heard such a tirade from him. Though Crispin spoke gently, reasonably, there was a tinge of something not very pleasant there. Bitterness, perhaps? No, not quite that; more like just plain irritation, Oona thinks. In a way that is even worse; it is more insidious.

She glances into the shop window of the Sandpiper gallery, collecting her thoughts. She notes one of Molly's paintings there, a small one of an old granite gatepost in high summer, covered with ripe blackberries and with several foxgloves growing at its base like worshippers at a shrine. With her old experienced eye she can see flaws in the work, but she can also see talent there, that elusive spark that sets off the whole combustion. Inside the gallery the owner, Lance Giddens, sees Oona looking and waves. He is about to come outside for a chat, but she suddenly turns and begins talking to Crispin, the expression on her face severe, stern. Lance decides to leave them to it.

'All this running around the countryside seeking inspiration, doing the odd sketch, taking photographs, is not doing the actual work, I hope you understand,'

58

Oona says sombrely. 'Oh, of course, some is necessary, but the real work is in the studio, facing that blank or half-finished canvas, day in and day out. It is extremely easy to delude ourselves otherwise.'

Oona speaks as if she has had to wrestle with this problem for years, but as a matter of fact, she is disciplined and unbending in the application of her talent. She left her husband fifty years ago because she did not have time for both her painting and for him, and the fact that he was demanding, crass, and insensitive, was neither here nor there. They were totally unsuited, but Oona occasionally, throughout the years, has wondered whether she would have left him anyway, to get on with her life's work.

Now Crispin looks grim. 'I'm sure you needn't worry about Molly. She seems pretty dedicated to me.'

Again that flash of annoyance, of irritation. It troubles Oona, and she wonders if she should have a talk with her granddaughter.

Oona and Crispin change the subject and discuss the weather in a desultory manner for a few more moments and then part, Crispin heading for home and Oona walking into the Sandpiper. Neither of them are entirely satisfied with their conversation. Crispin feels that perhaps he should have said something about Molly needing a life as well as a career, and Oona wonders if she should have been more positive, emphasizing Molly's talents and the fact that she needs long hours alone in her studio if she is to realize her potential.

'And how are you today, Oona my dear?' Lance Giddens says as he approaches her. 'Have you decided to give me one of your paintings to sell?'

Oona merely smiles, inclines her head. This is Lance's little joke; Oona's paintings are all commissioned now; they go straight to private collections or to public galleries like the Tate, and others all over the world. 'I'm still trying to get Molly to sell that one of hers, the one you gave her. I think it's the best Oona North I've seen,' he teases.

'She's welcome to sell it if she wants,' Oona replies briskly. 'She ought to really, then she can stop all those ridiculous part-time jobs. Last summer she worked day and night at that café on the beach, and then in autumn she had that long stint of supply teaching in Penzance. Now it's yoga, and who knows what else will come up. She should be painting full time.'

'Shall I tell her you said that?'

'By all means. I will also tell her myself.'

They banter in this manner while Oona looks around the gallery. It seems deceptively small, but as well as this room there is a basement full of sculptures and a second floor crammed with embroidered rugs, pottery, and more paintings. Lance sleeps and works on the top floor. He paints strange intricate sea shapes, the blooms of ocean weed, the skeletons of fish: a kind of Georgia O'Keeffe of the sea. They don't sell but he doesn't seem to mind; his gallery is his passion, his *raison d'être*. Lance is divorced, with a grown-up son in London and an ex-wife who periodically sweeps down to Cornwall to check up on him, though they have not been together for fifteen years.

Oona looks around the gallery, Lance at her side with a running commentary on all his new items. 'Look at those boxes with the assortment of feathers in various bird shapes. Aren't they exquisite? A chap from Devon does them. I've sold two already. And those odd little wood carvings; they look like laughing Buddhas with huge penises. Several of the down-market tourists wanted to buy them for a laugh last summer, but I told them the sculptures were far too dear to take the place of smutty postcards.'

Lance chatters on while Oona looks, sometimes feels

60

a texture, lightly touches a surface. Much of the stuff is mediocre, she thinks, but occasionally there is a true creative work, a unique talent, and when she spots this she can feel her heart sigh once again, as if in relief.

'That's a good one of Molly's, don't you think?' Lance is saying. Oona nods. They go downstairs and look at the sculptures, and Oona stops by a favourite of hers, one of Esme Cochran's done in sandstone. It is a small crouched figure of a man or woman, bent and crushed except for one long elongated arm reaching out blindly, upwards. It's titled, simply, *Faith.*

'Fantastic, isn't it,' Lance murmurs, his monologue finally running down.

'She has talent. Let's hope now that Hugo is out of school, she will stop fussing so over her family and do some serious work. It's a pity, really, that both sons are still in St Ives; it distracts her.' Oona doesn't add that Molly too would be less distracted if Crispin were elsewhere.

'She loves her sons. And Richard too, of course.'

Oona glances sharply at him. There is a hint of regret in his voice. Lance has fallen into an uncharacteristic silence, and Oona studies him. He has long healthy silver hair parted down the middle, and an aesthetic face which reminds Oona of an ageing Jesus. He has dark circles under his eyes which are not unattractive, and rather tortured brown eyes which belie his sense of fun and mischief. He saves the dark brooding Byronic side of his nature for his paintings. There is something demonic and feral about them, but there is nothing like that in Lance. Oona quite likes the man, and wishes she could see some of his work. He had a small exhibition some years ago which was thoroughly panned by those who saw it. Oona was abroad at the time, though some of the comments she heard later were so outrageous she was intrigued. Oona knows from long experience that

61

sometimes the more vitriolic the criticism, the more genius there may be in the painter.

Since that unfortunate episode, Lance paints in secret, and neither exhibits nor displays his work even in his own gallery. Oona respects this determined privacy, and rather admires it. So many of the artists these days seem to thrust their paintings at you whether you like it or not.

As she leaves the gallery she is almost knocked over by a boisterous child who is accompanying his mother into the Sandpiper. 'Oh, Lord, I'm sorry. Oh, it's Ms North, Christopher, do apologize. I'm so sorry, he should be in school; I kept him home because of a stomach ache and he seems fine now, the skiver.' The woman, who is slight and fair and wearing a long green skirt patterned with half moons, is carrying a rather large parcel, obviously a painting, wrapped in cardboard and string. Oona recognizes her as Alice Culpepper, Molly's friend, the one who sits on the quay every summer doing hasty sketches of holiday-makers for easy cash. They exchange greetings, then Oona goes down the street and Alice enters the shop.

'Well, well, well, it's Alice in Wonderland,' Lance says for the hundredth time, making Alice think crossly that she must either change her name or cut off her long straight blond hair. 'That certainly doesn't look like one of Jordan's seascapes, unless he's suddenly escalated in size in a big way.' Lance handles Jordan's work, though he wishes he didn't have to. He doesn't like the man, and those miniature watercolours that Jordan does are not his type of painting. They are competent, far better than a great many of the paintings of the sea and boats and harbour that proliferate in the town, but they are certainly not great art. They sell particularly well to a certain type of tourist, the ones with a bit of money who fancy themselves as patrons of the arts, meaning that they buy a painting of the sand or sea to hang in the guest bedroom back home to remind them of their summer holiday. Lance needs the money he gets from Jordan's paintings, so he stocks the man's work. He supposes they are not that bad, merely mediocre. He is glad that his own work is not mediocre. It is either horrendously bad, or so amazingly brilliant that he will not be discovered until long after he is dead. He is quite content to let history decide his fate as an artist.

'This isn't Jordan's, it's mine.'

Lance looks at Alice with interest. The only works he's seen of hers have been the sketches she does on the sea front; sometimes the day-trippers come in with them and say rude things like, 'This is real art, mate, none of your stuff that looks like a kid has been scribbling all over it.'

She is unwrapping the painting carefully. Lance is watching the child, Christopher, stalking around the gallery, poking, prodding. 'Here now, I don't think you should touch the works of art, lad. How would your mum like it if you stuck your sticky fingers on *her* painting?'

The boy sticks his tongue out. Alice, flustered, reprimands him and apologizes to Lance, then nervously goes back to her package, delicately peeling off the thick brown paper. She is slow, meticulous. Lance thinks she is the most frail and prim young woman he has ever seen, and wonders irrelevantly how every small bone in her tiny body is not ground to shards in the act of making love with that great ox Jordan.

Finally the picture is free of its wrapping and Alice stands it up against Lance's desk in the corner. It is a portrait in oils of a fisherman with a gaunt face, a high forehead as carved and pocked as the granite cliffs. The background is the sea, with vague surreal shadows swimming just under the surface which Lance sees are the creatures that belong there: a dark crimson lobster, an elongated conger eel, other fish. Snaking around the man and the fish is just a hint of a net, but it is so delicately done, so opalescent, that it could be the mist, or a figment of one's imagination.

'I call it *The Sea Captain*,' Alice says, to break the silence.

'It's Percy Prynne, isn't it.'

'Yes. Crispin took a photo of him, years ago, before he retired, on the boat. I used the photo for the portrait.'

'It's very fine, Alice. Very fine indeed.' Lance could say more, but for once he isn't effusive. When a painting is as good as this one is, words sometimes almost demean it.

Alice waits while he studies the painting. 'I started it ages ago, but then you know how it is. The kids—' She breaks off and looks despairingly at Christopher, who has stuck his finger in one of the boxes on the table. She grabs him away and goes on, 'They're a handful, as you can see. And then there's the guest-house, and in spring and summer I'm down at the harbour all hours sketching the visitors. Jordan can't help; he keeps telling me he has to keep painting to make a living, which of course is true. Anyway, I dug it out, saw there wasn't much left to do, so I worked on it a bit, and – well, here it is.' She finishes in a rush of words and will not watch as Lance scrutinizes her painting.

The next few moments are extremely painful for Alice. She feels, irrationally, that her whole life, her whole self, is being judged and may be found wanting. She wonders what possessed her to drag out that old painting and finally finish it. It was something to do with seeing Molly the night before. As always, Alice felt churned when she talked to Molly. She dismissed it as envy of Molly's freedom, her ability to go where she wanted, paint what she wanted. And then there was the way Molly grew quiet and rather grim when Alice's pastels of the tourists were mentioned. Molly was too polite to say anything, but she was also not able to dissemble. The look on her face told Alice only too well what she thought of the drawings.

Finally she dares to glance over at Lance, who is looking at her oddly. 'I'd like this, Alice. It's bloody good.'

Alice knows by his voice that he is impressed. She feels reprieved, like a victim of a horrific accident who thinks she is going to die as the car spins around and around but then finds, when it hits the ground, that miraculously she has survived. She cannot speak but nods gratefully.

They discuss a price, which is far higher than Alice had anticipated, but Lance knows quality when he sees it. It's not only the tourists that come into his gallery; there are also many serious buyers, dealers from all over the world.

Alice leaves the Sandpiper gallery in a daze, forgetting to admonish Christopher for his appalling behaviour. *The Sea Captain*, begun years ago, was the first serious painting she had attempted for years, but she had hidden it away and stopped thinking about it until last night, after Molly left. Though exhausted, she was too restless to sleep herself, so she had taken the painting out, looked at it for a long time, and then got out her oils. Luckily, she had put them away carefully, the caps all on, so most were still usable. Working most of the night, she had fallen exhausted into bed at five a.m., shattered, but oddly at peace.

Alice slowly wanders outside, going along the pedestrian walkway that skirts the sea behind the houses. She stops for a moment and hangs over the railing, while Christopher spits at the rocks a short distance below, trying to make each spit go further and further. The tide

65

is out, and the sea makes a slurping noise as it recedes from the rocks. Over in the harbour Alice can see the boats stuck listlessly in the sand like abandoned water toys after the bath has been drained. Though it's late January, it feels mild, almost spring-like, and the sun is shining. Out over the sea a cormorant dives under the water for a fish and soars out again. Alice feels she ought to point this out to Christopher, who is sticking out his tongue at a seagull perched on the railing, but decides she can't be bothered with him at this moment. The thought shocks her; she has always prided herself on being a good mother.

Not today. Today, she decides, if only for this one day, she will be an artist first, a mother second. The thought is so satisfying that she takes the long way home, stopping first for an amble along Porthminster Beach to enjoy the unseasonal sunshine, much to the disgust of Christopher. He'd far rather be at home playing his computer games, but Alice doesn't care. For the first time in a long time, she is doing exactly what she wants to do. She wonders if this is addictive.

On this same January day Richard Cochran is having lunch at the Swordfish pub in Penzance, with a friend of his wife Esme's. The friend is a woman of Esme's age with a pale wide face, high cheek-bones and attractively slanted eyes. Her dyed-black hair is pulled up in a topknot with a long fringe covering her eyebrows and eyelashes. She is made up artfully, with dark-red lip-stick, deep-green eyeshadow, and long black mascara'd lashes that flit out from her fringe like the legs of a spider. The result is not unattractive, rather like an oriental Barbie doll. Her name is Harriet, and neither Richard nor anyone else ever calls her Harry, or Ettie, or any other diminutive. Perhaps this is because of her slightly foreign, slightly haughty look which she cultivates diligently. But she is English through and through, having been born in Dorset to parents who came from London.

The lunch is tasty: fish pie, fresh vegetables. Richard and Harriet have lunched together once or twice before on a Monday since the winter term began; Richard has a free lesson after the dinner break on this day, and Harriet does not start work on Mondays until two o'clock. She works for an estate agency in Penzance; she finds it tedious and boring, but cannot support herself with her painting and sculpture, which is what she longs to do. Her paintings are small abstracts usually in black and orange; her sculptures she prefers to call constructions, for they are constructed rather than sculpted, with soft metals such as sheet lead, which is malleable and easy to work with. They are composed mostly of angles rather than curves, rather like Harriet herself, who has slim sharp hips and flat breasts with pointed nipples.

Harriet has known Esme and Richard for several years. They have supported her through more than one crisis in her life, usually over a man. Harriet is single, with an appalling track record in men. She would like nothing better than to have a long loving marriage like Richard's and Esme's, or so she thinks (and voices persistently), but none of her many relationships have lasted longer than a few short years. Sometimes she wonders if she spends so much time at their house because she wants something to rub off on her: some stability, some permanence.

Harriet, finishing her food, takes a cigarette from her bag and lights it, offering one to Richard. He hesitates, then takes it, and at the same time looks around surreptitiously. He has given up smoking but has the odd one now and again, knowing he shouldn't, but not really giving a damn at this moment.

'Hm, naughty boy,' Harriet says. 'Does Esme know you've started again?'

Richard smiles at her through a smoke ring. 'Are you going to tell her?' he says. He is aware that he is flirting.

'It's pointless giving up something you enjoy,' Harriet says, looking at him with frank appraising eyes.

'Esme wouldn't agree with that. She'd give me a lecture on heart and lungs and so on. And men my age.'

Harriet laughs out loud. 'A man of a certain age, eh?' she says. 'Esme has every reason to lecture you, but personally I don't see the point. A little of what you fancy does you good, or so they say.'

Richard nods, thinking of Esme, working so dementedly on her new sculpture that he sometimes wonders if she knows or cares where he is, what he is doing. Defiantly, he takes a deep lung-destroying puff on his cigarette.

Harriet thinks of Esme too. Ever since the two women met at a lecture in one of the galleries, Harriet has pursued the friendship, enjoying Esme's company, but also learning from the more experienced artist. Harriet has always found Esme restful; often, after yet another horrific row or rejection by one of her lovers, she has found solace in Esme's serene garden, in the woman's composure, her sympathetic understanding.

Lately, however, Harriet has been thinking more of Esme's husband than of Esme. If she were honest with herself, she would admit that she has been thinking of Esme's husband for a long time. Harriet, desperate for love, looks for love everywhere. She knows she is not fulfilled; knows her work, her creativity, relies on love. Harriet is addicted to it, the rush of blood to the head and heart, the mind-blowing sex with a new body, the agony and ecstasy. She feels hungry, predatory without it.

She thinks of Esme again. How lucky Richard's wife

is, to have a husband like Richard. Harriet is getting on; she's been around long enough to know that good men are not easily found. She thinks that Esme is exceptionally fortunate to have found a man that does much of the cooking, a great deal of the washing-up, and even hangs the clothes out to dry on weekends. Richard is a good listener, too. Already she has told him about her last unhappy relationship with an antique dealer in Penzance called Bernard. Richard's shoulder, Harriet has found, is lovely to cry on. It is not surprising that she is fast getting over Bernard, with such a sympathetic shoulder on hand.

They order coffee and Harriet lights another cigarette. She flicks ash over her smart ecru jacket and brushes it off carefully. Her nails are painted red, matching her lips which have mysteriously stayed a deep crimson despite food and cigarettes. The black fringe of her hair shines and glitters in the subdued lights of the pub and her cheeks have two perfect round rosy patches on them, whether by nature or design Richard cannot tell.

Recklessly he takes a second cigarette. Harriet, eyes glued to Richard's face like a barnacle glued to the bottom of a boat, says, 'You seem preoccupied. Is it this new sculpture Esme is doing?'

Richard marvels at her intuition, not knowing that Esme, feeling low one day recently, rashly confided to Harriet that she was worried about Richard's resentment of her work. Now Harriet stares at Richard with such genuine concern, her black eyes in that pale face never leaving his own, that in a rush of gratitude he tells her about Esme's intense love affair with stone and wood. Harriet, sympathetic and understanding, listens. Though Esme is her friend, though she has always preached sisterhood and solidarity between women, she feels such compassion for this warm and sensitive man that impulsively she puts her hand over his, grips it warmly.

Richard, his spirit lightened by this generous woman, thinks how understanding she is, how much more so than Esme. Basking in her warm empathy, her encouraging smile, the black eyes that look into his as if he were the only man in the world, Richard grips her hand back, and the two smile at each other somewhat deliriously.

The slippery slope has been reached. Richard and Harriet stand on it obliviously, not knowing what a long, long way down it is.

Much later on that same day Crispin glances in the window of the Sandpiper gallery, looking for one of Molly's paintings, and sees a large portrait of Percy Prynne dominating all the other work. He recognizes the photograph behind the portrait, but comprehends that the painting has far outreached and extended and transformed the photo. It has captured something primal in the man, some deep need, some basic longing. Crispin has seen Percy look like that on the boat, staring at the sea as if it were his soul, as if he would soar down into it like a sea-bird joyously plunging into the depths. Alice has captured that look, which is not, never was, a desolate or desperate need; on the contrary, it is powerful, even ecstatic, as if the man and the sea were one, as if the sea needed Percy as much as Percy needed it.

Crispin stands staring at the portrait for a long time. He wonders if that look will be in his own eyes in twenty years' time – or whether it is there now.

The gallery is shut, or else Crispin would have gone inside, bought the painting there and then, whatever it cost. He is determined to have it. The bass have been running well for weeks; the other night he came in with forty stones: he can afford it. Even if he couldn't, he'd have had that portrait somehow. It is, he feels, too stark, too like Percy's very soul to be sold into the hands of strangers. He is obliged to buy it, to keep Percy's spirit safe in St Ives.

Crispin forces himself to stop staring at the portrait and moves on, wondering what his mind is coming to, endowing paintings with souls and spirits. None the less, he knows that as soon as the gallery opens he'll be there.

Someone else gets there before him. It is getting on towards eight in the morning, the sun already creeping up over the bay, the nights pulling out at last in these last days of January. Percy Prynne, unable to sleep, has been aimlessly walking back and forth on Smeaton's Pier for an hour. The tide is in and he saw the fishing boats off, after the bass again. It's been years since the catch has been so fine, and Percy is bereft that he's not out there, sharing the excitement, the thrill of it all. It's not the money that he's lusting after – though God knows he could use it. Bass fetch good prices, and good luck to them, Percy thinks. It makes up for the bad times, when the catch is low, the season slow, when mackerel is all you get and that fetching a mere eighty pence a stone over at Newlyn fish market.

Percy lives on his pension, and the bit of savings he has left from the sale of his boat. Crispin tried to pay him more than he asked for the *Fair Celt*, but Percy got angry, told him *he* was the seller, and he'd name the price. In truth, he'd have given the boat to the lad, so keen was he to have Crispin take it on. The thought of the *Fair Celt* going to strangers was more than he could take.

It's going to be another fine day; the winds have dropped, the clouds high and soft, unthreatening. Percy wanders down the pier and stops before the medieval fishermen's chapel, St Leonards, no more than a tiny stone room at the base of the pier. Percy can't remember when he was last inside; the days have long gone when

71

the fishermen used it as a meeting and sheltering place, and he can't recall it ever being used as a chapel.

He pushes the door and goes inside. There is only stone and a dark wooden bench. He sits on the bench gingerly, his hip troublesome. He has forgotten why he came in, but it doesn't seem important. He remembers playing here as a lad with the other boys, playing their games of marbles, or swinging happily from a rope on the beams in the ceiling. It was a good place to lark about on a rainy day.

Thinking of these things, dreaming, reminiscing, Percy suddenly opens his eyes. He sees that the chapel is full of fisherfolk, smelling the good clean smell of seaweed and fresh fish, of salt, of spray. They mill about him, the men smoking their clay pipes and greeting him kindly. He sees his father amongst them, ginger-bearded, clasping him on his shoulder, and his older brother who drowned in a lifeboat accident fifty, sixty years ago now. Percy's wife Maggie is here too, young and laughing, sleeves rolled up to her elbow and her hands and arms red with gutting the herrings in the big wooden barrels. He laughs with her, smells her tangy salty hair, hears her light lilting voice.

It is almost an hour later when Percy comes out of the little chapel. At first the sun, bright and assertive, disorientates him, and he is not sure where he is. Slowly he limps down to the quay and walks alone down the Wharf which is already lively with pedestrians meandering along the harbour, taking advantage of the cheerful morning. There are pensioners walking dogs, youngsters ambling recalcitrantly late to school, early shoppers carrying baskets and bags, and a few old seamen like himself, drawn to the harbour every morning as if mermaid sirens were calling them.

In front of the lifeboat station Percy runs into Sid Hocking coming down off West Pier, his face – what can be distinguished under the sideburns and moustache – red and gleaming in the unseasonably warm early morning sunlight. 'God's truth, 'tis a beaut of a morning for January, my bird. Warmer than a whore's bottom!'

Percy looks vaguely at Sid. He doesn't seem to recognize the man. He realizes Sid is talking to him, but he can't make it out, for Maggie and his father are still laughing and singing in his head.

'What's up then, Percy my handsome? Cat got your tongue, my lover?'

Something clicks inside Percy's head and he says, 'Oh, mornin', Sid. Fine day, eh?'

'The bugger's woke up! That's what I was saying, Percy. It's a bloody fine day.'

Percy and Sid exchange a few more words and then Percy walks slowly away. He hasn't any direction; he doesn't want to go home, but he feels slightly dazed, as if he were floating on a warm sea with the hot sun glazing him like icing sugar on a bun. Wandering up St Andrew's Street and from there up the Warren, he makes his way past the terraced cottages with the sea behind them, the little tea-houses, the bed and breakfasts, until suddenly he is standing in front of the window of the Sandpiper art gallery. It does not open until ten, but Percy does not want to go inside, has never been inside. Yet here in the window is an image of *him*, Percy Prynne, sea captain. Or no, not quite. Here in the window is Percy Prynne himself, and the old man with the bad hip and the wheezing lung standing outside is only a shadow, a bad dream from which Percy now feels at last he is waking up.

He stands staring for a long time. When he finally turns to trudge up the long hill back home, he is somehow comforted, knowing he has found something important, something he must never let go of again.

As he gets to his house, fumbles with the lock, opens

the door and confronts the lonely unfulfilling day ahead, Percy knows that the old man now putting on the kettle, taking down one solitary cup and saucer, is only a shadow, a vague spirit unconnected to the salty earth of sea and sweat and the scales of fish and the singing of men. The real Percy Prynne is down near the harbour, staring out that window of the gallery for the whole world to see his power and his strength and his glory.

As he switches on the gas fire with its imitation coals, Percy hears his father and brothers singing like the sea, like they used to when he was a child and the fishermen went sailing out of the harbour in the herring or pilchard season, sometimes forty or fifty boats going after the catch. Their strong male voices roar like the tide, and he knows they are calling him, knows it will soon be time to listen to their song, to join them at last in the singing of it.

Chapter Four

'Hugo, I thought you were going to hoover this bloody hallway.'

'Chill, Dad. I'll do it later, no sweat. The surf is like, wow!'

'Bugger the surf. You get out of that wet suit and put on some work clothes,' Richard says crossly, and adds irrelevantly, 'You look like a bloody great cockroach in that thing.'

'Come on, Dad, have a heart.' Hugo, carrying his surfboard, his shoulder-length hair tied back in a ponytail, looks appealingly at Richard.

'Why?' Richard mutters belligerently. 'What good does it do me to have a bloody heart?'

Hugo knows he has won. 'I promise I'll hoover as soon as I get back, OK?'

'Too right you will. No going out tonight if you don't, Saturday night or not.'

Hugo leaves the house and races to the beach. It has been a fantastic month for surfing so far, this February. There must be about forty-five, fifty surfers out at Porthmeor Beach today. The weather is colder than it was those unseasonal days at the end of January, but it is still dry and sunny, the surf perfect.

'Hey Hugo, don't forget tonight!' A girl of about

seventeen with long shiny hair the colour of fine red wine calls out to him with a sexy smile.

'Would I ever, Cara?' Hugo grins. He runs into the water, begins paddling on his board, duck diving a few breakers, waiting for the right one. It comes and there he is, standing on his board, flying on top of the ocean, skimming the waves, powerful, sublime, at one with the sea and the sky and the gods. He *is* a god; for this moment, he owns the universe.

Richard, at home, does not realize that his nineteen-year-old son is a god, ineffable and out of reach of ordinary mortals. He is putting a load of clothes in the washing-machine and thinking that his son is a hopeless layabout. Richard had had great hopes for Hugo, who, unlike Crispin, stayed on at school to do A levels. Hugo says he will go on to university eventually, but why hurry, he says? The surf is good, he has a part-time job in one of the surfing shops. 'Chill out, Dad,' he says to Richard. 'Everything in its time, man. Stay cool.'

Richard wonders if he ought to call Esme up from her shed for lunch. She has been there since early morning, still working on her latest sculpture, the one she started in December. She has gone totally out of control over this latest piece, Richard thinks; she seems to have been working on it for ever. He feels neglected and unloved; he feels put upon and taken advantage of.

It hasn't helped that his own work is going badly. Perhaps not so much badly as boringly. Richard, years ago, deliberately chose to stay at the grass roots of his profession, refusing to apply for department or year headships when the opportunities arose. He wanted, simply, to teach, not to administrate, nor did he want to relocate, which cancelled out any deputy headships he could have applied for.

Now, he wonders if he has made a mistake. He is

feeling stale as a teacher, and dull. He doesn't think the students find him so, not yet at any rate, but he wonders if in a matter of time he will bore himself so much that they will be bound to catch on. Richard resents the fact that he is bored, resents the students, even though he knows the fault is within himself. He has done the job too long, he often thinks. There are no more challenges.

'Why don't you change, then?' Esme asked once, last autumn when he was trying to describe his apathy to her. She had listened quietly, aware of the lack of direction in Richard's life, silently grateful that in her own life she still had so much she wanted to accomplish, so much she needed to do, so much she still had to learn.

'Change to what?' Richard said. 'I'm too old.'

'That's ridiculous. I don't mean get out of the teaching profession, I mean it's not too late to begin applying for other things within the profession.'

'Hm.' Richard, noncommittal, had clammed up. He didn't want to admit to Esme that he felt too old, too tired, too past it, to have the energy needed to apply for anything. They are after all approximately the same age, and Esme certainly doesn't feel too old for anything.

Richard sighs, disgruntledly. It is such a lovely day he had been hoping that he and Esme could go for a long walk along the coastal path, maybe even to the village of Zennor where they could have had a pub lunch before walking back across the fields and farmlands. Esme, though, had been up and at work long before Richard had even got out of bed, and he knew it was useless to ask her. She would look bemused, then distressed, then go into a long-winded explanation as to why she couldn't possibly leave her work now, not at this moment. Then she would suggest he went alone, without her, which is what he should have done, he realizes. He used to like walking alone, once, but he has got used to hiking the cliffs with Esme, and now prefers company on his walks.

Hiking alone, like so many other things, he is beginning to find boring.

Esme comes into the kitchen, the old cloth overall she wears for sculpting covered in fine white dust as is her dark wiry hair. 'God, my shoulder aches, and my elbow is killing me. Should we have some lunch?' she asks.

'You mean, have I made lunch?' he says tersely.

Esme, preoccupied, doesn't hear the tension in his voice and says, innocently, 'I suppose that is what I did mean. I'm starving.'

Something catches fire, combusts inside Richard and he says dangerously, 'I'm afraid I haven't had time to make the lunch yet. I've been doing the washing, changing the sheets on the bed, and I went out and did all the shopping.'

Still Esme doesn't sense anything wrong. She does these things all the time when Richard is at school, and, on days when her work is less pressing, she has a meal ready for him when he gets home. 'Perhaps I'll go back down then and carry on,' she says, not even looking at him. 'Give me a shout when lunch is ready.'

Richard takes off his glasses and wipes them carefully with a handkerchief. Esme is already walking back down to her workroom when he puts them back on. He calmly goes to the refrigerator, takes out a lump of cheese, goes to the kitchen door, and hurls the cheese across the garden where it lands with a thump at Esme's feet. 'Here's your lunch,' Richard shouts, and a head of iceburg lettuce joins the cheese, flying over Esme's head and rolling down the lawn, coming to a stop at the door of the studio.

Esme, stunned, waits to see if any more missiles are going to be hurled, but Richard is no longer standing at the kitchen door. She races back into the house and shouts, 'Are you crazy? What the hell is the matter with you?'

78

'You don't know? You really don't know?'

'I'm afraid I don't,' Esme says coldly. 'I'm afraid you'd better explain.'

But Richard can't. He knows it would sound churlish to complain of a morning doing household chores, to accuse Esme of taking him for granted, assuming there would be a meal prepared, the domestic work done. After all, he assumed it for years when he was the primary wage earner, when Esme was raising the boys and struggling with her sculpture, coping with a part-time job, running down to her shed between school runs, between PTA meetings, between shopping and hoovering and helping with homework.

And so he says nothing, though Esme is standing there patiently, waiting for an explanation. Turning his back on her he grabs a denim jacket and walks out of the house. He feels the aggrieved one, the injured party, but he'd never be able to explain why to Esme. He couldn't even explain to himself, so how would she ever be able to understand.

There is only one person who would, he thinks suddenly. Walking quickly into the town, he heads towards her house.

Crispin, letting himself into Molly's house with his own key, feels as if he is suffocating when she shouts down from her studio, 'Be a sweetheart and make me a sandwich, love. I just want to finish this one section on *The Four Seasons* and then I'll be down.' Crispin has just witnessed his father throwing an iceburg lettuce at his mother, and the scene was not edifying. He had seen his father grim and silent more than once in the past ten years, recognized it as a growing resentment of Esme's emerging fame, but he has never witnessed such overt anger.

Neither Esme nor Richard had heard Crispin come in

79

with a large bass for their dinner. Crispin had left the bass in the dining-room adjoining the kitchen and fled, before Esme had stomped back into the kitchen to confront Richard. Crispin was appalled, and when Molly again calls down from her studio asking him to make her some lunch, it is uncomfortably reminiscent of Richard throwing Esme's lunch down towards her studio.

Crispin pulls himself together, tells himself that Molly is not Esme, and he is not Richard. Despite his occasional irritation at Molly when she becomes obsessed with a hedgerow, he is really quite proud of her work and her dedication to it. It's just that he worries sometimes about whether it will get out of hand, and if it does, whether he'd be able to cope without resentment or annoyance. It is for this reason that he can't totally commit himself to Molly. He has been around Richard and Esme for too long not to know exactly what price there is to be paid for artistic success.

And yet, Crispin muses as he goes downstairs into Molly's jaunty pine kitchen, opens the top of the stable door to let the cat, Witch, in before making some sandwiches – and yet, in spite of it all, Esme and Richard love each other, have always loved each other during their thirty-odd years of marriage.

Esme was pregnant when they married. She was only seventeen when she found out, in the middle of an Art A level which she had to abandon. Richard was not much older, just starting his teacher training. Years later Esme told Crispin she often wondered what would have happened to her, career-wise, had Richard's first job not been in Penzance and they had not chosen St Ives to settle in. Here, she was able to continue with the art apprenticeship and the education the birth of Crispin had disrupted; here, she had studied and worked with some of the greatest artists of the day, had been fortunate

80

enough to carefully observe the sculptor Barbara Hepworth herself, who was working just down the road until the day of her death twenty-odd years ago.

'I had a much better education here in St Ives than I ever would have had at art school,' Esme had said to Crispin many times. 'Thank goodness you came along, or I might not have come down here with Richard; I was dead keen on going to the Slade.'

Crispin, slicing cheese, tomatoes, thinks about his parents' marriage. By all odds it should have failed years ago, given their youth, the fact that they 'had' to get married, as it was put in those days. Crispin had grown up believing his parents to be happier than most of his friends' parents; they quarrelled sometimes, but never seriously; usually, they seemed to get on fairly well, at least on the surface. He had never really noticed anything wrong until after he had grown, and Esme's work suddenly became not just a little hobby in the garden that Richard and he could share a matey tolerance of, but something to be taken seriously, not just by the family, but by the world outside.

Crispin puts on the kettle and makes tea. Witch is yowling for milk so he feeds the massive great cat, muttering that Witch should be strictly on the skimmed stuff. Crispin is still deeply disturbed by the scene he has just witnessed in his parents' garden; he finds he is horrified at Richard's childish yet violent reaction. For perhaps the first time, he distances himself from Richard, understanding with sudden clarity Esme's difficulties, and even feels slightly uncomfortable himself over his churlish peevishness with Molly's work.

'Oh, how wonderful you look, how domestic!' Molly says as she runs down the kitchen stairs, looking both fresh and shambolic in faded jeans and her latest jumble-sale bargain, a baggy shapeless jumper knitted like a rainbow, in soft fine wool. She hugs him, spills Witch's milk and causes Crispin to burn himself with boiling water from the kettle. 'Oh no, sorry Crispin. Here, stick your hand under cold water.'

This done, Crispin says firmly, 'There, Molly.' He points to the corner of the tiny room at the table and two chairs. 'Sit. Do not move. This kitchen is not big enough for both of us. I'll finish the lunch and put it right in front of you. All you'll have to do is eat it.'

Molly obeys meekly. Crispin lays the table, putting down mats, plates, and a pile of cheese sandwiches on a platter in the middle of the table. Molly waits until Crispin has joined her before saying, quietly but firmly, '*Yours* is.'

'What? Hm, these are good if I must say so myself. Go on, Molly, take one. You said you were hungry.'

'Your kitchen,' Molly says. 'It's big enough for both of us.'

Crispin stops eating, looks at her. She is not looking at him but at her cheese sandwich, with such concentration that he realizes what an effort it was for her to say that. This is so unlike Molly, who is blunt and forthright and says exactly what she is thinking most of the time, that Crispin feels strangely moved.

'Molly,' he says, going to her. 'Molly, love.' He stands behind her, turns her around to him, makes her look up at him. 'What are you saying?' he asks gently.

'I was hoping *you'd* say it.' She looks away from him, but not before he glimpses the dark tinge of pain in her eyes. 'You can't, can you,' she says harshly, moving away from him, leaving the table and pouring Witch another saucer of milk distractedly. 'You can't bring yourself to say move in with me, or suggest you'd like to live here, or pool our resources to buy a place together.'

'Molly, love—'

'We've been together a year now, Crispin. Relationships don't remain static, you know. They change, alter. They grow or diminish. I'd like ours to grow, I'd like *us* to grow, together.' She gets out a tin of cat food, begins to open it.

'Molly, for God's sake, stop fiddling, that cat does not need any more food. Sit down, please, OK?'

Molly sits, sucking her finger where she has cut it on the cat-food tin. She looks like a recalcitrant child, Crispin thinks, like the younger sister he wishes he had had – maybe then he'd understand women more. As a matter of fact she's a year older than Crispin, but he feels decades older. He constantly worries about her, like you would about a kid sister always dashing about climbing dodgy cliffs trying to photograph a wild flower, or hitch-hiking in the middle of the night across Bodmin Moor. Molly has done these things and more, driving Crispin frantic. Perhaps, he thinks now, if they lived together, he could keep a better eye on her? But he discards that idea immediately. He'd worry more, not less, if he knew what she was up to all the time.

'Molly, listen to me,' he says, facing her across the kitchen table. 'I love you, OK? Do you believe that?'

'Hm. I suppose.'

'That's not good enough, love,' he says gently.

'OK, OK, I know you love me, and I love you. But that's my whole point, if we love each other, it's natural to want more, to be together all the time, when we're not working. To set up house together.'

Crispin smiles, and Molly immediately takes umbrage. 'Do I amuse you, Crispin?' she says coldly.

He smiles again. 'That's just what your grandmother said to me. And as a matter of fact I was thinking of her, that's what amused me. Oona thinks we see far too much of each other anyway. She's quite proud of you, that you haven't moved in with me, or married me.'

'Who's talking about marriage?' Molly snaps. 'Who says I want to marry you? Stop rushing things. I only want to move in with you.'

Now Crispin laughs out loud. 'You see, it's my *house*, not me that you lust for. You just want that bed with the sea view.'

Molly is up and at the cat food again, fumbling and shaking. 'You can't even discuss this seriously, can you?' Throwing down the tin-opener she opens the kitchen door and goes outside, brushing her eyes with her sleeve as she does so. The back of the house leads into a narrow stone-cobbled alley-way, not the best place to be alone and have a good cry with the old stone terraced houses crammed together and some of the top halves of kitchen doors opened because of the sunny afternoon. Molly runs down the alley-way, cuts down Salubrious Terrace into Fore Street, and is on the harbour, which is not very conducive to the solitary weep she feels coming on because even though it is mid-winter, the sunny weather has brought out day-trippers and weekenders, and the quay is quite lively.

Crispin, meanwhile, has grabbed the cheese sand-wiches, slammed the kitchen door, and is running after Molly, who has decided to go down the ramp into the harbour itself, for the tide is right out. Here there are people walking dogs, some families with children meandering about the sand, but there is a bit more solitude than on the Wharf or the West Pier. Molly, crying copiously now, walks amongst the fishing boats, stuck forlornly in the sand, and goes past them to the end of the other pier, Smeaton's Pier with the two lighthouses, the old original one in the middle, and what is still called the 'new' lighthouse at the end, built a hundred years ago when the pier was extended. Rushing past the end of the pier, Molly runs along the sand behind it, where there are no curious eyes to stare, no

84

Sid Hocking or Crispin's fisherman friend Tom, who is in the harbour doing repairs on the *Girl Lizzie*.

Crispin catches up with her here. She is sitting crouched up against the wall of the pier, facing the sea which is not that far away.

'You'll have a wet bottom,' Crispin says, squatting next to her. 'Here, have a cheese sandwich.'

Molly takes one and looks at it dispassionately. Her tears have dried and the sandwich looks tempting. Crispin knows the crisis is over when she takes the first tentative bite.

'Look, love,' he says when they have munched in silence for a few moments. 'We've got such a good thing going, you and I, the way we are now. I'm so afraid of spoiling it. It seems to me we have the best of all worlds: we're together much of the time, but we still have our own space to return to.'

Molly finishes her sandwich, takes another from Crispin. Several young seagulls which have been walking along the sand at the water's edge begin to fly around them, squawking for a crumb. 'I'm not going to crowd you,' Molly says sadly. 'Just because people live together, it doesn't mean they are on top of each other.'

Crispin waves away a particularly obstreperous seagull and says, 'So what is the difference, Molly? If we live in two houses or one? We'll still do the same things we've always done together, so what's the difference how we work our time and space apart?'

Molly is quiet. A fishing boat glides serenely towards the horizon across the still water and in the distance a seal pokes his head out of the sea for a few moments before diving under again. The water is turquoise today, iridescent. The sands of the bay opposite look luminous in the welcoming sunlight. The day is deceptively spring-like.

Two houses or one – what *is* the difference after all?

85

Molly asks herself. But there is, there is. It has to do with commitment, with taking a chance on each other, on the future. Crispin's way is safer, she knows; but she also knows how much they will lose if they don't take some risks.

'Come on,' Crispin says gently, getting up from where he was squatting on the sand against the pier and reaching down to Molly. 'You must be wet through, sitting there. The tide's turning, too; we'd better go.'

Molly, still silent, takes his hand, and they walk slowly around the pier and back into the harbour. There is, she decides, nothing more to say. If Crispin is not ready to commit himself fully to their relationship, she must wait. The other alternative she cannot contemplate.

It is still February, but the weather has changed: it is cold, damp, bitter. Harriet and Esme are in the Tate gallery looking at a new exhibition: a collection of prints by the early printer Guido Morris. Esme has, at last, finished her sculpture. She would have liked to celebrate with Richard, with whom she has made an uneasy truce after the scene last week in the garden. But this Sunday afternoon Richard is visiting his mother who is in a home in Bude; she is frail and ill and can only tolerate visitors one at a time, even family. And so Richard has gone alone, leaving Esme at a loose end. Hugo is upstairs in his room playing his throbbing music, which Esme secretly rather likes, though she would never admit it to Richard, and Crispin is, of course, either out fishing or with Molly.

Harriet arrived unannounced about an hour ago, returning a book Esme had lent her. Esme showed her the finished sculpture. 'Why . . . it's wonderful,' Harriet had said, but the words were an understatement. It was by far the best thing that Esme had done. It was magnificent, all elegant and moving swirls and curves as if it were flying, soaring above the earth, above the sea, into the sky.

'I'm pleased with it,' Esme had said simply.

The two women stared at the sculpture. A flash of envy struck Harriet with such explosive force that she had to turn away, hide her face from Esme. The woman had Richard, had two gorgeous sons, and now *this*, for God's sake.

As soon as these thoughts struck, Harriet, guiltily, tried to eradicate them by insisting that they celebrate, mentioning the new exhibition, saying she wanted to treat Esme to lunch at the Tate restaurant. And so here they are now, admiring the prints, wandering happily from room to room, commenting on what they see, relaxing in the tranquil atmosphere of the gallery, which is all curved and undulating like the sea and sand it faces, with great round windows everywhere, through which the green or grey of the water, the blue of the sky, the incandescent sand, can be seen throughout the year.

'I love this place,' Esme says as they sit down to lunch. The restaurant has windows all around and the two women are sitting facing Porthmeor Beach, which is nearly empty today. The surf is bad, and it is too cold and blowy for all but the most intrepid dog-walkers to brave a walk along the shore.

'It's a beautiful gallery,' Harriet agrees.

They talk about the exhibition, gossip a bit. The food comes: pancakes with a spinach and mushroom filling, and as they begin to eat Esme says, 'Well, I hope Richard will be a bit happier now that I've finished the sculpture.'

Harriet nods. 'Until the next one,' she says with foreboding.

Esme frowns. 'He seems more and more resentful of my work. He seems to feel that I only have a certain amount of love and energy to give, and that my sculpture

87

takes all of it. He doesn't understand that the deeper I become involved in my work, the greater my capacity for other things.'

Harriet nods again, but feels uncomfortable. She has heard all this from Richard, at lunch not long ago in Penzance, and then more recently, a week ago as a matter of fact, when Richard stalked out of his house after his lunchtime row with Esme. It was Saturday afternoon, and Harriet was working on a clay maquette for one of her sculptures, in the small spare bedroom which she uses as a studio.

'Fancy a walk?' he said.

Harriet dropped her tools without a moment's hesitation and said, encouragingly, 'I'd love one,' and Richard knew then that he wanted this woman.

They left Harriet's terraced house behind the centre of town and walked along towards Carbis Bay, up the hill on the narrow tarmacked road, the sea always beside them, a deep blue-green today, and still. They got as far as the old pilchard lookout, a stone shelter built on the hill, open towards the sea, where all the townspeople used to sit waiting to spot the shoals of pilchards that used to swim into the bay. Sitting on one of the wooden benches they relaxed and enjoyed the view.

'What a perfect day!' Harriet exclaimed. Richard thought how exotic she looked, in loose crimson trousers and a padded silk jacket of the same colour. He could not help comparing her to Esme, with her sensible dark trousers or skirts, her neat tasteful jumpers and blouses, her unmemorable hairstyle. This was unfair, he knew, for when Esme dressed up, made an effort, she could look stunning, far outshining Harriet, he had to admit. Unfortunately this made him angrier, for it seemed the only times Esme made an effort these days was for an opening, an exhibition. Again, this was not strictly true either, but Richard was in no mood to be impartial.

Harriet leaned back against the stone wall of the lookout and closed her eyes, giving Richard a chance to admire her. 'Beautiful day,' she murmured again. Her normally pale face had a bit of colour all over, instead of the two rosy patches of blusher she usually wore, and her black hair looked soft and newly washed, the fringe angled appealingly over her spidery black lashes.

'Yes, it's lovely,' Richard said, and Harriet opened her eyes to see that it was her he was admiring and not the view.

She knew then that she was falling in love with him. She hadn't been in love since her affair with Bernard, and that had ended disastrously a few months ago. She had thought she would never love again, and she had said this over and over again to Esme as she cried all over her kitchen table, and sometimes to Richard if Esme wasn't available.

As they walked back down the hill Harriet felt odd and floaty, sure indications that she was in love. Richard was still looking at her in a way that precluded despair, even though he was married to someone Harriet considered one of her dearest friends. But the incipient guilt she might have felt over Esme retreated weakly in the face of her euphoria. Harriet genuinely liked Esme, but told herself that if everyone was sensible about this, Richard's wife would not be hurt. Harriet had no wish to cause Esme pain, but how could she say no to love, to that delicious madness that energized her, made her forget the difficulties of her work, made her soar and sing, made life meaningful again. She couldn't, just couldn't live without it. It was a pity love had come to her with Richard instead of someone a trifle more available, but to refuse it would be tempting the gods; it might never be offered again.

Richard, as if mind-reading, began to talk about Esme. This made Harriet wary at first, until she realized he was complaining about her, speaking the words non-chalantly but obviously troubled.

'I had hoped she would take some time off from her work to come out today, but no chance. It's a pity, the break would have done her good. And she doesn't seem to realize that I need to relax too. It's one thing having a career, an interest, it's another to become so obsessive about it that you ignore everything else, even your family.'

Harriet listened sympathetically, trying to crowd out of her mind the knowledge that this was not strictly true. She had talked and empathized and agreed with Esme often enough in the past, but now she was shifting sides, edging over to Richard, hardening her heart against Esme. She did not see this as treachery, merely advantageous. You could not side against a man you were falling in love with. Besides, maybe Richard had a point; listening to his side of the story put a different perspective on things.

When they reached Harriet's house she was about to invite him in when a loud voice said, 'Ah, Harriet, I was just looking for you. You asked me to pop by sometime and see what you're doing. Here I am!'

It was Jordan Culpepper, big and breezy and out-doorsy in a sailor's hat, striped Breton jersey, and a scarf tied around his neck, as if he were about to inhabit one of his miniature paintings of the beach and harbour and fishing boats. Harriet swore under her breath. She didn't mind Jordan; he was good for a gossip and a laugh. She knew he fancied her in a half-hearted manner, but kept him at a safe distance because, as she had said to Esme many times, she just wasn't into married men. In the past she had prided herself on the fact that the men she slept with were either single, divorced, widowed or separated, and she had nothing but scorn for women who did otherwise.

Richard, who vaguely knew Jordan but didn't much like him, had left at once, and Harriet has not seen him since. She was hoping he would drop in during the week, but there was no sign of him. Returning the book today was a ploy to see him, though she told herself she was happy to see Esme. Harriet believes wholeheartedly in friendship between women; she has talked often of the network of support women give each other. Sometimes she thinks it a pity that men are so likeable, so easy to fall in love with, so accessible. She wishes she didn't need them quite so much.

Esme is talking now, and Harriet plays with the remains of her lunch while she listens. Outside the sky looks black and unsettled, the sea cold, dark-grey, forbidding. 'Take last week,' Esme is saying. 'I was going to suggest that Richard and I go for a walk for an hour, after lunch. I do take breaks, despite what Richard says – I'd seize up if I didn't, and my back hurts like hell after too many hours hammering and chiselling and sanding. But he just stomped out of the house in a temper.' She doesn't mention the cheese or the lettuce thrown at her feet. Richard hadn't mentioned it to Harriet either: there are certain things one is too embarrassed to tell friends or potential lovers.

'I'm glad you were at home and went for a walk with him,' Esme continued. 'He said it was very pleasant. I was worried that he'd be out on his own, brooding all afternoon.'

This slightly annoys Harriet. The fact that Esme is glad that Richard sought out her company and does not feel in the least threatened by it, makes her feel insignificant, unattractive. She realizes that this is rubbish, that she should be pleased that Esme trusts both her and Richard, but something has shifted, altered in her relationship with Esme. For the first time she sees her as competition in something other than the art world.

'Anyway, at least this crisis is over,' Esme is saying now, sipping the coffee that the waitress has just brought. 'I feel so absolutely drained after finishing this piece; it's so different from what I've done in the past – far bigger, too. I won't be starting anything else just yet. Richard will be pleased anyway; I'll be able to give him more time.'

Harriet, pouring milk into her coffee, says, 'Isn't this just the time to start something else, when you're in the midst of such a productive creative phase?'

Esme looks rueful, troubled. 'You're probably right, but there's too high a price to pay sometimes. I've had to learn to juggle my energy. I do love Richard and my family, despite what Richard thinks.'

Harriet suddenly takes the bill, makes a move to leave. 'We'd better go,' she says abruptly. 'I want to get home before it begins to storm.'

Outside the clouds are black, ominous. It is colder, windier, and though it is only just after two, the afternoon is dark. 'Thanks so much for lunch,' Esme says, embracing Harriet. 'And thanks for sharing the completion of my latest effort.'

'Don't thank me,' Harriet mutters, breaking from the embrace and walking away. 'For God's sake, don't ever thank me.'

Esme, waving goodbye, does not hear her last words. She walks home feeling not quite as bereft as she did this morning. She will cook Richard and Hugo their favourite pasta dish for dinner tonight, and later she and Richard can curl up together in front of the television, something they haven't done for a long time.

The rain hits her before she gets home, but she doesn't even notice. She can't wait to see her sculpture again, see if it really is as good as it seemed when she finished. She looks forward to Richard's return, hopes that now the work is done, he will share the joy of it with her.

Harriet also gets soaked before she reaches her own house. Walking into the empty living-room, she takes off her coat, throws it on the sofa, and swears softly. The only thing that cheers her up is that tomorrow is Monday. She sits down at her desk and writes a note to Richard, asking him to meet her for lunch at the Swordfish in Penzance, if he is free. She will go into work early and drop the note at his school well before the dinner break.

Feeling better, Harriet goes to her studio and begins to work. The soft lead she is using on her latest construction is malleable and satisfying. She is making one of her animal shapes, distorted and grotesque, powerful and sinister, resembling neither man nor any known beast, but containing elements of both. She feels high, charged with energy, on a creative roll now. Love has done this for her she is sure.

The hours go by and still she is working. Only Monday lunchtime will stop her, but then she'll be on another, more heady roll. It's time my life changed, she thinks as the construction takes shape in her hands. It's time for something new, something lasting, something strong and permanent. It's time I take the separate pieces of my life and work them into shape, as I am doing with this metal.

The sculpture grows, dark and unsettling, all jarring shapes, warring angles, the animal figure emerging with two heads, three legs. It is the eeriest thing Harriet has ever done, but she's pleased with it. When she finally collapses into bed in the early hours of Monday morning, she knows without a shadow of a doubt that she will be seeing Richard in a few hours.

Chapter Five

Oona, in her black painter's smock, a scarf holding the fractious white hair away from her wrinkled forehead, looks out the window of her Porthmeor studio and sees the surfers out in droves today, making up for the past few days when the waves crashed dangerously on the beach and the sea was too rough for anyone to go near it.

Oona quite likes to watch the surfers. She sees them as great black sea-birds, or a cross between a fish and a seal. She imagines that riding a wave would be like dying, soaring down a great unending roll, out of the body and one with the wind and the sea and the elements. Oona thinks about dying quite often, but not with any particular melancholy. She believes that anyone her age who *doesn't* contemplate the subject is a fool who will be caught short when the time comes. Oona believes in being prepared for every eventuality.

She allows herself one more look at the surfers before going on with her painting. She recognizes Hugo, Crispin's brother, though she is too far away to see his face clearly. But there's no mistaking the style, the grace. She watches him catch a fine wave, standing up on his board for what seems to be for ever. She is painting Hugo now, though not in any recognizable manner. He is a swirl of black on her canvas, surrounded by splashes of blues and greens, crests of frothy whites and greys.

Out of the water now, Hugo waves. He seems to intuit when Oona is watching him, for he can't see that closely into her studio from the beach. Hugo has known Oona for years, has been doing odd jobs for her since he was fourteen or fifteen. He thinks she's slightly mad, but he's fond of her, is quick to defend her when his surfing mates make derogatory comments. He can't blame them – Oona does look crazy sometimes, wandering on the beach seeking inspiration, long white hair flying, black trousers wet from the sea, for she is usually too oblivious to jump away from the more ambitious waves as she ambles along the water's edge. But Hugo thinks she's quite sound. She listens when he talks about surfing, which he doesn't to anyone else, not even Cara, his burgundy-haired girlfriend. Oona listens and seems to understand, and though Hugo doesn't like abstract painting much, there is one of hers in the Tate that he loves, for it looks just how it seems to him when he falls into the sea in the middle of a wave, all dark and deep-green and churning and crazy.

Oona goes back to her painting, works for another few hours, then locks up and heads back to her house in the Warren which overlooks the harbour and the bay and the sea beyond. Unlike Percy Prynne, who walks into loneliness and desolation every time he enters his house, Oona is welcomed by all the things she loves: the well-chosen paintings hanging on her walls, many gifts from friends whose other paintings hang in galleries all over the world; the window- seat with its velvet cushions where she sits for hours at night, looking out at the lights on the pier, the flicker of Godrevy lighthouse in the distance; the piano in the corner which her mother owned and on which she sometimes plays.

Oona, contented, turns on lights, switches on the

central heating. She is entirely self-contained and self-sufficient, and realizes how lucky she is to be able to be so. Sitting down in the window-seat, she rests for a bit after the short walk home, knowing there is plenty of time before she has to prepare her simple solitary meal.

And even if there isn't, she thinks calmly, even if there is no time at all, that is all right too. If she can't die riding the surf then right here would do fine, she sometimes thinks.

The green beacon of the lighthouse at the end of Smeaton's Pier catches her eye, and she sits for a long time, staring at the lights and at the darkening sky.

Crispin, just a street down from Oona, is also looking out at the lights on the sea. He set out his nets earlier and is about to take a shower and meet Molly at their favourite Italian restaurant for dinner. He likes this time of evening, the twilight time when the harbour lights start to go on but it is still light enough to make out the sea, the boats, the jumble of houses cluttered around the harbour in a random haphazard manner.

The shrill of the doorbell makes him jump; he is not expecting anyone. Going downstairs and opening the front door, he is surprised to find Percy Prynne standing there. 'Are you all right?' Crispin asks, for the old man seems pale, dithery.

''Es, my boy, I'm right as rain.' Percy stands there, but makes no move to do or say anything else.

'Come on upstairs,' Crispin says patiently, though it's getting late and Molly will be waiting if he doesn't hurry.

The two men go up the steep wooden stairs to Crispin's large main room with the beams and the wall of windows facing the sea. There, in a prominent place on the wall opposite, is Alice's portrait *The Sea Captain*. Crispin, as he had promised himself he would, had gone back to the Sandpiper gallery to buy it the next day, surprising Lance Giddens by not even raising his eyebrows at the price.

Percy, also going back to the gallery the next day, was befuddled not to see his portrait in the window. He was too shy and taciturn to go inside; instead he wandered over to the fishermen's lodge and sat there for a long time, feeling lost and bereft. He had lost Percy Prynne once years ago, when age and illness had forced him to retire; now he had lost himself a second time. Sitting in the lodge he thought he heard Maggie singing again, but this time it was only the wind whistling around the small shelter.

A day or so later, at lunch in the Union, Crispin told Percy he had a surprise for him, and took him to his house where he showed the old man the portrait. Percy didn't seem at all surprised, merely nodded and said, ''Tis a fitting place for me. Looking out towards sea.'

Since then Percy has come twice to look at the portrait. This time he does exactly the same as he has done on other occasions: he looks hard at the painting, as if it could speak to him, tell him something; then he turns abruptly and walks downstairs, out of the house. The first time Percy did this Crispin ran after him, invited him to stay for a cup of tea, but something in the old man's eyes, some lost vision, something important but elusive, stopped him. Now he just lets Percy look, then lets him go without a word.

When Crispin is alone again he strips off his clothes and gets into the shower. When he comes out his brother Hugo is there, sitting on the platform bed looking over the sea.

'How did you get in?' Crispin asks good-naturedly.

'You left the door open.'

Crispin dries himself vigorously, throws the towel on top of Hugo's head, and the two of them wrestle playfully for a few moments. 'That's enough, you idiot, let me get my clothes on,' Crispin says finally. 'I've got a date with Molly in a minute.'

'Where're you off to?' Hugo asks.

'To the Italian place, for a meal. Didn't you know this is Valentine's Day, you little toad?'

Hugo looks sheepish. 'Actually, I do, as a matter of fact. That's why I'm here.'

Crispin is pulling on clean jeans, a warm brushed cotton shirt. 'I'm your Valentine, right? C'mon, Hugo, out with it. What do you want?'

Hugo looks appealingly at Crispin. 'I thought, see, that maybe I could use your place, bring Cara here, since you'll be out. I got some wine; I thought I could cook her a meal. I've even got the prawns, bought them this afternoon at Stevens the fishmonger. Cara loves prawns; I thought I could do her some in a special cream sauce.'

Crispin smiles, making sure his back is turned so that Hugo cannot see. This is indeed love; what else could it be with prawns from Stevens and a special cream sauce? 'Why here?' he says.

'Where else?' Hugo says eagerly. 'The folks are home, so are Cara's. It's too bloody cold to sit on the beach and have a barbecue, you know. We get no privacy, not like you and Molly with a house each you can go to.'

Crispin understands. He is many years older than Hugo, but he has not forgotten what nineteen is like. 'OK, you can come here. I'm staying the night with Molly, so lock up and lights out when you go. I don't need to lecture you about condoms, contraceptives, Aids, pregnancy, and so on, do I?'

'Sod off, Crispin. And thanks, man.'

'I'm off, now. Here's the key, drop it in the letter-box when you leave. I'll use Molly's to get back in.'

Hugo is running down the stairs, long blond hair flopping, graceful even in his haste and excitement. 'Just

98

be careful, you hear?' Crispin shouts after him, knowing he sounds exactly like Richard or Esme.

Hugo pays no attention. Like a man who has just glimpsed heaven, he soars like an angel to collect Cara.

Alice Culpepper is surreptitiously painting again, a nude figure in oils. She has no model – Jordan would be livid if she spent money on one, and anyway, where would they work? – so she stands naked herself for hours in front of the mirror, drawing herself in charcoal first, then transferring it in oils onto canvas. She works in the laundry-room, the hum of the washing-machine and tumble-drier the piped music in the background, for there is no other place. Jordan's studio is sacrosanct; no-one is allowed in it (except for Molly's yoga class); and Alice has no studio of her own, as in the past few years she has worked mostly on location, sketching the tourists on the beach or pier or harbour.

Jordan, though he tried to hide it, was livid over *The Sea Captain*. For one, he was furious that his wife never showed him the portrait, not years ago when she painted it, nor the day she got it out and finished it. More importantly he was miffed because it made far more money than his miniatures. Jordan judges art by the amount of money it brings in, which is the reason he has encouraged Alice to do her pastel sketches all these years. Art should sell, should get real, enter the commercial world, Jordan feels. That he was wrong about Alice, and that her large unwieldy oil should fetch such a high price, annoys him like hell. When Alice said, quite reasonably, that if money were the object, Jordan should be encouraging her oils, he muttered that *The Sea Captain* was a one off. It sold purely for sentimental reasons and had nothing to do with either art or commerce.

'You'd be a fool to give up your sketches, and turn to

oil portraits, darling,' Jordan had wheedled, trying another tack. 'I thought we could raise the price this year considerably. The visitors will buy them regardless, they're so good. That's real art, you know; creating something that people want enough to pay hard cash to own. Anything else is bullshit, pretentious crap, and don't let Molly or Lance or any of those other so-called artists who sell either nothing, or very little, tell you different.'

Alice had not argued. She had heard it all anyway, and she wanted Jordan out of the house. Convinced that Alice had paid attention to his words, he had rewarded her with a brief kiss on the lips and said he was going out. Alice knew that he was probably going over to see Harriet, to try and worm his way into her bed, but she was too tired to care much. She knew Jordan didn't even like the woman particularly, but merely needed diversion. Harriet, single, unattached at the moment, constantly craving male company, filled this need perfectly. Jordan had decided, early in their marriage, that he and Alice would have what was euphemistically called an open marriage. Alice assumed that this meant one could have sex with whom one pleased, as long as one didn't do anything as daft as falling in love. Unfortunately, by the time Jordan had announced this, Alice had already had two babies a year apart, was running the guest-house, and trying to earn extra money by sketching the odd visitor. She was far too shattered at the end of the day to even contemplate extra-marital sex, let alone do it: it was hard enough to keep awake with Jordan. Besides, she didn't like the idea much. She told Jordan this, but he went on at great length about spontaneity and creativity and a host of apparently unrelated things, until finally Alice fell asleep in the armchair. They have not discussed the matter since, and Alice, by now, neither knows nor cares what Jordan is up to when he is not in the house. At least he is discreet, which she supposes counts for something. And he works hard at his miniatures, is generous with the money they make. The children adore him as well. Alice supposes that all in all, her marriage is as good as most.

So Alice listened, and said nothing. But she had surreptitiously replaced some of her dried-out oils, and spent money on a new canvas. Now in the cramped laundry-room Alice works, sometimes breaking off in her contemplation of her nude shivering body to throw a load of clothes into the washing-machine, or run to the kitchen to peel vegetables for dinner, not even bothering to throw a robe over her goose bumps. Alice is used to being naked, having posed for life drawings for years in art school, finding the money handy. Clothed, she walks, talks, laughs, smiles, primly; naked, her body loosens, becomes itself, natural.

Luckily there are no guests this month – the winter visitors have their pick of bed and breakfasts, and usually take the ones nearer to the beach or harbour – but after Easter the three rooms in the guest-house will be full much of the time. Alice will have no chance to paint then; by the time she has served breakfast, seen the kids off to school, washed all the sheets and cleaned the rooms, the day will almost be gone. She must work now and quickly.

Alice stands in front of the mirror she has set up in the laundry-room, her teeth chattering, her naked flesh icy to the touch. She stares at her small puckered nipples, needing some detail for her painting, but the room is unheated, and so cold that her lips are trembling. 'Shit,' she says as the doorbell rings. Jordan is out sketching on the harbour, not that he would answer the door if he was in. His attic studio is too far away, and besides, he refuses to be disturbed.

Alice only just remembers to put on her ancient gold

silk dressing-gown, the one she bought second-hand at an antique market stall in her student days, before going to the door.

'Sorry, Alice, did I get you out of the bath?' Lance Giddens, owner of the Sandpiper gallery, looks apologetic, but does not hesitate to come inside.

'You must be joking. I can't remember when I last had a long soak, especially in the daytime. I just about have time for a quick shower every morning before anyone else gets up, and that's it.'

Lance looks at her sympathetically. The dark circles under her eyes are prominent today and her whole demeanour conveys weariness. 'I wondered if you have any more work on the go. The portrait of Percy Prynne was good, Alice, very good. I'd like more for the gallery.'

Alice feels flushed, suddenly warm despite the cold in the house. She takes Lance into the laundry-room and shows him her latest work. 'It's a self-portrait. Not finished yet, but nearly, I hope.' Unself-consciously, forgetting about Lance, she slips off her dressing-gown and stands posed in front of the mirror, looking at her body with detachment as she studies the painting.

Lance, oblivious to Alice, stands very still and lets that old familiar tingling, more elusive these days, course through his body; that prickly sensation that tells him he is looking at something good. Not commercial good, like Jordan's watercolours, but something else, something that conveys with colour and form and texture the magic and mystery of life. This is what he tries to do in his own paintings, but standing here, looking at Alice's, he's not sure he achieves it. It doesn't even matter right now; what matters, he thinks, is that *someone* does.

They are standing like this, Alice naked in front of Lance, both of them looking at the painting, when Jordan walks in. 'What the fuck is going on here?' he says.

Neither Lance nor Alice are nonplussed, which annoys Jordan. Lance says calmly, 'Alice was showing me her self-portrait.'

Alice is putting on her dressing-gown as Jordan grabs her shoulder and turns her towards him. 'Showing him yourself as well, eh? Becoming an exhibitionist, are you? What are you doing? Trying to sell yourself to him?' He turns to Lance. 'And you eyeing my wife like some kind of voyeur. What the fuck is going on?' he repeats.

Lance sighs, inaudibly. They are, all three, artists; the nude body is as familiar to them as the sea, as natural as the sky. Lance did not feel at all surprised when Alice slipped off her silk robe and stood in front of her painting; she was still in the grip of it, comparing, noting, making mental adjustments. He had looked at her body as he would a model's, which indeed was all it was at that moment.

Jordan knows this, but Jordan is irritated. First Lance Giddens and his wife collude on *The Sea Captain* behind his back, now here the man is again, looking at yet another one of his wife's paintings that he himself knew nothing about. Though Lance buys and sells Jordan's own work, the man has never come to the house looking for more, nor has he ever encouraged Jordan. Now here he is, deliberately steering his wife away from her lucrative pastel drawings, urging her to spend all her free time on something which may not bring in a penny. The nerve of the man outrages him.

Jordan knows it would look churlish to complain of his wife's new oil painting – which he realizes, to his annoyance, is quite good – so he lets his temper loose with a display of sexual jealousy. It occurs to him, somewhat guiltily, that this is rather hypocritical, but it doesn't stop his tirade.

'What are you up to, Lance?' he snarls. 'What am I to

think, coming in here and seeing my wife standing naked with another man?'

'Give over, Jordan,' Lance says wearily. 'As Alice said, we were looking at her self-portrait.' He turns to Alice, who is standing quietly by the washing-machine. 'I'd like it when you're finished. I'd also like to have an exhibition of your stuff when you have more, downstairs in the gallery.'

Jordan is torn between greed and rage. Lance rarely lets an artist have his whole downstairs room for a single exhibition; Esme was the last one, a couple of years ago, and it turned out to be enormously lucrative. Yet Jordan has always told Alice her oils are not commercial; if they sell well, he'll be made to look a fool. Rage wins; Jordan hates being in the wrong. 'There won't be an exhibition for years,' he says viciously. 'Alice hasn't time to churn out paintings like pasties.'

This is so unhelpful that both Lance and Alice stare at him, speechless. You nasty pathetic bastard, you sad man, Lance would like to say, but he manages to restrain himself. 'I'm off,' he says instead. 'See you, Alice. Stop in at the gallery sometime and we'll have a chat about the exhibition.'

He leaves the house, and Alice runs upstairs to put on jeans and a jumper. Before Jordan can follow her the doorbell rings. 'Yes, can I help?' he asks ungraciously.

The young man standing there is taken aback. 'I was looking for a bed and breakfast,' he says. 'You have a vacancy sign . . .'

Jordan becomes both businesslike and unctuous. 'Yes, yes, of course, would you like to see the rooms? There is one with a sea view . . .' The man picks up his rucksack and follows Jordan inside.

Upstairs, Alice glows. Whatever scene Jordan is about to make (and he has a nerve anyway, with all his open bloody marriage ideas), it is all worth it. Her paintings are *good*. She is on her way.

'Lizzie, can you not flop so? Yoga movements are supposed to be controlled. You terrify the life out of me when you just collapse out of a posture.'

Lizzie giggles. 'Do you think I'd be better at aerobic classes? I tried one once, but I got that whacked I couldn't do a thing the next day.'

Molly smiles. 'You're fine, Lizzie. Just try a bit of control, OK?'

She looks over her class fondly. There are twelve of them, including Lizzie and Oona and Jordan. She rather likes her part-time jobs – the café work in summer, the supply teaching when it comes up, the yoga – though her grandmother is always telling her they interfere with her real work. Painting is solitary, often lonely; Molly likes the contact she gets through her classes with other people. Oona has several times offered her money to help support her while she paints, but Molly has always refused. She feels lucky enough to be getting her house rent-free from her parents; she doesn't want to accept anything else.

Jordan is raising himself up on his forearms in the Cobra posture, eyes closed, movements controlled, breathing rhythmically. Molly wonders why she prefers watching Lizzie, whose plump body in the lurid pink track suit is sweating with exertion and whose fair curly hair falls haphazardly over her eyes. As she watches, Lizzie groans, then collapses in a heap on her belly. 'Phew, that's a toughie, Moll,' she gasps.

Oona has already come down from the posture and is relaxing quietly on the floor. One by one the students relax, all except Jordan who is still extended, back curved, head up, deep into the posture. Molly

105

suppresses the desire to shout, to scare him out of his wits so that he collapses like Lizzie. She really wonders sometimes if she should be a yoga teacher.

Jordan is hoping that the yoga class tonight will calm him down after the scene at noontime with Lance Giddens and Alice. Jordan is still furiously angry, not because the man saw his wife naked, but because he has seen her painting and pronounced it good. Lance has never commented on Jordan's paintings. He has bought and sold them, but never once has he said they were good. Jordan reminds himself that what matters is the fact that his paintings are the bestselling items in Lance's gallery, but for once this does not console him. Uncomfortably, he remembers more original work he has done, remembers the promise of his younger years when he was willing to attempt failure in order to create something new, exciting; those heady days before the lure of financial success led him to concentrate solely on his miniature seascapes.

Finding these thoughts distracting him from his yoga, Jordan tries to concentrate on his breathing while arching his back supinely. 'Whoops, sorry!' Lizzie, attempting the Cobra again, falls over and knocks Jordan out of his reverie. Damn silly girl, he thinks with annoyance as Lizzie tries to disentangle herself. Her full breasts under her sweatshirt brush against his back where she has fallen against him, and then press down hard as she slips while trying to get up. The sensation is not unpleasant, and Jordan looks at her more benignly as she again says, 'Sorry.'

'That's all right,' he says magnanimously, making her blush. She has always been nervous with Jordan, painters do that to her sometimes; they seem so out of this world, on a different planet, always looking and drawing and, she has to admit, sometimes posing. She doesn't think Jordan is a poser; his paintings at least *look*

106

like something, instead of great blotches of paint or meaningless scribbles.

Jordan eyes her appreciatively as she rolls over onto her own blanket. He likes her roundness, her fleshiness. He preferred Alice when she was pregnant; she is far too small and slim for him now. When she was pregnant he wallowed in her great heavy breasts with the protruding veins, the swollen nipples; he buried himself in her fat belly and buttocks. It's time Alice was pregnant again, he thinks as he looks at Lizzie's corpulent pink-clad buttocks. Three children are such an odd number; they may as well make it four. Not only would his Alice be chubby and chunky again, like the models in the Renaissance paintings he adores, but she'd also be far too busy to paint those huge oils that Lance Giddens seems so interested in. It's not as if he wants to stop her from painting, he tells himself. He is an enlightened man, a painter himself; he knows a creative woman like Alice needs fulfilment outside the family. That is why he encourages her drawings of the holiday-makers.

Lizzie, on her tartan blanket, catches him looking at her and smiles tentatively. Her round face is pink and damp, her lips full and moist. She looks like a Rubens maiden, or a Botticelli Venus. He wishes she were naked, so that he could see her voluptuous beefy body.

Closing his eyes, Jordan starts to meditate. Instead of the candle he usually tries to envisage, he sees Lizzie's mountainous nipples, red-tinged like a flame, taking him flying into a state of nirvana.

The first week in March is foggy. The mist rolls over the sea and headland, filling in the crevices of the cliff and the vast spaces of the horizon, so that everything is enclosed, intimate. Crispin puts out his tangle nets to catch ray, lobster, crab, monkfish, plaice. He goes away

107

from the bay now, steaming out two, two and a half hours to get ten or eleven miles out to sea.

One gentle misty morning Crispin is bringing in a catch of plaice. Both Percy Prynne and Sid Hocking are on the pier watching through the mist. 'S'truth, ain't much of a catch, Crispin, my lover,' Sid exclaims. 'I seen better at a bankrupt fishmongers.'

'No, not very good,' Crispin agrees, loading up his van with the blue plastic bins containing the meagre catch. 'It's hardly worth the trip to Newlyn.'

Newlyn, around ten miles away, near Penzance, is the nearest fish market for the St Ives fishermen. Crispin and the others have to bring the catch there themselves, because the town no longer has a fish market of its own.

The *Girl Lizzie* is moored alongside the *Fair Celt*. 'Bloody waste of time even going out,' Tom says as he climbs the stone steps to the pier. Tom and Crispin load up their vans, helped by Crispin's boy, Pete. The two boats came in just in time, for the tide has ebbed now and both the *Fair Celt* and the *Girl Lizzie* are berthed in sand, tilting like the locals coming out of the Sloop Inn on the Wharf on a Saturday night. The fog creeps around them, shrouds them like a cloth of grey gauze. On the pier Percy Prynne shivers, feeling hollow, evanescent like the mist swirling about the light-house at the end of the pier, one minute covering it completely, the next blowing tantalizingly out to sea. Percy is like the fog, sometimes there, sometimes not. He loses himself like a boat lost in the mist, like Godrevy lighthouse out beyond the bay, now lost to the low hanging clouds.

'Right then, Lizzie, my maid?' Sid shouts to Tom's wife who is climbing down the steps of the pier, her baby strapped in a pouch in front of her. 'That's a lusty looking babe, my handsome. The spitting image of his dad.'

'Bloody good job too,' Tom grins, following Lizzie down the steps and across the wet sand to his boat, where he starts to sort out his nets. Lizzie has brought him a flask of tea and a slice of saffron cake. Perched on the bench at the back of the boat, she undoes her yellow cardigan, pulls up her bra, and begins nursing the baby.

'S'truth, I wouldn't half like to be that infant,' Sid mutters to Percy, chuckling to himself. 'That maid's got tits like a jellyfish.'

Someone else feels that way too, though he would pride himself on not putting it quite so coarsely. Jordan Culpepper, dressed in a navy-blue mock seaman's jacket with a jaunty red and white striped silk scarf around his neck, is sitting on a bench on the Wharf right opposite the *Fair Lizzie*, sketching. He began by drawing the boats in the mist, but he became distracted when Lizzie began nursing her baby. It reminded him excitedly of a Tintoretto painting he had seen in The National Gallery, called *The Origin of the Milky Way*, where the god Jupiter holds the infant Hercules to the breast of a gloriously fleshy naked woman. Lizzie could be that paunchy, pot-bellied, magnificent woman, Jordan thinks, and he could be Tintoretto, painting her in all her meaty splendour. He's not done life drawings since art college; perhaps he should hire a model, go back to it now.

Lizzie sees him and waves tentatively. Jordan waves back enthusiastically. He puts his sketch pad away and decides to walk down into the harbour, maybe sketch some of the boats at closer range. He curses himself for not wearing boots as he hops over pools of sea water left over from the outgoing tide, ending up with a wet shoe and a bad temper. The mist has thickened, and the harbour seems still and eerie. A weak sun can barely be discerned through the fog and the boats look like lost ghosts, the brightly coloured flags of the buoys like forgotten banners from a long-ago war.

'Hello there,' Jordan calls up to Lizzie when he reaches the *Girl Lizzie*.

Lizzie, embarrassed, tries to cover her exposed breast by pulling her cardigan around her. The baby is still suckling; when she tries to move him, he howls like a banshee. Hastily she clamps him back on and says, 'Hello,' to Jordan, not knowing where to look.

Jordan knows where to look, and does so, much to Lizzie's consternation. Tom luckily does not see all this, for after giving Jordan a cursory glance, he has dismissed him as a poser and is busy bending over his nets.

'Well,' Jordan says, at a loss for words, which is most unlike him.

'See you at yoga,' Lizzie says, flustered. She wishes he'd stop staring at her like that.

'Blimey, if that's the sort that go to yoga, you must want your head read,' Tom snorts as Jordan ambles away.

Lizzie says nothing. She wouldn't give up her yoga for anything, she thinks with determination. After all, she's lost three and a half pounds since she started.

Over on the pier Sid Hocking sighs with disappointment as Lizzie does up her bra, buttons her cardigan, and hoists her sleeping baby over her shoulder. He decides he'll go home to his wife, maybe have a cuddle or two before lunch if she's in the mood.

Chuckling softly to himself, he slaps Percy on the shoulders as he bids him goodbye, and heads home to his wife.

Eventually, when Tom finishes straightening out his nets, he and Lizzie go home too. They live in a cramped flat above a raucous pub overlooking the town. The two rooms are furnished with hand-me-downs from their respective parents, and cheap bargains from local junk-shops. Lizzie has tried to tart up the place, as she puts it, by hanging framed pictures of cuddly puppies and winsome kittens found in charity shops. No pets are allowed in the flat, so Lizzie makes do with animal knick-knacks, which sit on every available surface. Tom has promised to make shelves eventually, high up, so that when the baby is toddling, the glazed dogs and cats, the perky hedgehogs and smiling cows with ribbons around their necks won't be broken.

Tom switches on the telly, which is overlarge and unreliable, but at this moment in working order. Lizzie hands him the baby while she goes into the minuscule kitchen to heat up some frozen chips to eat with the warm pasties they bought on the way home. Mindful of her diet, Lizzie limits herself to ten chips which she counts diligently, making sure she chooses the largest ones.

Tom doesn't look at the telly, which is tuned in to some kind of talk show, but makes cheerful idiotic faces at his son, Michael, who squeals and grins in un-abandoned delight. Lizzie, bringing in the plates of pasties and chips, watches Tom bouncing her strapping lad and is filled with contentment. She loves her little home, the first one of her own. She's enjoyed fixing it up, like the doll's house her mum was never able to afford when she was young. She takes pride in Tom's comments as he admires her latest acquisitions, bargains found in market stalls, jumble sales, along with the second-hand toys, plastic bricks, stuffed teddies and rattles for Michael.

Pushing some of these toys away, Lizzie clears a space for herself on the stained beige sofa and sits down next to her two men. Tom eats with one hand, the plate on a rickety varnished coffee-table, and keeps bouncing the baby, so that Lizzie can eat in peace.

'Hm, tasty. Bloody good pasty, that. Best in town.'

Tom looks at her affectionately, pats her knee, gives Michael an extra hard bounce which makes him gurgle excitedly, a big smile showing his healthy gums. Lizzie feels so happy she polishes off Tom's left-over chips along with her own.

Percy Prynne does not go home. He watches everyone else wander off for lunch or to the pub, mutters good-bye to Lizzie and Tom as they wave and go off to their own place. Percy stands on the pier for a long time, motionless as the lighthouse. The mist is wet and damp now, and he is soaked through. Crispin, were he here, would have taken the old man to the Union for a pint, but Crispin is in Newlyn selling his fish.

After a time Percy leaves the pier and wanders around the narrow cobbled streets, finally heading towards Porthgwidden Beach and then cutting up Teetotal Street and around the corner to the Island, which isn't an island at all now, but used to be in some long-forgotten past before recorded history began. What is still referred to as the Island is now the headland, a grassy hillock leading to the old stone church – St Nicholas' chapel – standing on the cliffs overlooking rocks and sea.

The Island is empty today; the fog has changed from a gentle mist to a cold bitter dampness that permeates the lungs and makes Percy cough. As he trudges slowly up the hill, limping badly, he remembers other days when he was young, when the headland was covered in white – not foam or sand from the sea, but the white of Monday's washing, strewn over the grassy slopes and pegged down with large stones. Everyone in Downlong was allotted a bit of the Island for their washing, and it looked, on those Mondays, as if white summer clouds had descended and settled on the grass. It was not only the Island that was covered in drying laundry, all the streets in Downlong were too. Washing-lines were

112

thrown across the cobbled roads from house to house, and on a fine Monday you couldn't walk down the street because of all the sheets and clothes hanging on the lines.

Percy walks, reminisces. He remembers the games of football he used to play with his brothers at the base of the headland, in the meadow, now a car park. When he reaches the top of the Island he meanders slowly down around the coastal path, stopping at a wooden bench overlooking the rocks and sea. After a while figures begin to appear to him in the mist, old wrecks of ships torn upon the rocks, sailors and fishermen swept off their boats and into the water, and he hears voices calling, crying, begging him to join them. His brother's voice is the loudest, the most plaintive, and the lines and hollows in Percy's cheeks fill with salty tears as he listens to his brother's lament.

After a time, Percy stiffly gets up and wanders around the grassy slope, painfully climbing to the stone chapel at the top of the incline. There is a bench outside the ancient church and here he sits, scanning the misty horizon before him with an expectant frown. Percy is looking for the light of a lantern, the one his father told him about when he was very young. The story went that there was a ship wrecked here, long long ago, with a young woman, a babe in her arms, standing on the deck as a storm raged around her. The St Ives lifeboat managed to get out to the sinking boat and a sailor tried to take the baby from its mother's arms to get it to safety, but the mother refused to let go. As mother and child were being helped onto the lifeboat, the woman passed out, the babe fell from her arms into the sea and drowned.

Later, the mother came to, but when she found her child had died, she died too, and was buried in the churchyard. She still roams the Island, though, looking for her baby, and at night many a person has seen her lantern. It doesn't bode well for those that do, though: it means death or disaster.

Percy looks around him, doesn't see anything. It's not time yet, though he saw the woman and her child. They were out in the harbour, on the *Girl Lizzie*; Percy saw them, the mother looking like a madonna suckling her babe. She's around now, Percy thinks. She can't be far away, but he doesn't see her lantern, not yet.

Percy sits and watches the fog for a long time, looking for the light, knowing it's just a matter of time before he sees it. When he finally makes his way home, he is wheezing so much he can hardly get his breath, but he doesn't seem to notice. Maggie is singing to him again; she started with the gulls over on the Island, and is with him now, humming like she used to when she was a young girl hanging the laundry out between the houses and on the headland.

Percy sings too. His voice is old and cracked like the cliff face, but he knows Maggie wants him to join her. Together they sing and for a moment Percy finds him again, the man in the portrait, the man he used to be, the man Maggie loved with all her heart.

Percy sings and sings. The fog curls around his house like an eel, but in his soul the sun shines and shines and shines.

The town is cloaked in mist for the next week or so. The surf is flat, and Hugo resorts to his second favourite pastime: making love to Cara wherever or whenever they can. They spend hours in Hugo's attic room, or borrow Crispin's house if possible. Cara, who is in her last year of the sixth form, has applied to various universities to study marine biology, and is nagging Hugo to come with her.

'We could share a flat; it would be such fun!' Cara

says for the hundredth or so time one night as they sit in the cinema, waiting for the film to begin. 'You can cook for me, be the house-husband, while I get my degree.'

'Oh great,' Hugo says.

'But what else are you going to do? You can't just hang around here surfing for the rest of your life.'

Hugo takes a handful of buttered popcorn and hands the container to Cara. 'Why not?' he asks. 'I work enough to earn a crust, keep me in beer and house music.'

'Aren't you ambitious?' Cara cries through a mouthful of popcorn. '*I* am.'

The lights dim and the film begins. 'I'd like to get out of my parents' house,' Hugo whispers. 'Get my own place, where you and I can be alone. There's an ambition for you.'

Cara sighs and slumps down in her seat. She adores Hugo, but can't cope with his life. She can't wait to leave Cornwall, get an education, a prestigious job, preferably in a decent-sized town or city. Her whole life has been organized to attain these goals.

She starts to brood, but Hugo's greasy hand encloses hers and she feels suddenly content, at least for the moment. Putting the empty popcorn container on the floor, she settles down with Hugo to watch the film.

Esme and Richard are also watching the movie, though sitting on the other side of the cinema from Hugo and Cara. They have been doing a number of things together for the past few weeks – having friends over for dinner, going on long weekend walks, going out for meals. It is all part of Esme's campaign to help Richard cope with her growing success in the art world.

Her sculpture, titled *Grace*, is going to feature at a major exhibition she is having at a prestigious art gallery in London. Knowing that as the time draws nearer she

115

will be exceedingly busy getting her sculptures together, deciding which ones she should exhibit, finishing the new one she has just begun, Esme wants very much to keep Richard from feeling abandoned.

Sometimes she resents having to do this, and then immediately feels guilty. But all her life she has, like many women, juggled a family and a career, always making sure that her family came first. Always, as she struggled with her work, she tried to make sure that her sons weren't neglected, that they knew they were loved and cherished. She had thought, at first, that such care would not be necessary with Richard, reasoning that, as he was an adult, he would be able to understand things better than the children. She found out before very long that she was wrong, that where her work was concerned, Richard was outside of reason. She has often despaired of this; she loves him and cannot understand why he will not let her love her work as well.

The film is banal and Esme cannot concentrate. In truth she would like to be at home, or rather in her studio, working on her new sculpture. She has just been awarded a sponsorship from a distinguished arts committee, and has used some of the money to buy a block of special marble for her next piece. She has also been commissioned to do a work for a new college building at a south-east university, and though there is time for this, the ideas are whirling in her head and she longs to get them onto stone.

Richard is also not concentrating on the film. He is thinking about Harriet, about the lunch he had with her a couple of weeks ago. It was not like their usual companionable lunches; Harriet, dressed in a short black skirt, a skimpy sleeveless white jumper, and a smart black jacket, seemed restless and nervy, smoking far too much and eating very little. The pub was crowded and conversation was difficult. Some tension seemed to be hovering in the air, some conflict that needed resolving.

At one point Richard remarked that she looked tired, and indeed she had hollows under her eyes which the mascara and long black fringe only seemed to emphasize. 'I was up all night working on a construction,' she said shortly. 'But it doesn't matter, it's not important. Let's not waste this lunch talking about it.'

And indeed it wasn't, not at that moment. What was important was Richard himself, sitting there facing her; his longish fair hair newly washed and falling softly on his face; his candid blue eyes, wrinkled at the corners, looking appraisingly at her through his tortoiseshell glasses. For Harriet was in love, of that there was no longer any doubt.

She had tried half-heartedly to exorcize it that day after her lunch at the Tate with Esme, throwing herself into her constructions, her dark heavy animal shapes, telling herself it was dangerous to become involved with a married man whose wife she knew, and who apparently trusted her. St Ives was a small town; people were interwoven, like an intricate tapestry. The risks of being found out were high, but the alternative – Richard leaving Esme – was impossibly remote. But by morning, the heady sensation of love had made all else seem meaningless. What she felt for Richard was the only thing that was real, solid. Trust, friendship, female solidarity, were as transient, as ephemeral to Harriet as the mist on the sea, and that Monday, sitting with Richard at the Swordfish, she knew that Richard was aware of this, as plainly as if they had discussed it thoroughly and at length. She was waiting for Richard to speak, to acknowledge their feelings for each other, and the waiting was beginning to grate on her. Sooner or later someone would have to make the first move; if Richard didn't, she would.

'I'll see you soon,' he had said as they parted at the door of the pub. 'I'll be in touch.'

And now Richard, staring unseeingly at the wide screen, his wife at his side, sits in restless frustration, for he has not seen Harriet since that day. He called in one night after work and the house was empty, and later Esme informed him that Harriet's father was ill and she had gone to London for a week. When Harriet returned, she called in to see the Cochrans one evening, but Richard was out and he missed her. He has not had a chance to see her since, for Esme has been organizing their lives just lately, spending a great deal of time with him.

Richard is not fooled by this. Squirming in his seat he loosens his hand from Esme's grip and tries to concentrate on the screen. Esme seems intent on what she is watching, but you never can tell with her. Richard knows that all this attention he is getting from Esme stems from guilt and not affection; he knows that she will be off again soon in her garden shed, abandoning him like a broken shell one picks up on the beach, shoves in a pocket for a day or so, and then chucks out. Richard, thinking in images again, decides this is an apt one: himself a broken forgotten shell in Esme's pocket. He loves her, but hardens his heart against her. As her fame spreads there will be more trips to London, to other cities, possibly abroad; there will be media attention, interviews; and in between there will be Esme herself, locked in the garden shed, locking him out of her life and her heart.

The film drones on. Esme and Richard impatiently sit through it, neither one of them suggest leaving because they think the other is enjoying it. When it finally finishes, they leave the cinema quickly, passing Hugo and Cara, waving to them as they hurry past.

'Your mum's getting quite famous,' Cara says to Hugo with some admiration. 'There was this article about her in the *Guardian*, about this new sculpture for the university.'

'Oh?' says Hugo, unimpressed. 'Mum?'

'Yes, it was all about how she works with—'

'Let's cut across to Porthmeor Beach, I want to see what the surf looks like. I haven't been out for days.' Hugo puts his arm around Cara and steers her the other way.

'Aren't you listening to me?' Cara asks. 'Don't you want to hear about your mum?'

Hugo kisses her soundly on the lips. 'She's my mum, right? I know all there is to know about her.'

Cara acquiesces. They walk along the beach languidly, part of the mist and the sea and the blackness of the sky.

'You're here at last,' Harriet says a few nights later, when Richard walks through her door and takes her in his arms.

After they have kissed for some time, Harriet says, 'And Esme? Does she know you are here?'

'She thinks I am out walking on the beach. She is locked in her shed again.' He kisses her once more, begins loosening her clothes.

'Won't she worry when you are late coming home? Won't she think you've fallen off a cliff somewhere?'

'I know Esme,' Richard says with both satisfaction and bitterness. 'If I walk in at two a.m., she'll still be in that shed, totally unaware of the time.'

'That's all right, then. Now, can we please stop talking about your wife?'

'Just one more thing,' Richard says, pulling slightly away from her and looking at her closely. 'You need to know that I love Esme and my family, even though I am

119

falling in love with you. You need to know I would never hurt them. Esme must never find out about this.'

'She won't, I swear it,' Harriet promises. 'No-one will.'

They look at each other solemnly for a moment. Then, arms entwined, they go upstairs.

Chapter Six

Spring is late coming to Cornwall this year, as it is in the rest of England. March is blustery and cold, the wind strong and bracing, the days filled with frequent squally showers of sleet and hail. When at last the weather suddenly turns fine and warm and still, Molly decides to walk across the fields and moorland to Zennor, on the coast.

The morning is sunny, balmy. Primroses butter the meadows and the hedgerows are alive with little creatures stirring after the long winter. Molly, though at first missing Crispin (he is out at sea, searching for lobsters), finds she is rather glad she is alone, for she has her sketch book with her and stops often to do drawings in coloured pencils of wild flowers, bits of twigs and leaves, a tuft of grass.

At the little village of Zennor she has a drink and a quick lunch at the Tinners Arms, then takes the coastal path back to St Ives. She walks past the majestic cove, stopping to do a quick sketch. The water is emerald green, sparkly. Regretfully, she packs up her sketch book and starts to head toward home. The coastal path is rougher, more rugged, and it will take her several hours even if she does not dawdle. She took a long time doing the five or six miles through the fields, for she stopped often, took diversions if something interested her. The weather is changing now, turning colder, and clouds are forming over the sea. Molly shivers. She has brought no waterproofs, and though her boots are adequate, her clothing is not. Shoving her sketch pad and camera into her rucksack, she walks as quickly as she can over the rough path, making good time and feeling more relaxed as she passes the halfway mark, though the wind is freshening from the sea and hitting her straight on.

It is a sudden gust of wind, fierce and wicked, that throws her off balance, just as she is negotiating a particularly dangerous bit of cliff. Molly has walked this path a dozen times or more; she is a good climber, a good hiker, but all it needs is a moment's lack of concentration, a second of unbalance. Molly slips and falls. Her last thought before she loses consciousness is not of the paintings she will never paint, but of the babies she will never have with Crispin. She wishes he were around so that she could have told him.

Lance Giddens has closed his gallery for the afternoon. He is having lunch with Esme Cochran, and this to him is such a sacred event that he wants the afternoon off to ponder it, secure it indelibly within his memory bank. The two of them buy cheese and onion pasties at one of the local bakers and take them outside to eat, sitting on the rocks on the edge of Porthminster Beach, enjoying the first sunshine of spring.

Lance glances surreptitiously at Esme as he eats his pasty. He secretly admires her rough chestnut hair, strewn with silver streaks; he likes her lean but tough body, her plain honest face. He thinks she is beautiful and has been in love with her for several years. No-one knows this, especially not Esme. He would not burden her with the knowledge, just as he would keep from her anything unsettling or painful. He would like to protect her from every danger, cocoon her in a web of love and tenderness so that she will always be free to create the wonderful sculptures for which she is, quite rightly, becoming acclaimed.

Lance not only loves Esme – body, soul, mind, spirit – he also loves her work. Esme would say they are inseparable, and so, in truth, would Lance. Esme should have been loved in this way by Richard, but nothing is perfect in this world.

Lance knows that Esme loves Richard, that they are happily married. In the sometimes hot, seething, insular artists' colony Esme and Lance are part of, not a breath of scandal has ever been heard of Esme. Lance loves her for this, even though it means he can hold out no hope for himself. He is content to love from afar, to worship at the feet of his beloved, as did Petrarch and Ronsard and the other courtly lovers of the continental Renaissance.

After they have eaten, Esme settles herself on the rocks while Lance, on the sand below her, sets up his easel and gets out his paints. Only Esme has seen him paint, seen his work in recent years. He wants her to know all of himself and, of course, his paintings are an integral part of his person. It goes beyond wanting her to like them; he knows it is somehow necessary for their friendship for her merely to know them. As a matter of fact, Esme thinks Lance's work is in a class of its own. It is disturbing, confused, sometimes even grotesque, but there is something compelling about it, something unique, something bordering on greatness. Right now he is painting the eye of a dead fish washed up on the sand, and Esme, watching it take shape, thinks it looks like the eye of a drowning god.

Looking away from the painting, Esme watches the noisy and argumentative oyster-catchers wading along the water's edge; their colours still rather dull and brown; their bill-tips dark. Soon, when spring finally arrives, they will turn a beautiful black and white, their beaks bright orange.

Esme sighs contentedly and turns her face to the sun. Lance is helping her prepare her exhibition; she relies heavily on him for advice, for support. Esme loves Lance, as she loves Molly and her other friends. He is a good listener and discreet; a perfect confidante. She feels comfortable and easy with him, secure. She would be distraught if she knew how he felt about her, for she does not reciprocate his feelings. Even if she did, she wouldn't. Esme has many old-fashioned notions: she disapproves of divorce, infidelity, dishonesty; she believes strongly in odd things like the sanctity of the family, of marriage.

'How is Richard these days?' Lance asks after a time, eyes still on his painting.

'Much better,' Esme says, opening her eyes just in time to see a cormorant dive into the sea. She watches until the bird reappears, then turns to Lance. 'He seems really lively these days, doesn't seem to mind how hard I'm working. Perhaps it's because his own work is going well; his fifth formers are putting on a play which he is helping to direct, so he's out late at least twice a week.'

'That must be easier on you, then.'

'Yes, I suppose it is.' Esme looks thoughtful. 'I miss him, though. Even though I'm busy, I miss not having him around at mealtimes, for he usually stays in Penzance for dinner when there's a rehearsal.'

'You can't have it all ways,' Lance says gently. 'You're working hard; so is Richard. When things slack off for both of you, you'll see each other more often again.'

Esme looks fondly at Lance. 'You're right, of course. And I really am truly happy for Richard, that he's enjoying his job at last.'

She really is, Lance thinks, looking at her again as she

124

turns towards the sea, smiling at a tiny sandpiper scurrying near the rocks.

And I'm happy for *her*, he says to himself, for she looks so much more relaxed now that Richard is off her back for a time, no longer sulking or brooding when she spends an hour longer than he thinks feasible in her studio. Lance gets terribly angry about Richard sometimes. He has known the two of them for years, and he always knew there would be trouble when Esme's work began to be recognized. As long as Richard's teaching career was of primary importance in the household, he was all right, but Lance could foretell ages ago what would happen when Esme's light began to outshine his.

The tide is coming in now, swirling with an ominous sound farther down along the rocks. A guillemot which had been perched on a reef, partially submerged by the rising tide, suddenly flies away with a great flapping of wings as a crashing wave covers the rock. 'We'd better go,' Esme says, suddenly disconcerted.

'It's all right, the tide's not going to cut us off, not for ages,' Lance smiles. He knows Esme's fear of the sea; he finds it sweet and touching.

'It just sounds so fierce, so relentless, coming up like it is now. As if nothing can hold it back.'

'Nothing can, I suppose. We try to contain it, but we can't stop it.'

They are silent for a few moments. Esme is thinking how ironic it is that someone who finds the sea so frightening should have sons so in love with it, Crispin in his boat and Hugo on his surfboard.

After a few moments Esme says she has to go back to work. She has been restless since the waves began their inexorable journey up the sand and over the rocks. Lance packs his paints and easel and carefully puts the dead fish in his rucksack. Together the two of them wander up the beach and Lance walks Esme back to her house, then heads for the gallery where he drops off his bundles. Later he will continue work on his fish-eye, alone in the privacy of his workroom, but now he just wants to drift and think about the last two hours with Esme. He meanders towards Porthmeor Beach and beyond, heading for the Clodgy, the outcrop of rocks on the coastal path. Because the sun is making him soporific, he stops at Man's Head, a cluster of rocks overlooking the sea, and finds a grassy nook in a cleft where he curls up like a baby and promptly falls asleep.

It is much colder when Lance wakes. Clouds have come up, and wind. The sea is lashing against the rocks below him and on Clodgy Point ahead of him. He feels stiff, uncomfortable, and decides he needs a brisk walk to clear his head, loosen his limbs. The euphoria he felt after his lunch with Esme has totally evaporated, leaving him bereft with unfulfilled longing. He remembers that his ex-wife is threatening to come and visit again, to discuss their son who is broke as usual and wants to borrow more money. Despite Esme's encouragement, he is also having a crisis over his paintings; past criticism and mockery still rankles, and he is unhappy with his last-finished canvases.

Lance doesn't like wallowing like a pig in the mud of self-pity, and walks faster to shake it off, putting on the jacket he had tied around his shoulders. It is threatening rain now, but he decides to walk on. Getting wet and cold and tired will alleviate his mental apathy, he thinks with grim satisfaction.

The path is rugged, broken, but Lance is used to it. He goes this way often, sometimes taking his sketch pad and making dark charcoal drawings which he uses as a basis for his paintings. In spite of the rain he wishes he had his sketch pad now; the sky is fantastic, black and eerie. He feels his spirits lift, his confidence return.

Later he will wonder how he heard the cry, weak and

nearly inaudible in the wind and the crashing of the sea. At first he thinks it is a sea-bird, a gull calling, or a cormorant. He stops, listens again, for he can't identify it. With horror he realizes it is a human voice, and then he sees her, crouched on a flat grassy outcrop, not very far down from the cliff path.

'Thank God,' she says, closing her eyes with relief and weariness. 'Thank God.'

'Jesus, Molly! Are you hurt? Hang on, I'll climb down.'

He gets to her in a matter of moments, though the rain is lashing down now and the rocks are slippery. 'What happened? Never mind, tell me later. Can you climb back up? I'll help.'

'It's my arm, I can't move it. I think it's broken; that's why I can't climb up, I can't get a grip. I must have passed out too, I don't know how long I've been here.'

Molly is wet and shaking. It has got a great deal colder in the past half-hour and she is chilled to the bone. Slowly they make their way up to the path. 'Can you walk?' Lance asks anxiously. 'I don't really want to leave you here while I get help; you'll die of exposure, even with my jacket over you. We're not far away anyway. You didn't get very far before you fell.'

'I didn't come from St Ives, I've come from Zennor,' Molly gasps. Her head hurts; she feels dizzy and there is an excruciating pain in her chest. But her legs, though wobbly, are all right, and Lance half carries her, half props her up, as they slowly and precariously make their way to help and safety.

Crispin is mad with worry. Molly was supposed to have met him at his house for an early dinner, and then they were going to see the new film on at the cinema. He has bought steak, prepared vegetables. Molly is an hour and a half late and he has been to her house; it is dark, empty. No-one has seen her; he has called by Oona's studio,

127

where she is working late, and found out, without frightening Oona, that Molly has not been there. Neither Alice nor Jordan have seen her, nor have Esme or Hugo.

Lance, phoning from the hospital in Truro, misses Crispin who is roaming the streets of St Ives looking for Molly, not knowing where to search for no-one knew where she was going. As Crispin calls in at yet another friend's house, Lance tries ringing Oona, but there is no reply at her home and her studio doesn't have a phone. Crispin, returning again to Molly's house and letting himself in, sits at the kitchen table and groans, head in hands. Witch, the cat, meows and howls indignantly; she has not been fed since early this morning. Suddenly the phone rings and Crispin, his heart pounding, answers it.

'Molly's in Treliske Hospital,' Lance's voice comes urgently over the phone. 'She's had an accident—' He starts to add, but don't worry, she's fine, but the telephone has gone dead, they've been cut off. Lance tries to phone again, but the wretched thing won't accept his coins, so he swears softly and races off in search of a phone that works. By the time he has found one, Crispin is on his way to Truro.

'Don't go,' Molly says weakly, holding on to Crispin with her left hand. Her right arm and wrist are wrapped in a plaster cast, only the tips of her fingers and thumb protrude. It is very late at night and Molly has come around from the anaesthetic following the operation on her arm which was broken in several places.

'I'm not going anywhere. I'll stay with you all night.' For ever, he almost adds, but Molly has drifted off to sleep again.

The half-hour drive to the hospital was not something that Crispin would soon forget. Not knowing the kind of accident Molly had had, whether she had been hitch-hiking and was in some stranger's car, or had been mown down herself on one of the narrow Cornish roads, Crispin was free to imagine, and this he did with terror and despair. He pictured Molly already dead, dying. The pain going through him as he sped along the roads in the driving rain numbed him, made him dizzy with shock and grief and mostly fear, an agonizing dread that drenched him in sweat, causing his hands to tremble uncontrollably at the wheel.

'She's in theatre,' Lance had said when Crispin found him in the waiting-room. 'She's all right. Broken arm, lots of bruises, a broken rib, possibly concussion. But she's all right.'

Crispin, weak with relief, had sat down on one of the bright-red plastic chairs and wept. When he had composed himself Lance said, 'Let's go and have some coffee, then I'm off home.' He was exhausted and damp and beginning to ache all over. 'I didn't want her to be alone when she came out of the anaesthetic. She's a brave soul, you know. She kept telling me I mustn't worry you.'

Now Crispin sits holding Molly's hand gratefully, thankfully, not wanting to let it go, not even when sleep overtakes him and he dozes off in the chair next to the bed, dreaming of himself and Molly entwined like ivy in a green forest somewhere beyond the sea, beyond themselves, beyond the harsh realities and practicalities of life, which sometimes Crispin finds difficult to get beyond.

Molly dreams too. In her drugged state she dreams she is tumbling down a cliff, her paintings falling with her, cascading drunkenly and haphazardly onto the rocks below.

A few days later, Molly's grandmother Oona, resplendent in a black wool dress with a high neck, thick black

129

tights, and dainty lace-up boots, sits with Crispin's brother Hugo in Oona's long wide window-seat facing the sea, watching the gulls shrieking over the rocks underneath the window. There are hundreds of them, crying and calling and shouting to each other, circling the sea and the rocks, then swooping down to land in the water or to perch on the edge.

'Noisy buggers, aren't they?' Hugo says languidly. He is holding a china cup and saucer with Darjeeling tea, as he does once a week when he goes to Oona's house to help with some of her heavier chores and housework. Today he has washed the huge picture window, taken out some rubbish she wanted disposed of, repaired a loose slate hanging over the door, and moved the piano to be nearer the window now that spring is definitely on its way.

'The gulls are certainly exceedingly noisy,' Oona agrees, sipping her tea appreciatively. The China tea is a reward for Hugo after his exertions; the ritual has been enacted for years, since Hugo began his odd-job work for Oona. Hugo was once awed by the grandeur of the occasion: the proper tea tray, the cups and saucers, the lumps of sugar with the silver tongs, the fancy cakes fresh from the bakery or the very best tea-shop. Now he is amused, finds it a light-hearted game. He half suspects Oona sees it as a game too, for when she is entrenched in the middle of a painting, the ritual vanishes, and in its place is a cursory note stating the chores to be done. By the note and Hugo's wages, there is always a mug with a tea-bag in it, telling Hugo to pour boiling water on it when he is finished and help himself to milk from the fridge and biscuits from the tin.

Today, however, Oona sits thoughtfully overlooking the sea which is especially calm and intricately blue, and somehow so endearing that Oona feels quite touched, as if the peace of the ocean is an antidote to

130

the turmoil inside her. She has not yet recovered from her granddaughter's near escape from death on the cliffs. Oona, resigned to her own death, is alarmed to face the possibility that others dear to her could go first; she cannot contemplate this. Though Molly is home now from hospital, settled in Crispin's house while she recuperates, Oona still wakes at night drenched in fear and perspiration.

'Have you seen Molly since she got out of hospital?' Hugo asks now, perceptively. He knows Oona has been shattered by Molly's accident; she seems paler, and he noticed how her normally steady hands trembled when she poured the tea. Though she is dressed elegantly, a necklace of silver and amber gleaming against the black of her dress and matching earrings firmly in place, her white hair is not quite secure in its French plait; a strand or two has escaped and is wisping forlornly down her shoulder.

'Yes, I visit her every day,' Oona replies, livening up a bit as she talks of Molly. 'She seems in good spirits.'

'Crispin waits on her hand and foot. I've never seen my brother miss the fishing like he's been doing lately. Pete's been giving Tom a hand on the *Girl Lizzie*, as Crispin hasn't taken the *Fair Celt* out since Molly's accident. It's a bloody shame, Pete says, because the nets are full again after the last disastrous month.'

'I heard the fishing has been bad for weeks, after the fine run of bass in December and January,' Oona comments. 'Of course, Molly can't do anything for herself with that arm. I've told Crispin I'd be happy to sit with her if he wants to work, but he said he was due a holiday anyway.'

Hugo sips his tea, adds another lump of sugar to it, and glances out of the window again. The seagulls are still crying imperiously; there must be a school of tiny fish near the rocks which they are after. 'I think Molly

131

and Crispin are having an ace honeymoon,' Hugo says with a grin. 'All alone, neither of them working . . .' He trails off, thinking of the vast double bed, raised on the platform looking over *this*, this incredible view of sea and sky. He has spent more than one night there himself, with his Cara, watching the lights shining from the pier and harbour, from the lone solitary ship at sea. Since Crispin has moved Molly into the house, he and Cara have found it difficult to be alone, to find space for themselves. Cara lives on the outskirts of town in a house packed with younger brothers and sisters; she doesn't even have a room of her own but has to share with a sibling. There is his own room, but Esme does not approve of Cara staying the night, and during the day and evening they are always aware of Esme downstairs, beavering away in her shed but likely to come in at the most inopportune moment to ask if they want a cup of tea, a meal, whatever. Hugo did hint to Crispin that perhaps they could use Molly's house, but Crispin drew the line at that, saying it would be an imposition to ask.

'Why don't you look for your own place?' Crispin had queried.

'Have you seen what the rents are around this town? I could never afford it.'

Crispin had shrugged. 'You'll have to get a full-time job, then.'

'Oh sure. Where?'

'Summer's coming. There will be jobs then.'

'What about the surf, man?'

'Well, that's up to you, mate.' Crispin looked at his brother fondly but with some impatience. 'You either have a flat and unlimited time with Cara, or you have the surf.'

Thinking of this conversation now, Hugo realizes that he has never seriously considered the possibility of a full-time job. He is willing to carry on with the odd jobs he does: working in the surf shop for the occasional morning or afternoon, doing chores for Oona and a couple of the other artists. In the busy season he works in cafés or restaurants, but always just enough to keep him in beer and house music. The surf, thank God, is free.

'Cara wants me to go with her to Plymouth. She's got an offer of a place at the university.' Hugo blurts this out to Oona without thinking. He is used to talking to her, ever since he was a child and she used to visit Esme's workroom, buying her first early sculptures in wood, encouraging her, telling Hugo, 'Your mother is quite a talented artist, young man. Don't you ever stop her from her work.'

Esme would just blush and smile, and later tell Hugo, 'You never stop me from my work, sweetie. I'd much rather be here playing with you than in my workroom.'

Hugo believed her, so much so that even now he still feels his mother would rather cook and clean for him than create form and symmetry from a dull block of stone. It doesn't occur to him that perhaps she has moved on, has tried to give him the reins of his own life so that she can get on with hers.

'Do you want to go to Plymouth?' Oona says this for the second time, since Hugo is in a dream somewhere and didn't hear her question the first time. 'Do you want to go with Cara? What would you do there if you went?'

'Cara thinks I should look after her while she does her degree.'

Oona does not find this at all strange. When she was in her forties she had a lover who did just that: kept house and cooked and cleaned and shopped while she painted. She accepts this as perfectly natural. After all, women have been doing it for men for years.

'Would you be bored, though?' Women have had that inflicted on them too.

'Out of my head!' Hugo exclaims. 'I'd be bored out of my mind. And I hate cities, I don't know what I'd do in one.'

'Well then, you mustn't go.'

Out in the harbour a fishing boat steams slowly away from its moorings, out to sea. 'Cara thinks I'm a bit of a deadhead,' Hugo sighs. 'She thinks I should go to college or something. Or get a proper career job.' He doesn't mention that his father's been nagging him to do this for months. Somehow it has never seemed important what Richard thought, but it does with Cara.

Oona looks fondly at the boy. She admires and respects the ease with which he floats through life, and the feckless way he feels that he is entitled to do what he likes. It seems to Oona to be pure innocence, something she does not encounter often. 'Hugo, what do *you* want to do, now that you're out of school and have done your A levels?'

'Surf,' Hugo says softly, 'that's all.'

Oona admires this too, the passion, the intensity that is there even though Hugo has spoken quietly, almost carelessly. Oona is not fooled by his tone of voice; she knows that when riding the surf, he feels the same joy and power and surge of unity and harmony that she feels when she is painting. Hugo searches for the right wave in the same way that she searches in her painting for truth, perception and beauty. Oona knows, like Hugo, that when the perfect wave finally arrives, it is never enough; it is only perfect for that one moment, that one ride. When it is over one must begin again, paint another picture, wait for another exquisite roll.

'Then do it,' Oona says. 'Surf. Until you're ready for the next thing.'

Hugo goes, and Oona stares at the sea. She pictures Hugo riding the waves, and imagines herself out there with him, surfing, flying, crashing through and above and over the waves like a seagull.

Not very far away in the Sandpiper gallery, Lance Giddens is having words with Harriet, with whom he is trying to be tolerant because he abhors scenes. It is actually Harriet who is having words, for Lance has, so far, hardly spoken. All he has said is, basically, that he does not want to take Harriet's latest sculpture for his gallery.

Harriet, knowing she shouldn't, is getting heavy and demanding to know why. 'You've never taken my work, and I know it's as good as anything else you have here. Is it because it's not commercial? I thought this was supposed to be an art gallery, not a souvenir shop.'

Lance, with years of experience in handling artists, controls his temper and tries to be tactful.

'They are just not my sort of thing,' he says, dissembling. In truth, he does not like Harriet's work very much. As she pointed out, it is also not commercial. This has not deterred him with other artists; if he has liked their work and felt it is genuinely good, he takes them on. He does not think Harriet's bizarre animal shapes are particularly good, for all their shock appeal.

'What the hell is your sort of thing, Lance?' Harriet says with mounting irritation. 'Other galleries like my work; I have stuff in places both here and in Penzance.'

'Good. Fine.'

'So what the hell are you looking for? What do you object to in my work? Maybe you just can't handle it because it's different, innovative. You're happy enough to take on other constructions in soft metals, like this abstract here.' She disdainfully picks up and dismisses one of Lance's favourite pieces, an elongated curve like the ripple of a wave. 'And that funny stone frog with the popping eyes. You think that's a better work of art than mine?'

Lance is silent. He hates these kinds of conversations, loathes getting into them with artists. Sometimes he thinks he dislikes artists in general, remembering Jordan and some of the others he has had to deal with. But he reminds himself that these are the exceptions; most of them, like Esme and Alice and Molly, are just fine, fine and easy.

Harriet is prowling the gallery like a thin white and black cat. Her hair is not tied in its usual topknot but is hanging straight and loose and dark against her pale neck and face. She is wearing grey pinstriped trousers and a white shirt with long jet beads hanging around her neck. Her black-rimmed eyes are darting disparagingly from object to object in the gallery, as, further incensed by Lance's silence, she makes derogatory comments on his collection. 'Look at the crap you have here,' she snaps viciously. 'Those fucking boxes are so primitive they're practically Neanderthal. And those small bronzes – I was doing them in my first year at art school. Some of us grow up, go on, develop.'

As she storms about, Lance still not saying a word but looking at her contemptuously, Harriet knows she will regret this later. It pays to be circumspect in the art world, to not make enemies, for one relies too heavily on others: critics, gallery owners, members of art councils, the like. She knows just as sure as the tide will go out tonight that when she gets home, she'll be kicking herself for losing her temper. But right now she cannot help it. Volatile, quick to anger, Harriet often does things without thinking, things she regrets bitterly later. She knows this will be one of them.

Lance has turned his back on her and is busy at his desk. He will never take any of her work now, even if it becomes the most sought-after in St Ives. He will

136

also talk about this encounter to others: to Oona, whom Harriet admires; to Esme, who will in turn tell Richard. Harriet swears under her breath. She cannot bear to seem a fool in Richard's eyes; this bothers her even more than Lance's rejection of her work. She will have to tell Richard a watered-down version of this encounter, blame Lance somehow so that Richard will not believe the true story when it is filtered down to him.

Harriet sighs, deflated, her anger suddenly gone. She tries to make amends by a token apology to Lance, but he says goodbye coldly, hardly looking at her. As Harriet leaves the gallery she sees one of Esme's wood carvings in the window, one of her earlier small mother and child figures. Stopping, she stares at the figure coldly, feeling hard, detached. 'You may be good enough for Lance and his sad gallery,' she mutters through clenched teeth, 'but you are no longer good enough for Richard.'

Cheered, Harriet walks briskly home, carrying her rejected sculpture like a trophy.

Richard, driving home from Penzance late that afternoon, looks forward with pleasure to his evening with Harriet. He is in love with her, or so it feels to him. Sometimes, because of the peculiar nature of the buzz this love gives him, he wonders if he has fallen in love out of revenge, to pay Esme back for the hurt she has inflicted on him all these years. He does not dwell on this for long, as he feels it somehow belittles what he feels for Harriet. He wants nothing to sully this feeling; he is alive, radiant, vibrant, all the things that lovers are supposed to be.

That Harriet loves him, he does not doubt. If she is working on one of her constructions when he walks in through her door, she immediately drops everything and goes to him. She rarely talks about her work, preferring

137

to listen to him talk about his. She is kind and sympathetic, warm and loving. He feels he is the luckiest man alive; he feels like he is the sea at night: rich, dark, mysterious, powerful. He likes that image and takes it further. If he is the sea, Harriet is the pale opalescent sand that the tide takes every day, covers with its deep mysteries, then departs, leaving the sand glowing, pearly and lucent and everlastingly docile, waiting for the next tide.

A honking horn behind him wakes Richard from his reverie. Coming into St Ives, he goes down the back streets and down a little-used alley-way to park his car a few blocks away from Harriet's house. This is a small town, and Richard takes care to be cautious, circumspect. He is, after all, supposed to be in Penzance, working with the fifth form on their play. So he slinks along culs-de-sac and hidden pedestrian walkways, a lie or two on his lips against the rare chance that someone he knows might accost him, and slips safely and surreptitiously into Harriet's house.

She is waiting for him with words of love, a drink, and a meal of Chinese sweet and sour pork which they eat with chopsticks. Wearing an embroidered red kimono, her black hair flat against her face, Harriet looks rakishly oriental, Richard muses approvingly. His own little geisha girl, he thinks with a rush of affection. His own sweet love, his own dear treasure.

'You are smirking,' Harriet says, passing over some hot noodles. 'Like the Cheshire Cat.'

'Am I? I suppose I'm feeling smug. Tucked away here in our little hideaway, the world miles away . . .'

The world is only straight across town, up the hill from Downlong, barely a ten-minute walk away, Harriet thinks pragmatically, but keeps her mouth shut. She wonders, disconcertingly, how Richard would react if Esme suddenly decided to walk over and pay her a

138

visit. She's never done this before, not without phoning first, especially in the evening, for Harriet's house is a bit out of the way. But there could always be a first time.

Harriet is not going to mention this either. She wants Richard undistracted and relaxed, not nervy and stressed. How easily it slipped over into *this*, she thinks, watching Richard's eyes as he looks at her. Not long ago she was crying desperately on Esme's and Richard's shoulders over that bastard Bernard, hanging out in his antique shop in Penzance hoping for a reconciliation, and now she is in love with Richard. How sweetly complex life is, she silently exults.

'More tea?' Harriet asks prettily, pouring herself some of the green tea from the squat Chinese pot.

'No thanks. I could do with another drink, but I suppose I'd better not. Esme would soon sniff out alcohol. I'm supposed to be at school working, as you know.'

Harriet makes an impatient gesture but keeps her mouth shut. She doesn't want Richard to talk about Esme, not now. But Richard, preoccupied, is saying, 'Sometimes I wish she would just pack her bags and move out into that bloody shed.'

'And then what would you do?' Harriet says lightly, as if the answer doesn't really interest her.

Richard looks at her carefully. He is replete and contented after the delicious meal, and Harriet looks alluring, fetching, in her red kimono. She leans over, pouring more tea, so that he can see the outline of her small pointed breast.

'I would move in here with you,' Richard says recklessly. He feels he has known Harriet for ever, loved her for ever. 'But it can't be, you know. Esme exists, and I could never leave her, never hurt her. I told you that from the beginning.'

139

'And what about me?' Harriet demands. 'Do you think I don't love Esme too? Do you think I want to hurt her? She's my friend, you know. Don't you think it hurts *me* to betray a friend like this?'

Richard is moved. Harriet, so good and kind and loyal; she has betrayed her friend for him, endured agonies of guilt and wretchedness for him. 'Don't look at it as a betrayal,' he says gently, going to her, holding her. 'We love each other, and we both love Esme. No-one will be hurt, I promise you.'

Harriet embraces him as the tide embraces the luminous sand, as the waves embrace rocks, as a woman in love embraces a man, Richard thinks as he clings to her. She is his work of art: his painting, his sculpture, his poem. Smiling with satisfaction, he strokes her black hair tenderly, grateful and humble that she should love him too.

Esme, in her workroom, has finished the small marble sculpture she wanted to complete before the exhibition and is wandering in a desultory manner around the house. Hugo is out somewhere with his Cara, and Molly and Crispin are nesting like love-birds. Esme wishes they'd get married; she'd like to see Crispin settled and happy.

Esme has finished a meagre and solitary dinner of pasta and spaghetti sauce out of a jar, for no-one is home to share a meal with her. She dislikes eating alone; even when working she has always relished the breaks for meals, finding the company of her family combined with nourishing food just what she needs to carry on again.

Richard is, of course, in Penzance, staying over for an early dinner, then the play rehearsal. Esme will be glad when the play is over; she misses Richard.

She turns on the television, then switches it off after

five minutes. She needs to talk to someone after all her solitary hours, needs to be in company, let the real world into her life again. Molly would be just right to talk to; she knows what it's like to finish a work, that feeling of exhilaration mixed with desolation. But Esme has already visited the invalid today; she doesn't want to overdo it, doesn't want Crispin to think she is pushing things.

Oona, perhaps. But Oona is now at work on another painting, out of touch and out of this world until it is finished. All her other friends will be settled at home with their families, except Lance, perhaps. She brightens up at the thought of seeing Lance, maybe even asking him to come around to look at her latest sculpture. Picking up the phone, she suddenly puts it down again as she remembers that Lance's ex-wife is there.

Esme decides to take a walk instead. She heads down to Porthmeor Beach, listening to the surf pounding like a demented drummer onto the sand. There is both wind and fog in the air, and Esme shivers. The lights of the Tate gallery shine like the beacon of a lighthouse, or like the prow of a ship coming majestically out of the misty night. Esme walks along the beach aimlessly, hardly able to make any headway against the wind. The tide is big and full, and she has to jump once to escape a far-reaching wave. The beach is deserted; even the dog-walkers have gone inside.

Esme leaves the beach but doesn't want to go home. She still wants to talk, and knows that Richard, if his other rehearsals are anything to go by, won't be home for a while yet. Suddenly Esme thinks of Harriet. She has not been to her place for ages, though Harriet often calls in to see her, especially during the weekends. She wonders why she did not think of Harriet before. Some-times, lately, she has felt uneasy around her, probably because Harriet seems to be calling in so often, and at such odd times – early evenings when Richard has just returned from school, when he hasn't a play rehearsal and can relax a bit; or Saturdays when they are sitting down to a quiet lunch together. Esme has, once or twice, almost resented Harriet's presence, thinking it was beginning to encroach on hers and Richard's time together. She dismissed the thought as soon as it occurred, however, thinking herself selfish and petty.

Esme wanders through the quiet cobbled streets, pondering over her friendship with Harriet. There has always been a desperation about the other woman that makes her seem frantic sometimes, unable to cope with any world other than that of her emotions. When her relationship with Bernard cooled because he was finding it too cloying, Harriet went berserk, missed work at the estate agents, stopped her art work, vacillated between outraged temper tantrums and long spells of despondency. At one time the whole family, even Richard, rather dreaded her unannounced arrival, not knowing how long she would stay, what mood she would be in. Now she seems to have, fortunately, got over him, and Richard no longer seems to mind her frequent visits.

Really, she's a good person, Esme thinks, remembering how keenly Harriet listened when she had confided her worries about Richard and her sculpture. She feels guilty that she hasn't taken the initiative in their friendship for ages, and decides to make up for it now. Esme will go over there this very moment, have a good woman-to-woman talk, something they haven't done much lately as Richard always seems to be about when Harriet is at the Cochran house.

Esme wonders if she should stop by home and phone first, check that Harriet is in, but decides that she could do with the walk anyway. Esme would like to see her latest construction too; she hasn't seen Harriet's work for ages.

Feeling less aimless and mopey, Esme purposefully goes up the main street, past the shops, the banks, the library, and heads for Harriet's house.

Chapter Seven

While Esme has been walking aimlessly on the beach, the mist and sea spray covering her with a fine coating of dew-like moisture, Percy Prynne has been roaming the Island above her. For a long time he sat in front of the old stone chapel on a soggy wooden bench facing the sea and rocks below, listening to the waves crashing tumultuously, watching the white foam bubble and sizzle against the dark of the sea and the night. Once, he thought he saw the light coming from the lantern held by the poor dead shipwrecked woman looking for her drowned child, but the glow escaped him and there was nothing but blackness around him. He knows it won't be long, though. Percy often sees the mother wandering through town, or talking to Tom on the *Girl Lizzie*. Her baby is always clutched to her tightly, but Percy knows it won't be long before the poor infant is torn from her bosom and thrown into the sea. Then the mother will search the rocks with her lantern and beckon Percy home.

Finally moving from his bench, Percy limps painfully down the slope and onto the beach. He is coughing steadily, and the wind nearly knocks him over, so thin and frail has he become. Esme, her path crossing his as she heads off the beach and into the town, heading for

Harriet's house, hears the cough, sees the old man stumble and fall onto the sand.

'Percy!' she says, rushing to his side. 'Whatever are you doing out in this wind? Look at you, you are absolutely drenched through.'

She helps him to his feet, tries to brush the sand from his clothes but it is wet and sticking to him. 'You look ill,' she says. 'Come on, I'll walk you home, get you to bed.'

But Percy has got some of his wind back. 'No, no, my maid, not home. Take me to see Percy Prynne.'

Esme looks at him with alarm. 'What did you say?'

'Percy Prynne, the fisherman. I've gone and lost him, y'know. But I know where he be, don't you worry.' He looks at her cannily.

'Come on,' she says gently. 'Let's just go home.' She will get him to bed, then call the doctor at once.

But Percy won't budge. 'I ain't going home,' he mutters. 'Not until I've see'd him.'

Esme, humouring him, says, 'All right, we'll go find him. But you have to help me. Where do you think he is?'

'Why at Crispin's place. *You* know.'

Esme suddenly realizes what he is talking about. 'You mean you want to see the portrait,' she says with relief. 'The one Alice painted.'

Percy's voice, suddenly loud and strong and impatient, shouts, 'I want to see *him*, dammit!'

Soothing, cajoling, Esme steers Percy off the beach and through Downlong, heading up to Crispin's house.

Molly and Crispin, unaware of their impending visitors, are sitting at the plain unvarnished wooden table in front of the window listening to jazz on the stereo and enjoying a late dinner. Crispin is cutting up Molly's food, chicken and rice and a stir-fry of red and green peppers and mange tout.

145

'It's so maddening that it's my right arm,' Molly moans. 'I'm useless with my left.'

'I'm surprised Oona hasn't been lecturing you about that. It was very careless of you to break your painting arm.'

Molly smiles. 'I'm surprised too. She has been very restrained, hasn't she.'

Crispin, beginning to eat, says nothing. He knows that Oona, like himself, is so thankful that Molly is alive that neither of them would think about scolding her.

Crispin wanted to, after he knew Molly was safe and would make a complete recovery. Even now he feels an incipient rage when he thinks how irresponsible she was, going on a cliff walk without telling a soul where she would be. What if Lance had not happened to come along just then? It was already late afternoon; the day was foul; darkness would come early. Probably no-one would have walked that way until the next day, and Molly would not have survived such a cold wet night without shelter or provision, not in her condition. True, Crispin would have raised the alarm, but who knew where to look, where she might be? One day last October, when Crispin was ten miles out to sea fishing for conger eels, Molly suddenly took it into her head to go to London, see an exhibition there at the Royal Academy. She hitch-hiked in the early hours of the morning to Penzance, caught the first train to London, and was back by late evening, stony-broke – she had sold a small painting, and blown the proceeds on her excursion – but full of the joys of the afternoon at the Academy.

'Why didn't you tell me you were going?' Crispin had said. 'What if you'd got mugged in London, or simply disappeared, as people do? I'd never have known where to look for you.'

'Oh, don't be so dramatic,' Molly had laughed. 'I'm

perfectly safe when I go on one of my jaunts, believe me.'

Well, she wasn't, obviously. But Crispin could no more tell her, not now when she was subdued and still covered with purple and yellowing bruises, than he could reprimand a repentant child after a spurt of mischief. He just prayed that Molly had learned her lesson.

Watching her now, eating awkwardly with her left hand, he says, 'Does it hurt, Molly? Your other hand.'

'Hm, a bit. The fingers are still swollen and stiff; I can hardly move them.' She tries to do so and winces.

He looks at her fondly. Her face is pale and drawn, with a nasty cut on her cheek and a great bruise on her forehead. Her cinnamon hair, the gold highlights dulled and subdued, is fractious, as if she had made a half-hearted attempt to tame it, but had given it up as a bad job. Crispin had offered to brush it for her, seeing her struggle with her left hand, but she had brusquely refused, saying she had better learn to cope as her arm would be in a cast for a long time. She is wearing a luxurious green velvet dressing-gown, bought ages ago for a pound when the amateur operatic society had a sale of their old no-longer-used costumes. Crispin has just helped her in and out of the bath. Her legs are still stiff and painful, and her cracked rib bothers her considerably.

Molly catches him looking at her. Staring straight back at him she says, firmly, 'I'm quite well enough to stay on my own now, you know. I can do most things for myself, except open tins. Witch will have to live on dried cat food and milk for a bit, it'll do her good. She might lose some of that excess weight.'

She gazes fondly at Witch who is sitting on the window-sill, staring out at the black sea, the foggy night. Witch was brought over with Molly; unlike most cats,

147

she can make herself at home anywhere, and spends hours on the window-sill watching the gulls playing on the water.

'Nonsense,' Crispin says. 'You can't possibly be alone yet. Besides, what would you do? You can't paint, can't teach yoga, can't go hitch-hiking all over the countryside. You'd be bored rigid.'

'Well, you've got to get fishing again soon.' She looks up at him and suddenly smiles, and the smile is so wan and tentative in that poor bruised face that Crispin is moved to reach across the table and take her hand. 'You must get back to your boat,' Molly goes on. 'I do take your fishing seriously, you know, even though you accuse me and your mother of not doing so, when you lose your temper.'

Crispin looks at her thoughtfully. 'I suspect I do so because it has always been a struggle for me. Fishing as a profession was such an outlandish choice, with a teacher father and an artist mother. I feel that, even now, they'd rather I did something else.'

Molly shakes her head vehemently. 'You are such a fool sometimes, Crispin, though I love you dearly. Richard much prefers you being a fisherman than an artist any day, and Esme – well, she's so proud of you, haven't you sensed that?'

'My mother?' Crispin asks incredulously. 'She hates it when I go out to sea.'

'Because she's afraid, you idiot. She's a mother and she's frightened to death of the risks involved. But she loves the drama, the adventure, the romance – as she sees it – of what you do. And she's secretly proud that you chose something reckless and challenging, rather than safe.'

'Like you,' Crispin says with a grin. 'Choosing the precarious life of a painter rather than the steady one of a schoolteacher.'

'Exactly.'

Crispin and Molly look at each other and smile. The sounds of a lonely saxophone fill the room from the stereo speakers, and outside the window the lights from a solitary boat twinkle in the darkness.

'So to go back to what we were saying.' Molly looks up determinedly. 'About me going home, and what would I do there all day with my arm in a cast? You've got to get back fishing and it would be the same thing here: what would I do here all day long?'

Crispin is silent. *Wait for me*, he would like to say. *Be here when I return from the sea*. But instead he says, 'You might as well be bored here as anywhere else, and at least Oona is just a street up; she'd be glad to stop in to see you every day. And Lance too; he's not far. He seems to think he's responsible for you now that he's saved your life, like that old Chinese – or is it Indian? – belief.'

Molly has stopped eating and puts down her fork. 'And you?' she asks carefully. 'What about all your space you were talking about not so long ago? I don't want to be here because you feel sorry for me, because I've had an accident and can't cope.'

'Oh Molly, stop it! Let's just enjoy this time together, OK? I like having you here, all right? I *want* you to stay.'

Molly is just about to say, 'But for how long, Crispin?' when she suddenly thinks better of it. Her accident has left her weepy, exhausted, frail, and she hates feeling this way. She knows she cannot cope with a confrontation with Crispin about their future, not now. 'All right,' she says with a tremulous smile. 'I'll stay on for a little while.'

Her words unexpectedly fill him with relief. 'Would you like some ice-cream?' he says with a wide smile. 'Invalids always seem to be fed ice-cream.'

As he goes down the two flights of steps into the

149

kitchen to get the dessert, the doorbell rings. Stopping to answer it, Crispin is surprised to see his mother standing there with Percy. 'I found him coming off the Island, soaked to the skin as you can see for yourself. He insisted on coming here.'

Percy nods to Crispin but does not speak. He brushes past them both and climbs up the stairs, followed by the other two. Molly looks up in surprise, speaks to Percy, but he doesn't seem to see her.

For a long time, Percy stares at the portrait. His own eyes stare back at him, full of confidence and strength. Percy feels the power coming back into his body, his soul, and takes several deep gasping breaths, like a man who has been drowning but suddenly can breathe air again. He closes his eyes and feels Percy Prynne inhabiting his body, getting a grip on his spirit. He'll be all right now, he thinks with gratitude. He is himself again.

Crispin, Molly and Esme have been standing behind Percy, letting him be as he stares motionless at *The Sea Captain.* Finally Percy turns and acknowledges them. 'Right then, my maid?' he says to Molly. 'I heard you had a bashing. I wondered where Crispin had disappeared to, but Tom up at the pier told me.'

Crispin, guiltily, says, 'Sorry, Percy, I've not been in touch. I was worried sick about Molly.'

''Tis right and proper that you be so. Well, best be off now.'

He heads for the stairs, nodding to Esme who says, 'I think you should see the doctor, Percy. Your cough doesn't sound too good, and the drenching you got tonight won't help.'

'I'll drive you home,' Crispin says. 'Esme's right, you must see the doctor tomorrow.'

Percy insists on walking, but Crispin is adamant. He goes out to get the car while Esme and Molly wait with

150

Percy, who seems calm now, his normal self. 'I'll be a while,' Crispin says to Esme when Percy cannot hear. 'I'll get him settled, try to get him to bed, make sure he's all right before I leave him. Will you stay with Molly?'

Molly, overhearing, mutters, 'I'm perfectly capable on my own,' then smiles at Esme and goes on, 'but it would be nice if you stayed and had a gossip.'

'I'd love to stay. I've just finished a sculpture, and I've been dying to talk to somebody, be sociable. Richard's at a late play rehearsal, so he's no help.'

Crispin and Percy leave, and Esme, having forgot completely her sudden intention to visit Harriet, settles down with Molly, the two of them soon deep in a satisfying exchange of ideas and good gossip.

Richard, coming home from Harriet's place much later, is surprised to find the house dark, nobody at home. He is not worried, merely slightly annoyed. Esme could have left a note, he thinks with irritation. He supposes she is at the Tate, at one of those talks they have Tuesday evenings, about some artist or another. They go on for ever, what with coffee and wine and cheese and all that endless analyzing. Esme tried to get him to go when the Tate first opened, and he did once, but was unnerved by the cluster of people swarming around her, plying her with accolades over her latest exhibition which had just opened in the town. Sycophants, he had thought with disgust, unwilling to face the simple truth: that Esme's work was exceptionally good, and the praise and admiration were justified.

He is in the bath when Esme walks in. 'Where have you been? You could have left a note,' he says as she walks into the bathroom.

Immediately in the wrong, Esme starts to apologize, explaining about meeting Percy Prynne on the beach, taking him to Crispin's. 'Crispin's only just come back

151

now. Percy was feverish, so he got the doctor out right away; luckily he was in the area and came at once. The poor old boy has got bronchitis. I'm glad it's something curable; I thought he was losing his mind when I met him wandering about. It must have been the fever making him act so strangely.'

Richard closes his eyes, relaxing in the bath while Esme tells him about her day and evening. She doesn't think to mention her aborted plans to visit Harriet, and indeed, why should she? They were not important, and certainly not of interest to Richard or anyone else.

Instead, since Richard doesn't seem to want to talk about his play rehearsal this evening, she tentatively begins to talk of her latest completed sculpture, sensing that Richard is in a good mood and inclined to listen, something that happens rarely these days. They end the evening peacefully, with a drink of hot chocolate and a good book in bed. Esme, propped up on pillows beside her husband, gives his arm a squeeze and thinks how good life can be, how serene during these periods of contentment.

Richard, next to her, thinks of Harriet.

Jordan Culpepper misses his yoga classes. He tells himself he misses the discipline, needs it for his work, misses the spiritual vibes which are necessary for creativity.

And so when he wanders out to Smeaton's Pier with his sketch pad one sunny day at the end of March and sees Lizzie and her hulking great baby hitched on her hip, waving Tom off in the *Girl Lizzie*, it seems only natural to invite her to his studio on the night they normally have yoga class.

'But why?' Lizzie blurts out. 'Molly's laid up, will be for weeks with that arm.'

'Yes, it's a great pity,' Jordan says solemnly. 'We all miss her dreadfully. That's why I thought I'd ask a select few from the class to get together despite Molly's absence. We could go through the postures, keep ourselves in trim until she returns.'

Lizzie thinks about this. Since Molly's accident she has already put back on the three pounds she'd lost, and Tom is making rude jokes about changing the name of his boat to the *Fat Lizzie*. Besides, she rather likes the idea of being one of Jordan's select few. She didn't think she was that good at yoga, and to be singled out by someone who does the exercises as well as Jordan flatters and pleases her.

'All right,' she agrees. 'I'll come. Tomorrow night, right? Me Mum'll be glad of babysitting again; I think she likes getting away from her own mum one night a week.'

She gives Jordan a shy little wave and walks back down the pier, her fat baby bouncing on her hip and looking like a plump cherub right out of a Poussin painting. Jordan wishes Lizzie would sit with him in the sun, take out that delectable breast and begin nursing the babe again. Sitting on the stone bench against the back of the pier, Jordan picks up his sketch book and begins to draw the gulls floating tranquilly in the water of the harbour.

'Right then, my lover?' A booming voice in his ear forces him to look up into the whiskered face of Sid Hocking.

Jordan frowns, trying to look intense as he stares at the gulls and at the drawing, but says politely, 'Hello, Sid.'

Sid frowns too, wishing Jordan would call him Cap'n like the tourists do, and many of the artists as well. Of course he's not a proper sea captain, not a master mariner or anything fancy like that, but what do the

153

artists know? He's skipper of his own vessel, and that's what counts.

However Sid Hocking is not one to carry a grudge. He believes firmly that the fishermen and the artists should not only tolerate each other, but be on friendly terms, a view not popular over the past hundred years but gaining credence now. Sid feels that he personally has to make up for the days when the fishermen, staunch Methodists, used to throw the odd artist in the harbour at full tide, easel and all, when an unwary painter tried to work on Sunday. Besides, Sid rather likes the artists. He feels they give the town a kind of bonus, like a good run of bass on a wintry December day. He doesn't think much of most of their paintings, especially the ones in that Tate gallery which he had a look at once. He went out of curiosity, wanting to know what everybody was talking about, but never again. If he had fished like those blokes painted, his nets and lines would have stayed empty, catching only seaweed and the odd useless dogfish.

'Still at it, eh, my handsome?' Sid says with a snort and a chuckle, pointing a chubby finger at Jordan's sketch. 'You've drawn them boats a hundred times, sure as sea-birds cry.'

'These are gulls, Sidney,' Jordan says frostily, 'not boats.'

Sid roars with laughter at his mistake. ''Es, I see that now. The old eyes ain't what they used to be.' He puts his blubbery hands on his belly where they shake and tremble as he laughs and laughs.

Jordan ignores him, hoping he'll go away, but Sid likes Jordan, thinks his pompous manner is a huge joke and that underneath is a normal human being. He likes his paintings: at least you can recognize what they are, unlike some. Sid doesn't see the point of artists coming to Cornwall to paint the beauty of it

154

all, and then painting great blobs of nothing instead.

Thank the good Lord that some of them retain some sanity, like Jordan here, and that nice wife of his, Alice, Sid thinks. She comes down often in the spring and summer, to the harbour, with her huge sketch book, bigger than she is practically, to draw the emmetts, good pictures too, clear and simple and a decent likeness. He hopes she's not starting to get funny, though. Sid didn't like the portrait of Percy that she did with those murky fish lurking about in the mist, and Percy himself, all grand and full of himself. In truth, Sid was slightly miffed that she hadn't painted *him*.

'Do you ever do, like, those portrait things?' Sid asks Jordan. 'You know, like your wife does.'

'I haven't for some time,' Jordan says, thinking that Sid means the nude in oils, Alice's self-portrait, which is hanging in the window of the Sandpiper right now. 'Though I might just try my hand at it again.'

Sid beams, and leans back against the stone of the pier to catch the sun. Perhaps Jordan is thinking of painting *him*, Sid muses. That would be one up for old Percy Prynne, for Jordan is sure to do a better job than Alice.

The sun is warm on his face, the air calm and still. Even the gulls are not flying raucously about but are floating serenely in the water, bobbing up and down with the slight movement of the waves like little boats themselves. Crispin, who is back fishing again, is moored not far off the pier with a catch of sole that he and Pete are untangling from the nets. The old seal is around as usual, begging for a hand-out, and Crispin throws him the odd fish which he catches in his mouth and then dives back under the water.

Jordan pauses in his sketching and thinks about Sid's question and his own reply. Perhaps it *is* time for a change in his work, a new direction. Perhaps it is time to begin drawing the human figure again.

Sid Hocking, dozing in the sun, feels that his hour has come at last, that he will soon, like Percy Prynne, be immortalized on canvas. He would be dismayed to know that Jordan Culpepper is not thinking of a portrait of a crusty old seaman in a captain's hat and a whiskered face, but the tubby nude body of a young nubile female with a tangle of curly hair and swollen nipples leaking milk.

The next evening, promptly at seven-thirty, Lizzie lets herself in the back door of the Culpepper guest-house, which is opened on yoga nights, and makes her way up the stairs which go directly to Jordan's studio. Jordan is there alone, sitting in front of the drawn velvet curtains in the lotus position, eyes closed in deep meditation, though one lid surreptitiously flickers open for a moment to check who has come in.

'Oh, excuse me, Jordan. Sorry, didn't mean to barge in like this, only you did say—' Lizzie breaks off and looks around the empty studio. 'I must be early, I'm the first one here. And I rushed so, I thought sure I was late.'

'You *are* late, Elizabeth,' Jordan murmurs without opening his eyes. 'We've started without you.'

'We?' Lizzie asks, bemused. 'There's no-one here but you and me.'

'Me and the cosmos,' Jordan says enigmatically. 'The vibrant energies of the universe. *They* are all here, Beth.'

'Oh. Well, what about the others?'

'No-one has appeared but you, my dear,' Jordan murmurs, opening his eyes at last. He neglects to add that he has not told any of the others about this special yoga session.

Lizzie is disappointed. 'Well, I suppose I'd best be off then, go back to me mum.' The thought of sitting and talking to *her* all evening puts Lizzie in a gloom. Tom is out fishing and her mother will have her ear off, telling

156

her how to look after the baby, complaining about Tom, moaning on about her own mother who lives with her.

'No, don't go!' Jordan exclaims. 'It will be far better with just the two of us. Roll out your blanket and come lie here beside me.'

Tossing up between this and her mother, Jordan wins, and anyway Lizzie is getting a bit of her old confidence back. Jordan obviously thinks she is a serious yoga student, as graceful and supple as Molly herself. Peeling off her wet anorak, she spreads her blanket and flops down, all pink track-suited and glowing from the wind, on the floor beside Jordan.

Jordan looks at her critically for a moment, and is pleased at what he sees. The cheeks of both her face and her bottom are full and round; he imagines that the ones he can't see are as rosy and tempting as the ones he can. He'd like to gently pinch all four, and hopes that one day he will.

Lizzie, unself-conscious now, is lying flat on her back in the relaxation position, or corpse posture as Molly calls it. Her legs are apart, her arms relaxed away from the body, her palms facing upwards. Molly always starts her classes with a few minutes like this, to unwind them. 'God, I'm knackered,' Lizzie exclaims, then remembers she is not supposed to speak whilst relaxing and blushes, turning as pink as her track suit.

Jordan finds this fetching. Lying down next to her, he edges as closely as he can to her blanket, feeling his arm brushing against her plump little hand. 'Now breath deeply,' he murmurs as Molly would. 'In and out, in and out, slowly, rhythmically.'

Their breathing slows, deepens. Soon they are breathing in unison, harmoniously, and Jordan feels the cosmic energy radiating from their prostrate bodies. He feels deeply spiritual, yet at the same time physically excited. He feels he is linked with Lizzie on a higher plane, imbibing the vibrations of the universe. He knows Lizzie must feel it too: the vibrations are so intense, magnetic.

A sudden noise disturbs his reverie. Lifting up his head and opening his eyes, he sees that Lizzie is fast asleep and snoring. Somewhat deflated, he pinches her rather sharply.

'What? Oh hell, did I go to sleep again? Sorry, Jordan.'

Jordan stands up and motions Lizzie to do so. He begins taking her through the various yoga postures, which Lizzie obediently follows. Jordan decides that he could be as good a teacher, if not better, than Molly. He especially likes helping to adjust Lizzie's positions, putting his hands under her capacious bosom to straighten her ribcage, or at the very bottom of her fleshy spine to angle her hips correctly.

Lizzie, on the other hand, misses Molly. Jordan is too serious, too intense about this yoga stuff, and though she was flattered at first to be included, she misses Molly's fun and laughter, misses the comradeship of the rest of the class. When Jordan decides that it is time for the final relaxation, Lizzie plops down on her back gratefully. 'Phew, what a workout! I'm sweating like a pig.'

She closes her eyes and within moments she is asleep again. Jordan, sitting on the floor next to her, doesn't even pretend to relax, but takes the opportunity to study her soundly, taking in the ample breasts under the tight pink sweatshirt, the meaty thighs, the chubby chunky belly.

Lizzie wakes suddenly, to find Jordan looking intently at her. Embarrassed, she wiggles into a sitting position and says, 'Hey, aren't you relaxing too? It's not on, that! We do it together or not at all.'

'I can relax much better looking at you, Elizabeth,'

Jordan says seriously. 'Yoga always makes me creative, unleashes the muse, as it were.'

'Um, oh?'

'Yes, I very often get a strong urge to paint after a yoga class. I'd like to paint you, Lizbet darling. Here, now.'

'Oh. Oh my.' Lizzie wraps her blanket around herself and blushes for the second time that evening. 'The thing is, me mum, you know. She's expecting me home. And Tom will have come in by now, and he doesn't half get wild if he has to talk with me mum alone for more than ten minutes.'

'I see. Well, we certainly don't want Tom getting wild, do we.' Jordan is limp with frustration. 'What about next week, then? We can forget about the yoga until Molly is better and I'll just paint you on Wednesday nights. Then you don't even have to tell either your mother or Tom; they'll think you are just at your usual yoga lessons.'

Lizzie looks at him suspiciously, and Jordan hastens to add, 'So that you can surprise them, you know? Show them the painting when it's finished and hanging in a gallery somewhere.'

Lizzie ponders all this. She can't see herself bringing either her mother or Tom into one of those poncy galleries, but perhaps she'll keep it a secret anyway. Tom thinks Jordan is a poser, and her mother believes all artists are immoral. Neither one of them really appreciates a sensitive man like Jordan, who is not only a successful artist but also a very serious man. Unconsciously she straightens her shoulders, lifts her chin. If a man like that wants to paint her, she can't be *that* fat, she thinks with some satisfaction. She decides to stop at the off-license on the way home, treat herself to a couple of packets of salt and vinegar crisps, something she's denied herself for a month now.

159

Jordan, seeing her face light up like the Godrevy lighthouse, is satisfied. 'See you next week then, yes? Same time, same place.'

'Right.' Jordan helps Lizzie put on her anorak and rolls up her blanket carefully. 'Oh, I was wondering,' she adds as she goes to the door, 'That is, I'll have to wear my track suit again, you know? For my portrait, that is. I mean, if this is going to be a surprise for Tom and me mum, I'll have to dress like I was still going to yoga class.'

'That's fine, Beth darling,' Jordan assures her. 'It really doesn't matter in the slightest what you wear.'

Lizzie nods, waves an awkward goodbye, leaving Jordan smirking delightedly in the doorway. She makes her way down the hill, picks up her crisps and eats them hurriedly before she gets home. Luckily Tom arrives at the same time, so her mother leaves before too long and Lizzie can collapse on the sofa in front of the telly.

'Right then, love? How was the old keep-fit or yoga or whatever?' Tom squeezes her knee in the pink-clad track suit and changes the channel.

Lizzie feels a momentary guilt as she thinks of the fib she will be telling him next week, pretending to be going to yoga when really she will be modelling for Jordan. A cry from the bedroom – infant Michael awake and squawking for a feed – distracts her, and she rushes to him, taking the baby out of his cot and onto the sofa with her and Tom.

'Little blighter's just like his mum, plump and always hungry. Don't know how I'll keep you both in tuck.' Tom chucks Michael fondly under the chin, but the baby doesn't stop wailing. Lizzie pulls out her milky breast from under her track-suit top and stuffs the nipple in his mouth.

'I could kill for a cup of tea,' Tom says, getting up

and stretching his arms. 'Haven't had one since mid-afternoon. Like a cuppa, Lizzie?'

Lizzie nods gratefully, looking at Tom with a rush of affection. Tom grins at her and says, 'Get that stroppy lad to sleep, Lizzie, love, and let's you and me hit the sack. Not to sleep, mind.'

Lizzie's eyes glow. 'You told me mum you was dead beat,' she says, teasing.

'The things I tell your old mum and the things I tell you are not always the same.' He grins at her again, ruffles the almost non-existent hair of baby Michael and goes out to get the tea.

Lizzie, sprawled on the sofa, the reflection from the telly coating all her small animal figures with a soft coloured sheen, lets her baby suckle, forgetting Jordan Culpepper, and yoga, and artists, and everything else as she waits in a pleasant soporific haze for Tom and her cup of tea and the night ahead.

That same evening, while Jordan is still upstairs in his study doing a few yoga Salutes to the Sun after Lizzie has gone, Alice Culpepper is in the laundry-room with her lodger, Harlan Zayevich. Harlan is from Boca Raton, Florida, and is taking a year off from college to travel around decaying old Europe and learn about life. He is able to do this, not because he is young and strong and willing to take on anything – as he tells anyone who will listen – but rather because both his parents are very, very rich and he is their only child. Back in Florida, Harlan had fallen in love and was threatening to marry a most unsuitable young lady; that is, she was poor and of immigrant South American parents. His own parents prided themselves on being 100 per cent American, having forgotten somehow that Harlan's own grand-father had been a Polish immigrant. When Harlan's father could not buy off the young lady (he offered to pay for the rest of her college education if she transferred to another university, preferably as far away from Florida as was possible), his mother took a gamble and said that they would accept the girl if Harlan went away for a year and did not contact her in any way until he returned. Harlan's mother was both sage and sanguine; this girl was not her son's first love; he had been falling in love regularly since he was fourteen and she knew he would not stop now. To put it simply, if Harlan was not with the girl he loved, he loved the girl he was with, as the old song went.

However, this time Harlan was not running true to form. He had arrived in Europe last September, landing in Madrid (he had done high-school Spanish) and wondering why everyone in the city talked with a lisp. When he finally figured out that the South American Spanish he had learned at school was no match for whatever it was they spoke in Madrid, he escaped to Portugal, only to find they didn't speak Spanish there at all, something he had never known.

The French were somewhat better; they did speak English, or many of them did. Harlan very nearly fell in love with a lovely young woman on the banks of the Loire, in the town of Amboise, in the shadow of the great old castle where Leonardo da Vinci was buried. The girl was a waitress at the hotel he stayed in for several weeks, and Harlan had a few idyllic walks along the river banks with her, visited one or two châteaux. But before anything more than hand-holding and the odd kiss could develop, an old boyfriend appeared and claimed her back.

Harlan moped about for another few weeks, reverting to melancholy and a mournful longing for his lost Floridian love. He moved on to Brittany and got drunk one night in a Celtic pub in Lorient, where a charming Breton who spoke perfect English told him he must visit

162

Cornwall, in England, before surreptitiously lifting his wallet.

Harlan, unfazed by the theft (he only had 200 odd francs in the wallet; his credit cards and traveller's cheques were safe in a bum-bag wrapped around his waist), decided it was time to cross water again, and a few weeks ago appeared in St Ives, getting off the bus from Plymouth and wandering about until he spotted an interesting row of Victorian guest-houses and knocked on the first door. This was the Culpepper's house, and he arrived just in time to distract Jordan from pursuing his naked wife upstairs to chastize her for prancing about in that condition in front of Lance Giddens.

Harlan was not, however, to know this. What he did know was that they spoke English in this place, and with great relief he decided to hang out right there for a while. On fine days, which admittedly were rare, he could look out the window of his room at an expanse of ocean and pretend he was back in Florida, which he had missed like crazy in Spain and Portugal and France (except during his brief idyll with the girl on the Loire).

He's not missing Florida now, not in this damp cramped laundry-room where Alice does her painting. Harlan is looking at Alice's latest work, another self-portrait, only this time it is of her head and shoulders. Her face looks thin, harassed. 'It's not like you,' Harlan blurts out. 'I mean, you're a lot prettier than that.'

Alice smiles. 'You can't idealize people in portraits. I had to do that down at the harbour, make everyone young, attractive, or they wouldn't buy the bloody things. Have you ever seen Rembrandt's self-portraits? I love the last one, every line, every pouch, every agony and disappointment, is there.'

Harlan loves hearing her talk like this. He feels so

cultured, learning about art right at the door of an artist. He couldn't believe his luck when he realized he was in a real live art colony here, with an honest-to-God studio right on the top floor of the guest-house. Harlan's parents have always been devotees of art and culture, though sometimes he suspects his father collects paintings more as an investment than because of any affinity with them, and that his mother goes to the theatre and concerts in Miami more to be seen than to soak up any cultural vibrations.

Alice is studying the portrait intensely. Harlan watches her, secretly charmed by her little snub nose, the frown lines above it. He wishes she were working on a nude self-portrait again, like she was when he first arrived. He had discovered her stark fanny naked in this very room, on his second day there, looking for the dining-room and taking the wrong doorway.

'Oh, Jesus Christ, I am so sorry. Excuse me. I'm real sorry, OK? Excuse me.' He kept chattering on in this manner as he backed out of the doorway. Alice, hardly noticing, caught his eye in the reflection of the mirror and nodded. 'You'll be wanting your breakfast. Of course. To tell you the truth, I forgot. You said nine o'clock and it's that now. We haven't had guests for so long I forgot you were here.'

Oblivious of her state of undress, she turned and faced him, giving him a full-frontal view. Trying to look her straight in the eyes he stammered, 'Look, no big deal. I can go out and get breakfast. I want to go out anyway. You know, explore. I didn't do any yesterday; I was so god-damn tired I slept all day.'

'Nonsense. You can talk to me while I make your breakfast. It's nice and peaceful in the kitchen, with the kids all gone and Jordan in his studio.' She nonchalantly put on her old silk dressing-gown and tied it neatly around her waist.

Harlan didn't remember eating much breakfast. Though hungry, it was disconcerting to have Alice sitting in front of him, sipping tea with not a stitch of clothing on underneath that remarkable gold shimmering bohemian bathrobe.

Luckily, she is quite bundled up now, in a long skirt and turtle-neck, her hair tied back with a narrow yellow scarf. Harlan cannot help feeling a bit wistful, though, for he had rather got used to seeing her wandering about in her bathrobe, barely waiting until she had closed the laundry-room door before shaking it off and confronting her painting and her image in the mirror. When he had overcome his surprise and embarrassment, and she had explained what she was doing, he had felt quite sophisticated, incredibly European and decadent. He couldn't wait to get back to recount the story to the guys back home; they'd be green with envy.

Alice gives her painting another critical look and leads the way out of the laundry-room and into the kitchen. Harlan, following, is annoyed to find Christopher out of bed, in his pajamas, eating bread and jam and getting it all over the floor. He'd like Alice to carry on talking about her work; it is so inspiring to be in an artistic atmosphere. What with Jordan in his studio upstairs; and that old woman Oona North who is so famous, apparently, that probably his own parents have even heard of her; and Molly with the gorgeous red-gold hair who paints those huge canvases; and Esme Cochran, the sculptor, who is also getting pretty famous (he's seen her name in several books on St Ives); and that gallery owner Lance Giddens who knows everyone who is famous and maybe will be himself one day (for anyone who paints the weird things that people say Lance paints is *bound* to be famous). With such an illustrious lot, Harlan is beginning to feel quite arty, and almost famous himself, through association. He has even grown his well-cut sensible brown hair long – well, longer than it was – and bought several chunky wool fisherman's jerseys to wear instead of his fitted cotton shirts and cashmere sweaters. Harlan feels imbued with creativity, soaking it up by osmosis from the energy in the air, the sea, the breath of those around him. He has even modestly tried his hand at sketching, drawing the odd abstract line or two while sitting down by the harbour watching the fishermen bring in the catch.

Christopher is being a typical five-year-old, Harlan thinks crossly, whinging and demanding, and Alice stops being an artist and becomes a mother, which irritates Harlan. He wants his beloved Alice to be above all that, to be the madonna of the art world, to be the great earth mother of creativity, not of three obnoxious children and a bad-tempered husband, though Harlan can tolerate the husband because he is an artist. Harlan thinks of Art in capital letters these days, so completely has he been landed in the midst of it, like a poor cod hooked on a line of conger eel.

Alice doesn't seem to want Christopher out of the way, because she is cradling him in her lap, kissing his jammy forehead, her long fair hair getting sticky too as it escapes from its band and falls into the child's face. Harlan, looking at her, suddenly remembers how she looked naked, and has to turn away so that she cannot see his eyes.

He is in love with her, of course. He is totally besotted by her, but he knows beyond any doubt that she is definitely out of bounds. She is married, a mother of three children, fourteen years older than him, and a great artist – definitely out of his league. Harlan knows that he will spend the rest of his life loving her, sketching tragically under a palm tree in Boca Raton, never marrying, roaming the world aimlessly, always seeking something he will never ever find.

He sighs, audibly. Alice looks up and smiles; she knows Harlan is in love with her, and secretly finds it both sweet and hilarious, though she would never ever let him know this, or hurt his feelings in any way. She thinks he is rather endearing, and innocent despite his many girlfriends (whom she has heard all about, including the poor sod he is not now going to marry). He's quite nice looking too, with that squeaky-clean hair, those darling dimples and that healthy robust body. It is not unflattering to be loved by a young man, especially when one has been married twelve years and feels worn down with house, children, husband.

'Are you all right?' Alice asks, acknowledging the sigh, but pretending she doesn't know it is for her.

'Yes. Sure. Fine.' This is said darkly, morosely, enigmatically.

'Good.' Alice smiles at him again and leans down to kiss Christopher's blond hair. 'I was wondering, Harlan,' she says when she looks up again, 'if you'd like to go to an art auction in Penzance one day. It's quite a large showroom, and there are usually some interesting paintings there. Then, if you like, we can go on to Newlyn, as you've not seen the art gallery there and it's a definite must.'

'That'd be swell, Alice,' Harlan mutters, unable to believe his luck. Alice has been so engrossed in her painting that he's hardly seen her during the day, except for breakfast. In the evenings, when Jordan is sometimes working and Alice is alone with the kids, she'll ask him to join her, in the kitchen or in front of the telly. They've never had a day out together.

'We'll celebrate the finish of my painting. It should be done soon. Maybe take a picnic if the weather's fine, have it on the Penwith moors.'

Art auctions, picnics, wild romantic moors just like *Wuthering Heights* (he saw the film when he was an impressionable fourteen-year-old) – Harlan is ecstatic. 'I'd love that,' he beams.

Alice looks at his radiant glowing face and decides she'd better be careful: this lad is really infatuated, and she must take care not to tease him or upset him in any way.

Still, it will be fun going out with someone lively and enthusiastic for a change. Jordan has become so very critical lately, of everything: other artists, his children, Alice herself. He was terribly critical about her nude painting; he said he was surprised Lance wanted it for the gallery. Alice rightly attributes this to sour grapes, but it hurts none the less. Marriage and children and running a guest-house and sketching tourists on the beach is not conducive to enhancing one's self-esteem, and until she painted *The Sea Captain* it was at an all-time low. She has not shown Jordan the new self-portrait; she knows she'll have to, but she hates the thought of all the faults he'll find in it.

So a pleasant day out with an adoring young man will do wonders for her tarnished ego, she thinks contentedly. She must be very wary, that's all. She doesn't want to use him, to make him fall for her any harder, or to lead him on in any way, just so that she can salvage her own damaged confidence.

But a day out would be splendid. It will be April then, and hopefully spring will have arrived. Her painting will be finished – that will make three now in this new series – and it will be, she knows, simply beautiful up on the moors.

Hugging her son, grinning at the sweet young man who adores her, Alice suddenly feels young, vibrant and innocently happy.

Harlan, watching her, seeing this woman he loves so out of reach, feels old, stricken, and full of lugubrious angst. But he's innocent too, and because of this, slight trickles of pure joy penetrate his cloak of despair, and he can't wait, absolutely cannot wait, until he is alone with his Alice on the lonely wuthering (whatever that means) moors.

Chapter Eight

Fog slithers across the shining sands of St Ives for the next few days, sometimes deceptively gentle and soothing, like transparent pearls bubbling over the sea and land, and then suddenly changing, becoming damper, more opaque, dangerous, mysterious. At home, Percy Prynne stays in his bed taking his antibiotics with cold tea, scarcely noticing the skin sealing the liquid on the top of his mug. He is happy as he coughs and wheezes, for he is Percy Prynne himself again, skipper of the *Fair Celt*, as wild and strong and heady as the sea itself, as his sturdy reliable little boat that daily plunges, in his head, into the churning foam and depths. He can hear his wife singing as he takes the wheel of the vessel, heads miles out to sea, far away from land, from safety. The wind blows, the waves crash, but Percy is not afraid. Maggie sings and croons and hollers like the few intrepid gulls that have followed the boat instead of remaining, fat and lazy, on the harbour. She whispers in his ear like a mermaid, her long brown hair shining, falling in his face as he steers the boat, and wrapping itself around his neck so that he cries out in pleasure, gently chiding her to let him be so that he can steer the ship. Sometimes Percy sings too, his old voice hoarse and cracked, and he has to break off because of the wheezing and coughing

170

it brings about. But while he coughs Maggie carries on the song, and sometimes his father and brother join in, and with him the other fishermen, singing the familiar tunes he hasn't heard since childhood.

Crispin comes often to visit Percy, and so does Esme, but the singing stops when they arrive. Sid Hocking came once, with a bottle of rum which he thrust, embarrassedly, at Percy, saying, 'Here, my cock, that'll chase off the bronchials quicker than a shark can chase away a school of mackerel.'

Percy drinks the rum slowly, a sip or two out of the bottle along with his antibiotics. He is as contented as he's ever been lately; his bed is the *Fair Celt*, the woollen blankets crumpled over him are his nets, strong and well-handled; the wooden bedpost he grips in his fevers is the steering-wheel that he clings to as he rides through the storms.

Molly too lies in bed, feverish and bruised and pained, watching the fog snake across the sea and insinuate itself against the wide window-panes in Crispin's front room. She has succumbed to some kind of flu or virus; the doctor has been, prescribed rest and fluids, and left her, thankfully, in peace. Crispin has to leave her when the tides are right, for he has missed too many days already, but Esme comes for a day with hot home-made broths in a stainless-steel flask, with flowers, with her firm strong hands that straighten the bedclothes and cool Molly's brow. She apologizes that she's going away the next day, to London, but other friends pop in, bring fruit juice, make weak herbal teas for the invalid. Oona comes too, with just herself and a strong palpitating love that beats between them as she sits on a hard wooden chair beside her granddaughter's bed. Molly drinks Evian water and orange juice and watches the fog and the sea meet and merge, listens to the gulls outside her window, watches Witch watching the gulls flying ghost-like in the fog.

Other ghosts appear and disappear in this treacherous March mist. When the tide is low on Porthminster beach, Hugo and his Cara make love on the wet sand behind the rocks, hidden by the fog, the night and their own invincibility. More sedately, Hugo's father Richard makes love to Harriet on her plain hard bed, heady with deceptive freedom because Esme is now in London for the opening of her exhibition. If Hugo knew this, he would have taken Cara to the house, but he thinks his father stays home every evening, pining for his wife as he watches *Sportsnight* or the news on the telly.

Lance Giddens, alone in his attic, paints his deep fish eyes and salt-washed sea skeletons and thinks of Esme, far away in London. He'd have liked to go with her, but did not know how to offer without showing Esme the desperate love he feels for her. He is cross with Richard for not going himself; he feels the man could have taken at least a day or two off work, for something so important.

Alice and Jordan Culpepper do not notice the fog, for Alice is locked in her laundry-room while Harlan Zayevich lurks and pants outside the door, hoping for the odd glimpse of his beloved. Jordan, locked in his machinations, paints his harbour scenes but thinks of Rubens and Botticelli and Titian, and their naked ladies lying voluptuously on cushioned settees, or lifting their voluminous arms suggestively to heaven. He feels that he too is one of them, that the only thing keeping him from his goal is the right model, the right fleshy thighs and buttocks and breasts and shoulders that he thinks he has at last found in Lizzie. Creative inspiration, cosmic energy, and a certain striving ecstasy, which contains a great deal of pure lust, courses through Jordan, and he cannot wait for next Wednesday evening.

*   *   *

'How do you like the Cajun pork, Dad?'

Richard, contemplating the mixture of hot tomato sauce, noodles and bits of pork on his plate, says, doubtfully, 'Well, it looks good. I suppose presentation is important.'

'Absolutely. Now go on, try it.'

Hugo looks on with interest as Richard samples the Cajun pork. 'Not bad,' he says at last. 'Not bad at all.'

Hugo has taken over the cooking in the Cochran household since Esme left for London several days ago. Recently he got a job in a new restaurant on the Wharf, helping the owner, who is also the cook, with his speciality: rich spicy Cajun dishes. Hugo loves his new job, loves messing around in the kitchen, as he calls it, experimenting with spices and herbs and sauces. Because it is evening work he has all day to surf, and because the pay is good he has given up his part-time hours in the surfing shop.

Richard has mixed feelings about this new enthusiasm. He is delighted, of course, that Hugo is becoming more responsible, insisting on doing the cooking at home, but it means he has had to curtail his time with Harriet, which he senses is beginning to irritate her. Instead of going there straight after work now, he comes home, shares Hugo's latest culinary effort, and then goes off to Harriet's when Hugo leaves at six-thirty for the restaurant.

'Can't you tell him what you used to tell Esme: that you have to go back to Penzance for a play rehearsal?' Harriet said rather curtly one evening, when Richard phoned to say he wouldn't be over as planned, for Hugo had a night off and was at home.

'The play was put on two weeks ago, I really can't use that excuse any more,' Richard replied reasonably.

'Well, why isn't Hugo off with his girlfriend?'

'She's studying for exams,' Richard said, impatience creeping into his voice.

Harriet, wise enough to know not to push it, said nothing more. She sensed Richard was enjoying the companionship of his son, of the novel situation in which he was being looked after, so to speak, by Hugo. But she missed Richard. She had changed her part-time hours at the estate agency during Esme's absence, so they could meet after work, enjoy long languid dinners together, have time for talking, sharing their day, perhaps even, if Richard was particularly annoyed at Esme for some reason, dreaming of an impossible future which they could have shared, had things been different.

Richard was often cross with Esme these days. 'She's staying another week,' he told Harriet, pretending delight because it meant, of course, more time together, less risk of being caught out. But in reality he was angry. Esme should have been eager to return to him, sitting at home alone and lonely (well, Esme wasn't to know differently). Instead, she phoned to say that she was meeting gallery owners, being interviewed, was going to other exhibitions, and would he mind if she stayed on?

'Not at all,' he said, and vowed to spend even more time with Harriet. 'Enjoy yourself.'

Esme is enjoying herself. She is staying with an old friend, a woman recently divorced, and loving it. While Hugo sits with Richard in the kitchen in St Ives, watching with satisfaction as Richard not only cleans his plate but asks for more, Esme is drinking white wine at the opening of another exhibition, that of the friend she is staying with who is a painter of surreal still lifes which are all the vogue now in London.

Esme is, at the moment, being chatted up by an art critic, Samuel Tolling. 'You spend far too much time down in Cornwall,' Samuel is intoning in his husky voice, blowing smoke rings vaguely out into the chattering crowd.

'It's my home,' Esme says, amused. Samuel is skeletal and wears tight black trousers with dark turtle-neck jumpers, emphasizing this. He dyes his grey hair a glossy brown and wears it longish, combed sleekly straight back which reminds Esme of the seal in the harbour of St Ives.

'Your home is here, darling.' Samuel waves his stick-insect arm grandly, like the Pope giving a blessing. 'With us.'

Esme smiles. She enjoys her trips to London, but it would be the last place in the world she would choose to live. Samuel takes her hand and says, 'Dinner, afterwards?' He kisses her palm briefly with dry wispy lips.

Esme knows that Samuel is gay, so she accepts his invitation. Last night she went to a cocktail party with a well-known writer who had just bought one of her sculptures, a small stone sculpture of a woman and baby, one of her earlier pieces. Because the man had bought the work for his wife, away at the time, Esme assumed he was happily married but lonely, so she agreed to dinner later at his flat in Islington. It took her all the tact and diplomacy she could muster to extricate herself from *that* situation, and she vowed not to make the same mistake again.

Esme does not fool herself that it is her charm, beauty, sex appeal, that caused the writer, and one or two other men she has met here in London, to make a pass at her. She knows what men have known for ages, that fame, money and power are aphrodisiacs. Esme has been a minor celebrity in London since she has been here; her exhibition was written about in every major newspaper, her photograph has appeared in the glossy Sunday colour supplements.

'You are thriving on this adulation, darling,' Samuel

175

tells her later as he sees her home in a taxi. 'You look stunning.'

Esme knows this must be true, for Samuel is nothing if not objective about women. She has had her rough chestnut hair cut very short, and the silver highlights seem more a hairdresser's cunning art than the natural streaks they really are. Her eyes sparkle with excitement and triumph, and her skin is clear, radiant.

'You look like you have a lover,' Samuel exclaims as they leave the taxi to have a nightcap at the flat where Esme is staying. 'Do you?' he asks eagerly, avid for gossip.

Esme doesn't mind the question; she has known Samuel for years, still has his very first review of her work hanging on the bulletin-board in her kitchen at home. She sees Samuel often when she is in London, for she likes his company, likes the sensitivity she sees under his sometimes flippant manner.

'I'm happily married, Samuel, you know that. It's my work I'm passionate about,' she says.

He sighs. 'How disappointing. I'm passionate about my work too, but my skin has become dreadfully sallow.'

'You need some sea air. Why don't you come to St Ives, stay with us for a weekend?'

Samuel looks doubtful. 'I don't know, darling. All those Cornishmen.'

'Samuel! Don't be dreadful.'

'I suppose I could write another piece on the Tate St Ives. Or look up one of the grand old painters, Patrick Heron or someone, do an interview for one of the Sundays.'

Esme shakes her head. 'I meant come for a holiday. Take a break from work. We'll walk on the beach, sit in quiet pubs—'

'How dreary, darling.'

'And not go near the Tate this time. It will do you so much good, Samuel, I promise you.'

Despite his protests, Samuel lets himself be convinced, and they arrange a date in the near future. As Esme goes into the kitchen to find brandy and make coffee, Samuel is already planning the article he will write about her: the artist at home, surrounded by domestic details; the kind of thing beloved of Sunday-supplement readers. Esme is right, of course. The sea air will do him the world of good. He begins to look forward to his little jaunt to the wilds of Cornwall with gleeful anticipation.

And so as Esme flits about London, finding some things meretricious but others exciting and stimulating, Harriet kisses Richard goodbye after their times together and wishes he could stay longer, or even for the night, but he doesn't know when Hugo will be home from work, likes to be in before his son. Besides, Esme may phone, or Crispin may try to get hold of him – they mustn't be greedy, Richard tells Harriet.

As a matter of fact Richard is beginning to enjoy his evening meals with Hugo, and has to admit that the boy is becoming quite a versatile cook. Last night they had Spanish omelettes, with herbs and tomatoes and onions, and on Sunday Hugo had cooked roast lamb with mint sauce and all the trimmings. Cara was invited over on that day, and the two stayed on for the afternoon, for the surf was down, the day rainy and windy. Harriet had been annoyed, for she hated Sundays and had hoped Richard would spend this one with her. 'Can't I come too for this proper Sunday lunch?' she had asked, in a light flirtatious manner to show that it didn't bother her one way or another.

Richard was nonplussed at the question, for it had never occurred to him to ask Harriet to participate in a

Sunday lunch with his son and girlfriend. It was true that Harriet had taken to calling in more often than usual, and had occasionally been casually asked to stay for a meal when Esme was home, but this was beginning to unnerve him lately, though he had liked it well enough to start with. The lack of division between what was now becoming two separate lives was unrelaxing to say the least. So to Harriet's suggestion for an invitation to lunch he had said, vaguely, 'Hugo's planned it, it's his party. I'm not sure . . .' He trailed off uncertainly.

'Hey, no problem, that's fine, fine!' Harriet cried. 'I've got so much on, anyway; I've got some friends I haven't seen in ages . . .'

Richard, thinking how understanding Harriet was, how she never crowded him, never infringed on his family life and commitments, left her that night feeling benignly grateful and suffused with contentment.

Harriet, on the other hand, had three stiff drinks of gin and paced the floor until dawn, then stayed in bed the entire Sunday brooding on what bastards men were.

'Richard, you look wonderful!'

'So do you, Esme. Did you sleep all right on the train? Here, let me take your case.'

Esme has just arrived in Penzance, on the sleeper from London. It is eight o'clock on a Saturday morning in early April, and the day promises to be warm and soft and sunny. Richard and Esme get into the car and drive out of the town, Esme exclaiming at the familiar sights – the sea, blue and splendid; St Michael's Mount; the Penwith moors as they leave the main road and head towards St Ives. 'It's so good to be back,' Esme says as they drive into town.

When they walk into the kitchen, Esme is assailed by cooking smells: bacon, sausages, grilled mushrooms and tomatoes, eggs. Hugo, a spatula in hand, kisses Esme's

178

cheek and says, 'I thought you'd be hungry after your trip.'

'You're not surfing?' Esme asks. 'There are already four or five out at Porthmeor.' It is only eight-thirty in the morning.

'Wow, the surf must be ace then! Listen, I'll dish this out and then move, OK, Mum? I'll save mine for later. I'd love to hear about your trip and all but the surf has been bad for days, I don't want to miss a good one.' He begins hurriedly slamming eggs and mushrooms onto a plate.

When Hugo has gone Esme says, 'He's certainly keen, isn't he. This must be the earliest he's got up for ages.'

'He's missed you, I think.'

Esme waits for Richard to say that he has missed her as well, but he is helping himself to bacon and sausages, putting bread in the toaster.

So she says instead, 'I've missed you, Richard.' She goes to him, wraps her arms around his waist.

'That's good,' he says, feeling a sudden flush of affection, of love, go through him. He finds, despite Harriet and the freedom of their time together, that he is glad Esme is home, that the kitchen seems altogether warmer, brighter, more accommodating since her return. He turns to her and puts his arms around her and they stand embracing, face to face, for a few moments, until the doorbell, sharp and shrill, disturbs them.

Richard goes to answer it, and from the kitchen Esme can hear the chirpy bright voice of Harriet. Her spirits, lifted by the home-coming, drop sharply; she would like to be alone with Richard, at least for a short time, to savour their reunion. Doesn't Harriet have any sensitivity at all? she thinks crossly as the other woman walks through the doorway.

Richard offers her coffee, though, in truth, he too

is annoyed that Harriet has come over like this; he certainly did not expect it.

'How wonderful that you're back! I've brought fresh croissants and French pastries for you,' Harriet gushes. 'To celebrate your return, and your success.'

Esme thanks her, but her feelings of dismay do not leave. She tries to be friendly, telling Harriet about her trip, the exhibitions she saw, but she wants her to go, feels something has been spoiled. Richard, distracted, makes coffee, sits and listens. Esme at one point puts her hand on Richard's arm, but he moves away from her, which upsets her. Richard is also upset; he feels Harriet should not have shown her face so soon, feels it is a breach of good taste to do so.

Harriet, on the other hand, senses Esme's dismay, and Richard's discomfort, and is glad she followed her impulse to come. She suddenly could not bear being at home alone after her idyllic time with Richard, knowing that he was having a reunion with his wife. She is glad she is here, to reassure herself that nothing has changed, that she is still very much part of Richard's life. When, after about an hour, Harriet finally decides to go, Richard walks her outside where she surreptitiously whispers, 'Next week, as usual, all right?'

Richard, not liking this effrontery, none the less says yes, and Harriet is gone. He walks into the house to find Esme, but the mood has been broken. She has wandered into the back garden and down towards her workroom, and Richard's heart hardens against her. Home only a couple of hours, and there she is, unable to pull herself away from her sculptures, he thinks with irritation.

As a matter of fact Esme doesn't go into her studio. She has come into the garden to smell spring, see the primroses and the white flowers of the wild garlic in the borders, check if the camellia is still in bloom. She is waiting for Richard to follow her out, so she can tell him how very much she missed all this in London.

But Richard doesn't come. He is finishing off the breakfast dishes, clearing away croissant crumbs from the table.

Esme, in the garden, feels an incredible sadness go through her, making her shiver though the morning is warm. Her home-coming, which she has been looking forward to for the past few days, has somehow been marred, tarnished, and she doesn't, for the life of her, even know why.

On Wednesday night Lizzie comes to model for Jordan. A virile flu attack, similar to the one which decimated Molly, has kept her away until now, much to Jordan's frustration.

'I've lost five pounds, being ill,' Lizzie says proudly as she flops down on the plum velvet Victorian settee Jordan has set up for her in his studio.

Jordan studies her critically, relieved to find she looks exactly the same. Her pink track suit is still stretched tight and shiny over those gargantuan breasts, and her thighs still spread like a mammoth pink sponge when she sits down. She looks a bit pale, but this suits him. He likes the white chalk bodies of women in winter; he likes the mystery of it, of seeing skin that not even the sun and air has touched or witnessed, bodies hidden under thick muffled layers of clothing, that only he is allowed to glimpse.

Lizzie, seeing Jordan's sketch pad and pencils, sits up primly, suddenly nervous. 'What do you want me to do?' she blurts out. 'How do you want me to pose?' She moves stiffly, awkwardly.

'I'd like you lying back, just as you were, only you can lift your legs up, like this.' He goes to show her, brushing against her plump soft body with his huge solid

181

one. Lizzie gets comfortable. 'This won't be so bad. I can go to sleep here,' she says, relaxing now.

'Fine,' Jordan says. 'You need to be loose, at ease.' He smiles reassuringly at her, his broad bushy face crinkling like a hedgehog. 'You can undress behind there,' Jordan says, briskly now, strictly professional. He points to a discreet screen set up in the corner. 'There's a dressing-gown there,' he says.

Lizzie grows rigid with shock. He doesn't mean . . . he *can't* mean . . . nude? Naked as the day she was born? He wants to paint her *like that*?

Jordan turns his back and begins fiddling with his pencils, opens his sketch book. Lizzie sits immobile, terrified. She wonders if she can make a run for it, but Jordan is standing between her and the door. Jordan looks up and smiles kindly. 'We haven't that much time, you know. Hadn't we better get started?' he says.

Lizzie puts one arm across her breasts, the other over her lap, as if she were already naked. 'I . . . can't,' she whispers.

'Can't what, Elizabeth?' Jordan frowns, looking like Lizzie's old form tutor after she had been caught smoking behind the maths sheds.

'Can't . . . take off my clothes.' This is hoarse, strangled.

'You're cold?' Jordan asks politely. He promptly takes out a small electric fan heater and turns it on full blast, even though the studio is quite warm. 'There. Run along now and get ready, that's a good girl.'

Lizzie, as if hypnotized, gets off the settee and walks, zombie-like, behind the screen. Authority always defeats her when she is face to face with it, and Jordan is so like Mr Anderson back at school, that huge hulking presence, that deep commanding voice, that air of being completely in charge.

If the dressing-gown hadn't been there, Lizzie would not have been able to go through with it, but because it is practical and warm – white thick terry towelling – she seizes it like a lifebelt, wraps it tightly around her slightly perspiring but very nude body, and edges her way circumspectly back to the velvet settee.

'Ah, good,' Jordan beams. 'Warm enough?'

Lizzie is too nervous to talk or even nod. Jordan waits expectantly, and Lizzie knows she is meant to shed the dressing-gown. But this she simply cannot do. Embarrassed, terrified, unable to escape because her clothes are behind the screen, Lizzie does what she often did when her form tutor, Mr Anderson, scolded her once too often in front of the whole class: she bursts into tears.

Jordan is at her side in an instant, one long massive arm wrapped around her shoulders. 'Whatever is wrong?' he says, soothingly.

'I've never done . . . I've never . . .' Lizzie trails off, wailing.

'Done what, my dear Elizabeth?'

Lizzie's face, bright red with shame, nuzzles into Jordan's shoulder as she blurts out, 'I thought you were going to paint me in my track suit!'

This is so risible that Jordan nearly laughs out loud, but he knows he will lose Lizzie for ever if he does that. Instead, he says, rather pompously, 'The human form, Lizbet, is far too splendid to be cloaked in a pink track suit.'

Lizzie, subdued, sniffs, feeling quite chastized, as she used to be when Mr Anderson chided her about the cigarettes, going on about abusing the purity of her body, which she listened to in awe until she was able to get away and have a good giggle about it with her mates. Her friends are all either living with blokes or married now, many with babies like her, and she feels defenceless without their support. Jordan is embarked on a serious lecture, and she cannot help but be impressed, for he is on about other great artists who have painted the nude form, one of them someone called Rubens whom Jordan seems to admire.

'Look, Elizabeth darling, look at these,' Jordan exclaims, going to a nearby shelf and bringing over a large glossy book to the velvet settee. He opens the book at random, to a coloured illustration of an old-fashioned painting of three women, naked as jay-birds, flinging their arms about each other and twisting them around some kind of rope. They seem to be wading in an improbable watery spray, and it all seems to be suspiciously kinky to Lizzie.

'This is a detail from a Rubens painting, called *Marie Arrives at Marseilles*. Isn't it breathtaking? Look at those magnificent bodies. Look at the powerful stomach and breasts of the one on the left, the extraordinary buttocks on the dark-haired woman.'

Lizzie, cringing with embarrassment, looks. What she sees, however, begins to please her – the three women have bodies not unlike her own: the huge beefy thighs, the rolls of fat around the waist. Jordan is looking at them as if they were perfect, which is not the way Tom sometimes looks at her own body these days. Though he still fancies her, the last time she undressed for bed he made some smart-mouth remark about her excess weight, and since then he always seems to be making wisecracks about it. It's beginning to wear her down, erode her confidence, for he never lets up.

Jordan turns from the book and looks at Lizzie, smiling at her warmly. 'Elizabeth, darling, do you see why I want to paint you? You are the model I have been looking for all my life.'

This is not strictly true, of course, for Jordan has not been interested in life drawing since art college. However, it is true that the very voluptuousness, the massive grandeur of her body is what intrigues him about her. Some of this sincerity spills out in his voice and caresses

Lizzie, who has been starved for compliments since she had the baby, indeed since she became pregnant and she and Tom got married. Though Tom is a good sort, and she loves him like crazy, she also likes being called darling, though she knows Jordan uses it to everyone. Who knows, she thinks, perhaps one day Jordan Culpepper will be as famous as this Rubens person he is going on about, and she, Lizzie, will then be famous too, if she agrees to model for him.

Jordan is looking at her intently. Lizzie feels turbulent, unsettled, like the air over the sea before a storm. Jordan says only three more words: 'Please, darling Elizabeth?'

Lizzie capitulates. Taking a deep breath she undoes the dressing-gown, slips it off, and lies back on the settee with her eyes tightly closed, her cheeks flaming.

Jordan, looking at that rippling dimpled leviathan flesh, also breathes deeply, almost painfully. Then, not taking his eyes off that perfect ripe body, he picks up his pencil and begins to draw.

That night Sid Hocking, restless, leaves his own chubby adorable wife sitting by the television while he walks down to the pier. The days are drawing longer, though by now it is dark, but still remarkably warm. Spring is in the air, in the tides, in the high joyous calls of the seagulls, these days, as they prepare to nest. Sid finds he can no longer sit at home every evening with his wife, but drifts down more and more often to the harbour, to see what is going on there. It is the only time of year, these early embryonic days of spring, when he occasionally wishes he was still a full-time fisherman.

Smeaton's Pier is busy this evening. The *Fair Celt* has just come in with a large catch of ray, and Tom's boat, the *Girl Lizzie*, has been in for a while, by the look of it, for Tom has already loaded up his van ready to take to Newlyn.

'Right then, Tom, my bird?' Sid calls to Tom who is just finishing sorting out his nets.

'Can't complain,' Tom says.

'Just saw your Lizzie, coming out from that studio place, the Culpepper guest-house,' Sid says. He had bumped into her as she left Jordan's studio, and wouldn't have thought much of it if Jordan wasn't at the front door, saying goodbye profusely, and thanking Lizzie for something or other. Lizzie and Sid had walked part of the way down the town together, until Lizzie turned off for her own house. Sid, not normally that observant a man, had none the less noticed that Lizzie seemed furtive, ill at ease. This, of course, attracted his attention, made him wonder what exactly Lizzie was doing there at that hour of the night.

It never occurs to Sid to keep his mouth shut, or to at least be circumspect, if indeed Lizzie *is* up to something. He isn't being malicious, just avidly curious, which is why he mentions it to Tom. But Tom, disappointingly, says carelessly, 'Oh, she'll be coming out from her yoga class there. She's trying to lose a bit of weight, is Lizzie.'

Sid vaguely wonders why Jordan was thanking her so profusely if they were at a yoga class, and where, for that matter, were the other people in the class. But he soon forgets all this as Percy Prynne appears, shambling slowly with his perpetual limp down the pier.

'Percy, my handsome, good to see you out and about,' Sid exclaims, pounding him good-naturedly once or twice on the shoulder. 'Though God's truth, you look pale as the belly of an eel, and skinnier than a fish bone. Come up to my place one day; the wife'll feed you up a bit.'

Percy mutters something vague and wanders down the pier. His bronchitis is gone now, but it's left him with a sharp pain in the chest that nearly takes his breath away when he inhales too deeply. Crispin, from his boat, sees

Percy shuffling along the pier and calls out to him, but the old man doesn't seem to hear. Crispin watches as Percy walks to the very end, to the second lighthouse, and stands staring out to sea. Crispin finds this odd, for usually when he comes in with a catch, Percy is right there wanting to watch him and Pete unload, getting in Pete's way and in general driving the lad crazy. Crispin finds this strange disinterest of Percy's disquieting. They have not had their usual lunch at the Union for weeks now, first because of Molly's accident, then Percy's bronchitis. Crispin resolves to speak to the old man when he has unloaded his fish, but when he is finished, Percy has gone, no-one knows where.

'Wandered home, I reckon,' Sid says, unconcerned.

But Percy is on the Island again, looking for the light. He wishes the lady with the lantern would come soon, for he's getting tired, is Percy Prynne. He's getting almost too tired to wait.

Two days later, Friday night, and the Sloop Inn on the harbour is packed with people. There is a draw that night, and plates of food, fried whitebait and tiny garlicky potatoes, are passed around to the locals, and to the many visitors who are infiltrating the small community now that Easter is approaching. The quiet time, the winter season, will be at an end soon; already the weeks in March, and this first one in April, have brought a bustle to the town that was not there in January and February.

Molly sighs, thinking of this. She likes St Ives in those two winter months. It is never dead, like many seaside towns, because of the core of locals who use this time to relax before the hard months of the summer tourist trade, and, of course, the artists, who are always in residence. The opening of the Tate has also brought people to the town all year long, and January and

February is just right for Molly – lively but not unbearably overcrowded, like it gets in the summer.

Molly, recovered from her flu, is in the Sloop with Crispin. The pub, which dates back to 1312, is packed, but they have managed to get a tiny table near the door. Many artists have painted this inn in the past hundred years, and there are numerous stories of painters too broke to buy a pint, exchanging a picture with the landlord instead. Around the walls right now are delightful framed drawings of an assortment of characters, and in the adjoining room, where food is served, there is always an exhibition of local talent.

A number of fishermen are here tonight: Tom and his Lizzie, who is clutching the baby Michael in one hand and sipping a gin and bitter lemon with the other, and Pete and his girl, as well as Crispin, of course. In the next room, enjoying a seafood meal, are Esme and Richard, Esme fresh from her success in London and Richard looking as if he is coping with it, or so Crispin thinks. The four couples, all seated separately, happy in their own little worlds, look contented and peaceful, as befits a balmy Friday night at the beginning of spring.

'To us,' Molly says, clinking the glass of red wine in her left hand with Crispin's pint. It is her first night out since her accident, then flu, and she wonders if it is the beginning of life again, or the end of something.

At another table further down, Lizzie munches salt and vinegar crisps with abandon, no longer worried about losing weight. Jordan's admiration for her curves has taken the sting out of Tom's teasing barbs, and she is able to ignore them. Esme, in the adjoining room, orders a brandy after finishing her delicious dinner, for she feels celebratory.

The moment, for all of them, is as transitory as spring, and they will remember it clearly when, as inevitably must happen, it passes.

Chapter Nine

Crispin returns home one blustery morning a few days later to find the house oddly quiet. The big oak bed where Molly spent so many days convalescing and looking out over the sea is empty, the crimson quilt covering it pulled austerely over the sheets and pillows. Spray from a wild and turbulent sea whips against the glass of the window, and flecks of hail, tiny, like miniature marbles, hit the window with a sudden whip-lash. Crispin has been up all night setting out his nets; it was an unpleasant night with gusts of wind buffeting the small boat, the sea churning, unsettled. Crispin was seasick, something that doesn't usually happen to him after the first twenty minutes or so out at sea, and Pete was uncommunicative and moody, having had a row with his girlfriend the day before, and too many drinks later to compensate.

The fishing has been slack the past few weeks, and the few fishermen still at St Ives are disgruntled and unhappy. Many no longer have their own boats but have gone over to crew on the big trawlers going out of Newlyn, and the talk there is all of the Spanish being allowed into traditionally British waters. Only a handful of small fishing boats like the *Fair Celt* and the *Girl Lizzie* go out of St Ives now, and Crispin worries a great deal about the future of the industry and of his future as well, which is, of course, part of the same thing. Once St Ives was mainly a fishing community, with profitable herring and pilchard seasons, and Downlong busy and thriving with its smoke houses and net lofts and pilchard cellars. Now it's like the other seaside towns and villages in England: a lucrative tourist mecca. Crispin makes a living because he works long hours, seven days a week and in all kinds of weather, but weeks like this past one depress him.

And so coming home to a dark house (the storm has made the morning black and ominous), finding Molly gone, has a curious effect on Crispin. After the initial panic – since her accident, he worries about her more than ever – Crispin finds a note on the table in front of the window. 'Feeling so much better, so I'm moving back home. Could you bring Witch over when you finish work and I'll feed you both. Thanks for letting me convalesce at your place, I really appreciate all you've done. Love, Molly.'

It should not be unexpected, for Molly has always said that as soon as she is better she will go back home. Crispin has ignored these odd remarks, saying that there was plenty of time, no hurry. For some reason, he feels unsettled now, restless, and even a tiny bit annoyed. He knows Molly always does things spontaneously, at the spur of the moment, but he does think she ought to have consulted him, let him know that she was going.

Crispin takes a shower with a heavy heart. He tries to blame it on the storm, on the fact that he is tired, the weather appalling, but he knows that this is dissembling. In truth, the house, which has been exceptionally cosy these last few weeks, seems empty, dull and unwelcoming. Even the waves frothing outside his window, which he usually finds exhilarating, only remind him of his nets out there, probably getting torn to pieces by the angry sea, the sudden unforecast storm.

When Crispin dresses, puts on jeans and a heavy pullover, listening to the sounds of another hailstorm attacking his window, he decides he'd better go to see Molly now; make sure she has settled in all right. Though her flu has gone, it has left her weak and tired, and, of course, the heavy cast still covers her right arm. Crispin notices that the place is empty of all her belongings, and thinks ruefully that she must have been quite determined to pack everything with her left hand, lug her canvas bag down the streets to her own house. He decides against bringing Witch, for the cat is curled asleep in the middle of the bed and would not appreciate being dragged out in the rain and hail. Besides, he rather likes Witch sleeping on that bed, black and stark against the deep red of the quilt. It makes him feel that Molly is still around somewhere.

To Crispin's surprise, Molly is not at her house. Crispin leaves a note and runs back home, dodging pellets of white frozen rain, wondering what in the hell happened to spring. When he gets back to his place he is so undecided as to what to do that he stands just inside the front door for two or three minutes, trying to make up his mind. Finally he goes downstairs into the kitchen, deciding he needs coffee first, then maybe some food.

The next half-hour passes tediously. Crispin, unused to himself in such a flaky mood, drinks coffee, opens a book, closes the book, pours himself more coffee. He takes it upstairs and sits at the table, staring at the grey-black sea. He gets up and puts on the radio, finds nothing on it he feels like listening to, and so turns it off again. He is getting quite cross with himself; all this dithering is unlike him. He thinks of the many things he has to do – write cheques out to pay bills, sort out a small problem with his income tax, catch up on some

191

reading he's wanted to do, check the MOT on his car, and does none of it. When the phone finally rings, after he has finished his second cup of coffee, he leaps out of his chair like a snapped rubber band and answers it brusquely, 'Yes, hello?'

'Crispin? What's the matter?'

'Molly, at last. Where were you?'

'I went to buy bread, cheese, salad stuff. I thought you'd be back for lunch.'

'I am. I called round.'

'I know, I got your note. Are you all right? You sound a bit curt, and so was your note.'

Yours wasn't exactly a love-letter, Crispin thinks grumpily, but says, 'Uh, yes, yes, I'm fine.' Except you're not here, Crispin thinks. You're not here and I miss you.

'Well, are you coming over? I've bought all your favourite cheeses from the deli, Danish Blue and Brie, and I've made the most enormous salad, quite a feat with only one hand.'

Within minutes Crispin is back at Molly's house, sitting in her kitchen, and slicing a granary loaf she has just bought at the bakery. 'I can't handle a knife yet,' Molly says, frowning. 'I tried with my left hand, but I'm useless. I tried to paint, too, but it was hopeless. I've got to start on something soon or I'll go mad, but I can't even sketch with my left hand.'

'You'll have to be patient,' Crispin says maddeningly. He knows patience is not one of Molly's virtues.

'I can't even use my camera, not with one hand,' Molly wails. 'If I'm not sketching I should be taking photographs. This is such an exquisite time of year, and so much going on in the hedgerows and meadows and moors and woodlands. I'm missing it all!'

'There's plenty of time, Molly.'

'There's not! Before my accident I started that painting depicting the seasonal changes of a moorland – you know, you've seen it, that circular painting. I had just finished the winter section and was moving on to spring when *this* happened.' Molly waves her plastered right arm wildly, knocking over a cup of peppermint tea that Crispin had just made for her.

After Crispin clears up spilt tea, Molly hovering over him trying to help, and makes her another cup, he says, 'Look, love, when the weather gets better, I'll take you out on the Penwith moors and take the photos for you. You tell me exactly what you want, and I'll be your photographer. Then you'll have spring locked in an album, so you won't have missed it and can get on with your painting as soon as that cast is off your arm.'

Molly is so overjoyed about this that she nearly spills her second cup of peppermint tea. 'Oh Crispin, would you? That would be so brilliant. Oh, please, can we go now?'

'I said when the weather clears up. It's a foul day.'

Molly runs to the kitchen door, throws open the top half. 'Look, it's not so bad now. It's typical April weather, winds and rain and even sleet one minute, sun the next.'

The sky has indeed cleared, the clouds miraculously parted to reveal a breathtaking patch of blue. Molly is struggling into her faded wool coat, swearing at the cast on her arm as she tries to get it into the wide sleeve. Crispin knows that whether he comes or not, she'll be off, so he succumbs gracefully. 'Finish your lunch,' he orders with a smile, trying to establish some authority. 'Finish your lunch and drink that tea and then we'll go.'

An hour later Molly and Crispin are tramping across a patch of moorland not far from St Ives. Crispin has already taken a number of photographs and is crouched beside a slab of granite trying to get a close-up of a bright yellow clump of gorse. The April sun, which had flared warm and comforting for a short while, is now closeted up in a shelf of black clouds. 'I think we'd better get back to the car, Molly,' Crispin says, looking at the sky. 'It's going to rain again.'

'Just a couple more shots, please Crispin? Over there, behind that clump of rocks, see that craggy old hawthorn tree? I need a close-up of that, I've got a hawthorn for my winter section and I need to see if it's beginning to come into bud or leaf yet.'

Molly tramps along across the moor to the clump of rocks she has indicated. Overhead the sky is dark, ominous, and the wind has come up again, cold and sharp. Crispin catches up with her and they walk quickly, heads down against the wind. 'You shouldn't be out here,' Crispin says. 'You've only just recovered from a nasty flu.'

'I'm all right, honest,' Molly says, and smiles reassuringly at him. But her face is pale, pinched, and there are black circles under her tired eyes. Crispin silently curses himself for not being more forceful, insisting this trip be postponed until finer weather, but he knows nothing he might have said would have stopped Molly.

'Just the hawthorn, and then home,' Crispin says.

'We'll see,' Molly answers obliquely.

The pile of huge granite rocks are in a semicircle, forming a sheltered patch of rough grass and soft turf under the solitary, dwarfed old hawthorn tree. As Molly and Crispin clamber over and around the rocks they are stunned to find that they are not the first ones to have come here on this blustery April day.

'Good God! Alice, what are you doing here?' Molly exclaims.

What Alice is doing here is obvious. The sturdy legs of her lodger, Harlan Zayevich, are partially wrapped around her body which is lying horizontal on top of a torn thick brown sleeping bag, obviously an old one of the children's for it has cartoon elephants all over it. The remains of a picnic are scattered near the prostrate bodies of Alice and Harlan: a flask, some apples, the crusts of sandwiches, and a half-empty bottle of champagne.

Harlan and Alice struggle to their feet with some surreptitious and embarrassed straightening of clothes, and tightening up things that have been loosened, like bra straps and belts. 'We're celebrating,' Alice says brightly. 'I finished my painting, and I told Harlan I'd take him out. We've been to Penzance and Newlyn, and then came here for a picnic.'

There is an uncomfortable silence, which Alice breaks by saying, 'Uh, you know Harlan, don't you?'

Crispin and Molly and Harlan all talk at once, saying, Yes, of course they know each other, they have met several times, at the Sloop Inn once or twice, and possibly, yes surely, other places as well. They all search diligently in their minds for where exactly, and when and who was there, for it is a wonderfully safe topic at this rather awkward moment.

Finally Crispin says, 'You didn't choose a good day for a picnic. It looks as though it's going to rain again in a minute, or snow or sleet even. It's not very warm.'

Harlan and Alice, who actually look quite warm, even hot, with flushed faces and sweaty hands, mutter something banal about unpredictable weather forecasts. 'Would you like an apple?' Alice says suddenly, as if remembering this is her patch and she should be a good hostess. 'And we've got a flask with coffee in it, somewhere.' She begins rummaging in Harlan's rucksack. 'Oh, I forgot you don't drink coffee, Molly.' She looks distressed, as if she has made an enormous social blunder.

The hail comes suddenly, hitting them with hard nasty pellets like gunshot, and the wind is cold, intrusive. 'Come over here, under the rocks,' Alice says. 'The hail won't last long and there's plenty of room to shelter.'

The four of them crouch under the rocky outcrop, huddled together and silent, like sheep in a storm. No-one can think of anything to say. The thoughts of all four of them are scattered, disjointed. Crispin, who has inherited something of his mother's traditional values, is genuinely shocked. Though he dislikes Jordan Culpepper, Crispin has an idealized view of marriage. His parents, Richard and Esme, have, despite problems, remained loyal and faithful to each other, and he is deeply troubled at Alice's apparent infidelity.

Molly, on her part, does not blame Alice, does not condemn her, but is none the less shocked also, only because she had thought Alice slightly prim and a trifle sexless. She's known about Harlan's infatuation with Alice, has even giggled about it with her. Alice has never taken Harlan seriously, so what is she up to now?

Harlan, huddled and cold and wet under the rather precarious shelter, finds his mind so sizzled up over the events of the past half-hour that he doesn't know what to think. His lovely Alice, his beautiful unattainable little English rose, his love object, his madonna, had, only minutes before they were so crudely and cruelly interrupted, turned to him as they were sitting on the sleeping-bag, drinking the champagne from paper cups, and said, 'Harlan? Would you please kiss me?'

Stunned, he had, of course, obliged, and things were naturally progressing rather quickly before the interruption. Now, Harlan doesn't know what to think. Was this a sudden bit of whimsy on Alice's part, to be quenched for ever by the rain, by Molly and Crispin's untimely interruption? Will it never happen again then – or, to be more precise, will it never happen at all, since what was begun so fortuitously was never completed. Harlan, bemused and befuddled, sits miserably in the rain, thinking that picnics in Boca Raton were never like this. Every so often, in the midst of his desolation, a sharp flash of joy hits him like lightning, searing him to his toes. Whatever happens next, Alice loved him, wanted him for at least ten minutes or so. He knows he will never forget that, as long as he lives, even though, at this point, he feels he is going to die right here on this wet soggy moor.

And Alice? Alice is the only one of them whose mind is clear and calm and serene, unlike the turbulent air around them, and the turbulent thoughts of her companions. Last night, Alice had completed her painting, her new self-portrait of head and shoulders, and, knowing it was perhaps the best thing she had done to date, a quiver of pride and happiness shook her from head to toes, and she had to sit down to be able to breathe again. Suddenly, she wanted to see Jordan, show him the painting, share it with him. If she had thought rationally about it, Alice would have seen the absurdity of that, for Jordan's sole enthusiasm for her work was strictly for her pastel drawings of the tourists. But Alice, feeling that peculiar elation, not unmixed with the sadness and sense of loss that often comes with a completion of a work, wanted, illogically, to share it with Jordan, like she did in those early heady days of art college. Then, they shared everything: hopes, dreams, paintings, visions. They had planned a marriage based on this sharing, and suddenly Alice could not bear to remember that it had all gone horribly, hideously wrong.

And so, following her instincts, she ran up to Jordan's study to tell him her painting was finished, to ask him if he'd come look at it. It was Wednesday night and Alice knew that he was doing yoga, but assumed the class would be over by now. Alice knew that Jordan still had a few members of the class over on Wednesday nights – he was vague as to who exactly came – and although she never ever ventured up there on those nights (Jordan's studio was strictly off limits to her and the children, except by invitation) she felt today was an exception.

Neither Jordan nor Lizzie saw Alice as she opened the door of the studio. Lizzie, hugely naked and supine, had her eyes closed; though this was her second time modelling, she still felt shy and uneasy. Besides, Jordan was taking an awfully long time tonight; she had been here for ages. She wished he would hurry up so that she could get home before Tom, who was down at the Union with his mates.

Jordan didn't see Alice either, for his back was to the door. Alice had opened it quietly, surreptitiously, just in case Jordan and the others were deep in relaxation or meditation. But Alice had a glimpse of her husband's broad fleshy face: he was staring, not at his canvas which was now set up on an easel, but at the naked young woman in front of him. The look on Jordan's face was coarse, lascivious. Alice had seen that look many times before during the years of her marriage, catching Jordan as he looked at women he hoped to bed, women who turned him on, excited him by their availability perhaps, or their bodies.

Watching the scene before her, Alice had a heart-sickening feeling of *déjà vu*, and then something exploded in her head like a broken light-bulb. This is not what I want from life, she screamed silently to herself. There must be something more. Still unseen, she shut the door and walked quietly downstairs again.

'Everything all right?' Harlan, meeting her in the kitchen, noted her tense face, her trembling fingers as she tried to pour herself a cup of cocoa.

Alice nodded, unable to speak for a moment. Finally she said, her voice shaking, 'My painting is finished. Would you like to see it?'

She took him into the laundry-room. There, next to a pile of school shirts waiting to be ironed, was Alice's face in warm compelling oils: naked, vulnerable, un-adorned. Harlan fell in love with it as immediately and passionately as he had fallen for Alice, and said, softly, 'It's beautiful, just beautiful. Like you.'

Alice looked with new eyes at this sweet young man. Perhaps it was gratitude, or vengeance for the accumulation of twelve years of married hurt, or even just reciprocal infatuation – whatever, she felt herself suddenly, and without any warning, falling in love with him, then and there. 'We'll celebrate tomorrow,' she promised Harlan, slightly giddy at what was happening to her. 'We'll do the art galleries, the auction, have that picnic on the moor. I'll pack a lunch—'

'I'll buy the biggest bottle of champagne we can find; we'll drink to your painting—'

'Steady on, I have kids to collect after school, remember.'

Harlan looked so crestfallen at this return to reality, this reminder that Alice was a family woman, out of his reach, that she said softly and kindly, 'But we'll have all day, Harlan. Lots of time before picking up the kids.'

But not quite enough time, Alice thinks now, shiver-ing under the rock formation and wondering when the bloody storm will be over.

In about twenty minutes it is. The obstreperous sun is out again, the wind has dropped, the air has turned magically spring-like once more.

'We'd better get back now, while there's a lull,' Crispin says to Molly as they creep out from the rocks like some kind of crawly insects.

'We must go too,' Alice said hastily. 'It'll be time to pick up the children soon.'

They ascertain that their cars are parked not far from each other's on the main road and decide to walk back down together. Alice and Harlan pack the debris from their picnic, offer Crispin and Molly the remains of the forgotten champagne (which they refuse), and set off silently down towards the road.

'Well, I'm stunned, speechless,' Molly says when she and Crispin are alone in Crispin's house. 'Alice – and Harlan? Not that I blame her, Jordan is a prat and absolutely vile to her.'

'Perhaps, but the fact remains that she is married to him. And Harlan is just a boy, hardly older than Hugo.'

'That's neither here nor there. Hugo is a young man, in case you haven't noticed, and so is Harlan.'

'But she's married,' Crispin persists.

Molly is quiet for a moment. 'Yes, I suppose she is. Though Jordan hasn't acted like it for years.'

'Molly, no gossip, OK? I'm not overly fond of Jordan, but I don't particularly want to hear about his sordid love life.'

Molly sighs, and curls up on the bed next to Witch, who hasn't moved from the middle of the red quilt. 'It puts one right off marriage, doesn't it, all this. Your dad and mum warring over Esme's work, Jordan far more interested in Alice's earning potential than in her doing some real work, and now Alice having it off with an itinerant American.' She looks up at Crispin and smiles beguilingly. 'You were right, of course,' she goes on. 'Insisting that we live apart, don't commit ourselves to each other. It seems to bring only trouble and pain when one does.'

Crispin, joining Molly on the bed, feels that he has somehow been manoeuvred into an unfair position. He finds himself saying, 'I never mentioned anything about not being committed to each other. I just said that there is nothing wrong with having separate houses to go to sometimes.'

Molly sits up abruptly, picking up the cat who meows

200

indignantly as she is rudely wakened. 'And I am about to go back to mine,' she announces crisply. 'I only came back here to pick up Witch.' She looks at Crispin and softens. 'Thank you for looking after me when I was ill, for dropping everything and taking care of me. You do know, don't you, that I would do the same for you?' She smiles, then goes on. 'Don't tell Oona, but even if I was in the middle of my best painting ever, I'd drop it in a flash if you needed me.' She leans over, kisses him gently, and says, briskly now, 'I'm off to my own home. It's time I gave you back your house and your privacy.'

Crispin grabs her left arm as she starts to rise. Witch leaps crossly out of Molly's arms and rushes to the window-sill where she begins to wash herself, keeping one eye open for the gulls on the rocks below.

'Molly, don't be so impetuous. You don't need to go now, you don't need to go at all. You're still not well, you look ill, as a matter of fact. White and drained and tired. At least stay until the cast is off your arm.'

'Oh, I wouldn't dream of it, Crispin,' Molly retorts coolly. 'I've encroached upon your space for far too long.' She smiles stiffly at him and begins to put on her coat.

Crispin, suddenly devastated, remembers with sudden clarity how the house felt this morning, bereft of Molly. Taking her in his arms he says, without thinking, 'Stay, love. Please stay. Not just until your cast comes off, but always.'

There is a still silence in the room, like the moments before a storm. Even Witch seems to notice, and turns her eyes from the sea-birds to look at Molly and Crispin, who are staring in some kind of dazed amazement at each other. Then Molly says, with a funny numbed voice, as if she has just been run over by a bus, 'I don't think I'm hearing correctly. I thought I heard you say you want me to stay here. Indefinitely.'

Crispin smiles, hugs her like he's not hugged her since her accident. She winces a bit – her rib is still sore – and then pulls away, saying, with maddening logic, 'You're not making sense. All those lectures you gave me, about separate houses, our own space—'

'Can't a man change his mind?' Crispin asks. 'Or is it just a woman's prerogative?'

Molly feels a tightness around her chest, and finds she is having trouble breathing. There is a curious lightness in her head, but she just manages to say, 'Of course you can change your mind, Crispin. In fact, I can't tell you how happy I am that you did.' Then, to Crispin's horror and alarm, she passes out on the bed.

She is only out for a few seconds, and when she comes to Crispin is hovering over her looking so sweetly distressed that she closes her eyes again. 'I'll call the doctor,' Crispin says.

'No, no. It's just the tail-end of the flu, I feel fine. Just a bit light-headed.'

'All that walking in the rain and sleet,' Crispin moans, stricken with guilt. 'And you hardly had any lunch, just a bit of salad and cheese. That was ages ago.' As he talks he is fussing over her, slipping off her coat, taking off her shoes, trying to get her under the quilt. 'I'll get you a camomile tea, or would you rather have some soup?'

Molly, her head floating on a high cloud somewhere in the stormy April sky outside the window, says, weakly, 'I think, just before I fainted, that I was hallucinating a bit. Were we talking about anything important before I collapsed?'

Crispin laughs out loud. 'Oh Molly, yes, I believe we were. We were talking about the rest of our lives, I think, or something like that.'

'Perhaps I wasn't hallucinating then,' Molly says, and her smile is so luminous on her pale wan face that Crispin feels quite dizzy himself.

He settles Molly, gets her undressed and into bed, makes her a camomile tea, feeds Witch and lets her out to chase the sea-birds, and then rushes back to Molly's house to collect her canvas bag which is still packed with the clothes she had at Crispin's house. Then he calls by his parents' place, finds Esme in her workroom. 'I've got to go out soon and collect my nets, or I'll miss the tide,' he says. 'Molly's had a bit of a relapse today, do you mind calling in tonight to see if she's OK?'

'Of course,' Esme says. 'She's at her own house now, isn't she. I ran into her in the bakery this morning and she said she had moved back.'

Crispin runs his hand through his dark hair and says, almost shyly, 'She's moved back to my place again. Uh, for good, this time. We thought, well, what's the point of having two places, when . . . when . . . well, when we're together so often. So we'll try it out, anyway.'

The news cheers Esme like nothing has since her return from London. Richard has been vague, aloof, distracted, and Hugo seems preoccupied with more than his surfing lately. Esme has been suffering from post-exhibition, anti-climactic blues, so she is more than delighted to have something positive to celebrate. 'Oh, I'm so very pleased about this,' she beams, embracing Crispin soundly. 'I like Molly so very much.'

Later, out with Pete in the *Fair Celt*, steaming out to his nets which are about ten, eleven miles away, Crispin stands at the wheel of his boat feeling the sea surge under him, seeing the lights of the harbour receding in the distance, and feeling like the luckiest man on earth. All his qualms about living with Molly have totally disappeared, submerged under the bigger issues of life and death, of near loss, and he even lets the thought of marriage and children creep into his consciousness. After all, he thinks as he watches the beam of Godrevy lighthouse in the distance, his mother and father, despite their problems, have survived almost thirty three years together, in spite of Esme's passion for her work and Richard's insidious resentment. Crispin has learned much about himself through Richard lately, learned how destructive jealousy can be, and is determined now not to emulate his father.

When they finally reach the nets, Crispin finds, to his great relief, that they are not only intact, despite the sudden fierce storm earlier on, but are loaded with ray. Taking this as a positive omen for the future, he pulls them in with such a surge of spontaneous joy and exuberance that Pete wonders for a moment if he's on some kind of a drug.

The drug is love, of course. And more than one person has become addicted to it this spring, despite the foul wintry weather. It is a dangerous addiction, as many are soon to find out. But Crispin, unaware of this, pulls up his nets in the swell of the sea and neither a sudden brief hailstorm, nor the sudden heaving of the boat which makes him queasy for a few moments, can dispel his happiness. Molly is at home, at *their* home now, waiting for his return, and the knowledge fills him with more joy than he ever thought possible.

Chapter Ten

While Esme rejoices over Crispin's commitment to Molly and a shared life, her other son, Hugo, is wrestling with a commitment of his own.

'Come with me, Hugo,' Cara is saying, 'to Plymouth. We'll get a flat together, and I'm sure you can get some kind of a job. Then you can apply to the university for next year. You've got good A levels, you'll get in with no problem.'

It is Friday night, or rather the dawning hours of Saturday morning, and Cara and Hugo are meandering over the sand of Porthmeor Beach on their way to their respective homes. Last night they had been to a club on the outskirts of town, the one that plays the house music Hugo loves. It was a fantastic night; the DJs were brilliant, the lighting, sound, the dancing out of this world. Afterwards, about eight or ten of them had ended up at a friend's house where they had talked and listened to more music, until now, when the party had finally dispersed.

Hugo, checking out the surf as they walk along the beach, wishes he were out there now, with no decisions to make other than which wave to choose. Finally he says to Cara, who is waiting for him to speak, 'What would I study at Plymouth?'

Cara tosses her hair away from her face in a characteristic gesture which would annoy Hugo if she weren't so gorgeous and he wasn't so besotted with her. Her hair has grown longer and redder in the winter months, and there seems more of it than ever these days. Hugo thinks, irrelevantly, how he will miss that hair when she finally goes.

'What would you study?' Cara repeats incredulously. She cannot understand such indecision; she herself knew she wanted to study marine biology ever since she learned there was such a subject. 'You could do the same course as me,' she says, after giving it careful thought. 'You have two science A levels, and you love the ocean.'

Hugo considers this. It would certainly make his parents happy; Richard has been doing some serious nagging at him about doing something with his life. Hugo doesn't particularly want to do marine biology, but he supposes it would be better than some other science. He's really not interested in science at all, and only did the subjects because they came easy to him. He doesn't want to move to Plymouth either, but at least it is on the sea, and not far from home, so he could return every weekend to surf. And he doesn't want to lose Cara, which is a big plus for moving on to university. 'I'll think about it,' he says slowly.

Cara, knowing she has won, is ecstatic. 'Oh Hugo, we'll have such fun! The first year will be hard for you, with me at college and you working, but I'll introduce you to the others on my course, and when you get there a year later it'll be easy for you; you'll know me, know everyone.'

She carries on like this for some time, planning the type of flat they'll have, the kind of job Hugo should look for, how they'll pool their money. Hugo listens, entranced. Since Molly had her accident and moved in with Crispin, Hugo and Cara haven't had a place to escape to and they are missing it. Perhaps it won't be so bad, Hugo thinks. Having a place alone with Cara sounds fun, a game somehow, playing house. Strolling in the pink clear dawn, the sea lazy and accommodating at their side, the sand luminous and shining with that strange iridescent light that is peculiar to St Ives, Hugo drifts with the tide, and lets himself be persuaded.

But that night, at the restaurant, Hugo, who now has sole responsibility for making the Cajun sauce that is the speciality of the house, has second thoughts. He feels so very much at home here, with the smell of onions and garlic sautéing in a butter sauce, the sound of soft banjo music coming over the sound system from the restaurant. Next to surfing and Cara, cooking has become another great passion, and he feels almost a cosmic peace as he stirs and chops and mixes and smells the succulent aromas wafting around him. Perhaps he can get a job in a restaurant in Plymouth, he thinks idly as he chops up tomatoes, some green and red peppers. Though it seems pointless somehow, when he has a job right here, and the surf is only yards away, beginning to build and swell so that Hugo knows, just knows, that tomorrow will be a glorious day for surfing.

It is. By the time Hugo gets to Oona's house to do his usual chores, he has already done two hours' surfing, and his body and mind glow. The sun, still impossibly warm, as if trying to make up for its recalcitrant days in the first part of the month, has already dried and bleached his pale hair and the beginning of a tan is suffusing his face with a slight golden sheen.

'A good morning, I take it?' Oona says, noting with her painter's eye the colour on his skin, the whitened salty hair, the blaze in his eyes.

'Like, wow,' is all Hugo can say, shaking his head with the wonder of it all. It sometimes takes him many hours to come down from his high after a good day on the waves. He needs the surf like any addict needs a fix, be it drugs or alcohol or love.

'I hear you have made up your mind to go to Plymouth with Cara, and apply to the university there,' Oona says, arresting him in his attempts to get a ladder out of the broom cupboard so that he can put away some things for Oona in the attic.

'Holy shit,' Hugo says, then: 'Sorry, Oona.' He never swears in front of her if he can help it.

'My dear boy, I use that word myself quite often when I am painting,' she confesses with a smile. 'But why do you look so upset? Have I got the story wrong?'

Hugo abandons the ladder and faces Oona. 'It's just that Cara and I only decided yesterday. And now all St Ives seem to know. How did you find out?'

Oona, deciding that now rather than later would be a good time to have their tea ritual, puts on the kettle. 'I believe,' she says placidly, 'that Cara, in her excitement, told your mother when she ran into her at the newsagent yesterday afternoon. Esme, overjoyed, naturally informed your brother and Molly when she called round to see them later, and Molly told me this morning, just before you came.'

Hugo groans.

'Oh, the subject only came up in a roundabout manner, Hugo,' Oona says briskly. 'Molly is, after all, my granddaughter; she does visit me often and we chat about all manner of inconsequential things.'

'Oh man,' Hugo moans. 'My life, my whole life, you call inconsequential.'

Oona, smiling, puts Lapsang leaves and boiling water in the China pot and says, 'I just want to put it into perspective, my dear. Now come into the drawing-room and we'll have tea, and you can tell me all about it.'

A half-hour later, after Hugo has drunk three cups of Lapsang, eaten two large freshly baked macaroons from the tea-shop down the road, and told Oona all about Cara's plans for his future, Oona says, 'And what do *you* think? How do you feel about things?'

Hugo ponders this. He is sitting in his usual place, on the window-seat overlooking the sea, but he is not looking out the window. Instead, his eyes roam to Oona's paintings on the wall – none of them hers, but those of friends throughout the years. One very old painting is of a ship, riding the waves in a foamy storm. There is an eerie yellow light shining from the dark angry sky onto the boat, and the whole thing is slightly out of focus, shimmering. Hugo stares at the painting for several moments; he knows that light, that shimmering luminescent ark of colour, for he feels it surrounding him when he surfs, when he sails on the waves much as that ship is sailing high and proud on the crest of the storm.

'How do I feel?' Hugo repeats, somewhat dazed by the intensity of his staring. 'Like *that*,' he blurts out, indicating the painting, the extraordinary light. 'When I'm doing something I know is right for me, I feel like *that*. And it hasn't happened with this Plymouth stuff.'

The nice thing about Oona, Hugo thinks, is that she understands. Following his gaze to the ship in the storm, the extraordinary light, she says only, 'Ahh.' And nods her head.

They sit in silence for a long comfortable time. Hugo somehow knows that this is a very important moment in his life, though he cannot comprehend why or how. He only knows that he suddenly feels peaceful, in harmony with the world and with himself, exactly like he feels when he is surfing well.

Sid Hocking, getting his boat ready for the Easter tourists, feels a hum in the air and a song in his heart as he mends and paints in the April light. 'Morning, Cap'n,' the punters say as they walk past his boat in the ebbing tide, making Sid puffed and cocky like a cunning old seal at this deserved mark of respect.

Sitting on the sand at the edge of the harbour, on the dry bit, is Lizzie and her little Michael, asleep with mouth open in her arms. Sid looks her way and waves and smiles, then frowns as he notices that artist fellow, Jordan Culpepper, wander over the sand up to her and sit next to her, far closer than is decent. Sid automatically looks around to see if Tom is anywhere in sight, but the *Fair Lizzie* is gone, out to sea, and not coming back now until the tide comes in again.

Sid puts down his paint tin and brush and climbs down off his boat, walking slowly over the wet sand towards Lizzie and Jordan. Lizzie greets him cordially, but Jordan merely nods coolly at him and turns away again. This annoys Sid, who prides himself on his ability to get on with everyone, even artists, so he deliberately plants himself in front of Jordan like a stubborn tree and says, with a hearty chuckle, "Tis warmer than a gull's egg out here in the sun, eh, my bird?'

'Oh, I love it!' Lizzie cries. 'Roll on summer.'

Jordan says nothing, but closes his eyes as if bored by the whole conversation. This irritates Sid even more, and he remembers that Jordan more or less promised, ages ago, to paint his portrait. So he says, with a sharp little prod in Jordan's ribs, 'Well now, my cock, not working then? I've not seen you about with your paints for some time now.'

Jordan shifts on the sand and condescends to open his eyes. 'I work in my studio, mostly,' he mutters.

'Ah,' Sid says knowledgeably. 'So you do, so you do. And that reminds me, my handsome. I believe it was discussed between us some time ago now, that you wanted to do one of them portraits of me. You know, like the one your good wife did of Percy Prynne.'

'You must be mistaken,' Jordan says coldly, wishing the old man would go away so that he can continue chatting up Lizzie. 'I never do portraits.'

'Except for mine,' Lizzie says proudly, without thinking.

There is a sudden moment of silence. Jordan scowls at Lizzie, who is appalled when she realizes what she has said. 'It's a secret, Sid,' she blurts out, making everything worse. 'It'll be a surprise for Tom and me mum and all when they see it.' She refuses to even contemplate just what a surprise it will be; her as naked as the day she was born. She doesn't let herself think about this.

'Oh, 'es?' Sid says suspiciously.

'So don't tell, Sid, please?' Lizzie smiles winsomely at him, and he grunts noncommittally which Lizzie accepts as acquiescence. 'You're a sweetheart,' she blurts out, smiling innocently at him.

Sid Hocking likes being called a sweetheart, almost as much as he likes being called Captain. It almost makes up for not having his portrait painted, like Percy Prynne. Satisfied, he bids them both cheerio and wanders back to his boat.

Jordan turns back to Lizzie, whom he is trying to get to come to his studio two nights a week instead of one. But before he can persuade her, they are interrupted again, this time by Percy Prynne himself.

The warm soft weather has not altered Percy. Still dressed in scarf, woollen hat, and long brown coat, he looks pale and ravaged as winter itself, with great hollows under his deep feverish eyes. Lizzie, who hasn't seen him for weeks, is shocked at his extreme gauntness, and the distracted burning look in his eyes.

Lizzie smiles a cheery greeting, but Percy is looking at her strangely. 'When are you coming to look for your baby?' he asks.

'Sorry?' Lizzie says, glancing perplexedly at her infant Michael, still soundly sleeping in her arms.

Percy doesn't seem to recognize her. She wonders if his eyesight has gone bad, or if he is just going doolally like her own grandfather did years ago. 'The lantern,' he says impatiently, almost as if he is accusing her. 'When are you coming with your light, when are you coming to find Percy Prynne?'

Jordan, rolling his eyes at Lizzie, gives up and says he has to go home. When he goes, Lizzie stands up too, for Percy Prynne has not moved; he is still standing up staring at her in the same wild manner. 'Are you all right?' she asks with some concern. She wishes Crispin or Tom were around, to know what to do.

But Percy seems to recover his wits as quickly as he lost them, for he suddenly begins talking sensibly about the weather, about yesterday's storms, in a normal manner. Lizzie, relieved, chats with him for a few more moments until Michael, awake now and hungry and irritable, forces her to say, 'I'd best be off now, Percy. See you soon.'

'Cheerio, my maid,' Percy says, just like his old self again. Lizzie waves and walks away, not hearing Percy mutter to her retreating back, 'Damn right you'll see me soon. Over on the Island, over on the rocks.' He mutters this over and over to himself like a mantra, and begins to limp slowly over to the Island to sit and wait, like he has done all winter.

Crispin and Percy have not resumed their regular lunches at the Union since Molly's accident and Percy's bronchitis, though they have met there once or twice. Percy still comes occasionally to Crispin's house to look at his portrait, but since Molly has moved in, he has come less often. This is not because Percy dislikes Molly, it is because he needs to stand alone in front of

212

the painting, to find himself again, and since Molly has been in the house it is often filled with people: Oona and Esme, or Hugo and Cara, or Alice and any one of a number of Molly's friends. Percy is not quite sure it is dignified for *The Sea Captain* to be in such an unseaworthy group, but his fuddled mind doesn't know why. Molly and her friends also disturb the singing of his father and brother and Maggie; Percy cannot hear them quite so clearly when they are in the room.

Crispin doesn't mean to ignore Percy Prynne, but he has been so tied up with Molly after her accident he has had no time to resume their weekly lunches. He vows to himself to rectify this soon, but the days are now filled with moving Molly permanently into his house. There is a small room off the large main sitting-room/bedroom upstairs which Crispin is converting to a studio for her; it has a sea view, plenty of good light, and Molly is delighted with it.

'You're working so hard on this,' Molly exclaims, when Crispin has finished painting the walls a stark austere white, which Molly had wanted.

'Why shouldn't I?' Crispin asks.

'Well – my painting, my work. I thought there were seeds of resentment there. You know, like your father.'

Crispin thinks about this for a moment. 'I suppose that while I was afraid to be like Richard, in reality I was unconsciously imitating him. Until two things happened: first, I saw Dad go over the top in an argument with Mum, and I suddenly realized how unreasonable he has been; and then you had your accident. Do you know, when I first found out how badly your arm had been fractured, my first worries were about your painting. I brooded over it for days, until I talked to the doctor myself and learned that there would be no permanent damage.'

Molly is touched. 'I shall be impossible when this

bloody cast is off my arm,' she says after a moment, 'so be warned. I shall do nothing but paint and paint and paint, and work all hours of the day.'

'Thank God for that, woman,' Crispin says solemnly, surveying his effort on the studio walls with satisfaction. 'Maybe I'll have a chance to get some fishing done for a change.'

Molly looks at him with sudden apprehension. 'I'll know exactly when you are out at sea, now,' she says with fear. 'If you go out in some God-awful storm, I'll have to watch you go, and sit here waiting for your return.'

Crispin goes to her and looks at her with love. 'Like fishermen's wives have done for centuries,' he says softly.

'Wives?' Molly murmurs. 'Who said anything about wives?'

'I did. Like fishermen's wives waiting for their husbands to come home from the sea.'

Molly looks searchingly in his face. 'Husbands? Be very careful what you are saying, Crispin.'

'Oh, I am, I am.' Crispin grins. 'I was just testing. To see if we could say the words.'

'Words?'

'You know. Husbands. Wives. I think we've passed the first test rather well.'

Molly slowly smiles back at him, her amber eyes gleaming with delight. 'Oh my,' she says. 'When you change your mind, you do it in a big way, don't you.'

Closeted in Molly's new studio, the door shut, they don't hear the ringing of the doorbell as they wrap each other in a tight awkward embrace, trying not to crush Molly's bad arm. Percy Prynne waits for several minutes, and then gives up and walks away, limping up the hill towards the train station and Porthminster beach. A few tears trickle down his granite face but he doesn't notice

214

them, and they soon dry in the heat of the waning sun. He is mourning Percy Prynne, sea captain, skipper of the *Fair Celt*, husband of lithe Maggie and son of a fisherman and lifeboatman. Percy is gone now, he is sure of it. He walks and limps and coughs and cries until, finally, in a roundabout way, he finds his way home.

Lance Giddens sees Percy walking past his gallery but doesn't pay him much attention. Old fishermen abound in this town, he thinks ruefully, like old artists. Soon they'll all be crowded out by the tourist trade, he muses lugubriously, and the town will be one huge fish and chip shop, much to the delight of the seagulls who are becoming so aggressive that people are urged not to feed them.

The gallery door opens and Esme comes in. She is still sporting the new hairdo she got in London, her glossy hair burnished with silver, like the healthy fur of a sleek animal. There is a man with her, a tall skeletal man dressed in black, whom Lance recognizes as the art critic, Samuel Tolling.

Esme introduces the two men and explains that Samuel is visiting her for the weekend. 'To relax,' she says to Lance, with a smile at Samuel. 'I shouldn't even be bringing him here, but you have some lovely things, and I wanted Samuel to have a look.'

Lance is both touched and delighted that Esme should bring such a well-known reviewer of the arts as Samuel Tolling to his little gallery. As he shows them around, Samuel admiring the exquisite boxes with the bird feathers, and two of Molly's paintings, the door opens again and Harriet walks in, a small parcel wrapped in a soft cloth under her arm.

Harriet has had to swallow a good deal of pride to walk into the Sandpiper again. But she knows that Lance is one of the most influential gallery owners in town,

215

and has repented bitterly the fact that she lost her temper with him last time. She hasn't a hope that Lance will take her latest work now, but she feels she must at least offer it to him, to show that there are no hard feelings.

Harriet also recognizes Samuel Tolling, even before Esme introduces them. As she begins to unwrap her sculpture, she hears Esme telling Samuel about her constructions, how she works mostly in metal, and what she is trying to achieve. To Lance's surprise, the work she brings out now is far more competent than the other things she has offered him. For a start, it is not one of her grotesque animal shapes, but rather an angular abstract of fine proportions and symmetry.

'Why Harriet, this is wonderful,' Esme exclaims, and for one brief moment Harriet feels a stab of guilt.

Samuel Tolling is looking carefully at it. 'It's interesting,' he says finally. 'Unusual angles.'

'There, Samuel, you can mention Harriet in your article,' Esme says with a smile. 'Samuel will insist on working this weekend; he thinks I don't know it, but he's busily scribbling every time my back is turned.'

'Now Esme, don't be cross, darling. I thought a sharp, highly observant, gossipy little piece about your domestic life would go down a treat on a Sunday morning.'

'Sod that. You can write about the local artists instead, people like Harriet and Lance, who keep this community going. I'll tell you what, why don't you two come for dinner tonight? You can pick their brains then, Samuel. Lance will tell you everything that is going on in St Ives, and Harriet can tell you about her work.'

Harriet accepts with eager alacrity, and Lance, with more decorum, accepts also. 'Do you paint or sculpt?'

Lance hesitates, and Esme says, 'He is a painter, and his work is extraordinary. But he is very secretive about it.'

'Perhaps that's wise,' Samuel says. 'Too many artists show far too soon, when they are not nearly ready. I'm sure your time will come,' he finishes politely.

Lance looks at him gratefully, warmed by his tact. Esme and Samuel leave, and Harriet says coyly, 'Well, Lance, would you be interested in my latest creation?'

She knows he'll have it. With the greatest elation, Harriet feels that indeed her cup is at last overflowing. She attributes it to Richard, to whom she has opened like a flower, becoming not just more loving, but more creative as well. She knows, with a sudden fierce insight, that this is the man she must spend the rest of her life with.

Dinner begins festively that night, as Esme tells them about a letter she has just received from the Tate St Ives. The gallery wants to purchase one of her sculptures, particularly *Grace*, which was the most admired piece in her London exhibition. The Tate would like to commission a second piece too, to be permanently displayed with *Grace*.

'Darling, how rewarding for you,' Samuel says, kissing her chastely on both cheeks as Richard opens the bottle of champagne that Samuel brought. 'Though I must say, I think the Tate should have noticed your worth ages ago.'

Harriet, somewhat deflated by this piece of news and the knowledge that tonight is not to be, after all, her night, finds solace in Richard's eyes as they clink their glasses and toast to Esme. Richard, once again in the shadows, as he sees it, of his wife's ambition, finds the dark illuminated by Harriet's glowing presence. He rather likes this image: Esme, becoming shadowy and illusive in his life now, with her new fame, her new glory, and Harriet dispersing the shadows with the light

217

of her love, her jubilance, her life-force. Yes, that's good, he thinks pensively. The thought comforts him some-what for Samuel Tolling's presence tonight, which he is beginning to resent. The man is amusing enough, Richard reflects, but must he hover so around Esme, must he always pay her compliments, encourage her, egg her on with his constant comments on her work, as if it were a god on a high altar? Look at him now, pointing to one of her old sculptures in wood in the corner of the room, smiling at her, no doubt telling her how utterly brilliant she is.

She looks good tonight, Richard notices. Harriet, that is, not Esme. Though if he had looked at his wife closely, he'd have seen that she also looks good, her strong face serene and composed, her hair sparkling with silver, which reflects the silver of her long dangling earrings.

But Richard has torn his eyes away from Esme and looks now at Harriet, who is dressed in jade, her face-powder white, heightened by the two rosy spots on her cheeks, her lips a deep purple-red like rich plums. Her green dress swishes as she walks, and her ebony hair is pulled high on her head in that exquisite topknot, held in place by a jade clasp. Her black fringe shines on her forehead like polished lead or coal. He adores her for adoring him, for casting her bright powerful light on the dark cracks Esme's ambition is hacking in their marriage.

Two people watch Richard watching Harriet as Esme goes into the kitchen to check the dinner. Lance Giddens and Samuel Tolling, talking amiably to each other, find their glances straying more than once to the couple standing face to face in the corner of the living-room, sipping their champagne and looking covertly at each other, less discreet than usual perhaps.

Bloody hell, Lance thinks, suddenly comprehending. Once, a few weeks ago, he saw Richard's car parked in an obscure side-street in town, not far from Harriet's house, on the night when Esme had said he was in Penzance at a play rehearsal. It had mildly puzzled him, but he didn't think too much about it. But the way Harriet is smouldering at Richard, the way Richard is smirking like the damn stupid fool he is, makes everything suddenly uncomfortably clear.

Well, well, Samuel thinks, noticing these things too. So all is not as rosy as Esme paints it on the domestic front, he ponders with a slight streak of glee. Samuel is not malicious, but Esme's home life was sometimes just a bit too cloying to be true; all those macho sons, a devoted schoolteacher husband, a thirty-something-year marriage. It simply isn't on in the world Samuel frequents, and he feels rather relieved that it doesn't seem to be on in this little Cornish community either.

Sitting next to Harriet at dinner, which is a delicious seafood platter, Samuel begins to delve into her relationship with the Cochrans. Flushed with wine, with the success of her latest sculpture, but still slightly pricked by the envy she cannot help but feel over Esme's latest success with the Tate, Harriet expands like a balloon, blown up by Samuel's apparent interest.

'I've known Richard and Esme for years,' Harriet says in answer to one of Samuel's questions. 'They are both good friends.' Harriet believes this to be true. She has even convinced herself that her affair with Richard is not only good for him, but good for Esme too. Doesn't she need to concentrate on her work, not have to constantly worry about Richard? And if it should happen that Harriet takes Richard permanently off Esme's hands one day, won't it perhaps turn out all to the good? Harriet turns away from Samuel to smile at Richard, sitting on her other side. The two gleam at each other, like fireflies glowing in the shadows. Richard casually touches Harriet's hand.

219

Samuel, sophisticated though he is over these tricky marital situations – he has friends who pop in and out of marriage with the same nonchalance as they drop into their favourite designer shop – is not happy with what he sees. He likes Esme, and is sure she has no idea that this is going on. He is not about to tell her, of course, for she has been a good friend to him over the years and he would not want to hurt her, but he wishes he could warn her somehow.

Exasperated, he turns to Esme on his other side and ignores Harriet the rest of the evening, for he is certainly not, as Esme had suggested earlier, going to write anything about that silly female. He feels this celebratory dinner is spoiled now, and wishes that Esme's two sons were here, the ones he met briefly on his last sojourn to St Ives. He knows he cannot touch, but at least he could have feasted his eyes. It would have been a pleasant distraction.

Lance, on the other side of Esme, is stunned and angry. He, like Samuel, would not dream of saying a word to Esme about what he has just witnessed, but his hatred for Richard – and for Harriet – rings clear and cold and shrill in his head and in his heart. As he tries to eat the delicious shrimp and crab and smoked salmon, a feeling of such protectiveness for Esme rushes through his bloodstream that he feels quite weak. Then another feeling courses through him: helplessness. There is absolutely nothing he can do, nothing he can say. He can only stand by and watch. The thought fills him with such distress that Lance puts down his fork, grabs his wineglass, and drains what remains there. He wishes the evening were over.

Samuel continues to ignore Harriet, who finds consolation in Richard's loving attention to her at his wife's dinner table. Only Esme, tranquil and at peace, has no hidden agenda churning in her mind, no dark

220

clandestine thoughts fighting with the serenity of the candles, the gentle outward flow of conversation.

Esme, as always, is living entirely in the moment. She is surrounded by good friends and a decent husband; she has just completed a successful exhibition, and the Tate wants not just one, but two of her sculptures. Her son Crispin is not only settling with Molly, but has even hinted about marriage, and her other son Hugo will be going to university in a year's time and settling down to something serious at last.

Life is good, Esme thinks with pleasure and contentment. Life is so amazingly good.

Over the soft glow of the candles Lance and Samuel look at her with great pity, while Richard and Harriet don't notice her at all because they are totally wrapped up in each other.

That same night Harlan and Alice are alone together for the first time since their interrupted picnic on the Penwith moors. Jordan has gone to the Sloop where he is meeting some of his friends, and all three children are at an early-evening birthday party and will be delivered back home around nine o'clock or so.

Alice and Harlan are in the laundry-room. During their hasty snatches of conversation since the picnic, usually with the children around, Alice has asked Harlan if he would sit for her as she would like to paint him. Harlan is both relieved and elated at this request, for it means that Alice is not going to run like hell away from him, which he thought she might do when she had second thoughts about their last outing.

Alice has no intention of running away. After the initial shock, she feels free and liberated after witnessing Jordan and Lizzie in the studio. She is under no illusion that she is mistaken, that what she witnessed was purely and innocently an artist and model, for she knows Jordan too well for that. Besides, he has that furtive look about him these days, the one he always subconsciously develops when he is up to something nefarious. And this is not on the level, Alice thinks angrily: Jordan might insist on this ludicrous open marriage stuff, but Lizzie is young, not long married, has a baby, is probably out of her depth. Alice feels sorry for her, but she hardly knows her. She hopes Lizzie knows what she is doing.

Alice is stronger now than she was when Jordan first announced his decision to include extra-marital sexual liaisons in their marriage. She didn't like it then, and she doesn't like it now, but she was still very much in love with Jordan, still hoping for the ideal marriage: two serious artists, living and working and sharing their ideas and their lives together. Bullshit, she knows now. But, at the time, she was not only bound by love, but by exhaustion, hard work, and the babies that were arriving fast and furiously. Alice has been tired for so terribly long, but things are changing now. It has helped that Christopher started school last September; it has helped too that she is now freely painting what she has wanted to paint for years. The success of her new portraits beginning with *The Sea Captain* has given her a confidence she has never had before, not since art college.

Harlan, young and attractive and crazy about her, is the icing on this cake of self-sufficiency, but very tasty icing indeed. She feels heady and crazy when she thinks of him or sees him around the house, and assumes this is love, though it could, of course, be sheer euphoria now that life is starting to look up.

Whatever; the fact remains that Jordan's latest passion has been the final stone to destroy the tower of self-denial her married life has been lived in. She wants everything now, after years of doing without. She wants her work – *her* work, not that crap that Jordan

222

made her churn out year after year – and she wants her life. Though it is not in her nature to be promiscuous as Jordan is, she is not going to turn down any crumbs of love that may occasionally scatter her way; she wants that too.

And so, this first night in the laundry-room, after Alice has set up her easel and got out her paints, she suddenly finds herself not painting Harlan, but finishing what they had started that day on the moor. She is making love with him on the floor of the laundry-room, on top of a pile of fresh sheets and towels which are still warm from coming out of the clothes dryer.

Harlan, who has made love with his fiancée (he must remember to write to her and break off the engagement) under a palm tree on the sands of West Palm Beach, under a full moon on his father's yacht, and on top of an expensive Turkish carpet in front of a marble fireplace in his parents' house when they were out, thinks nothing has been as beautiful as this tiny cramped room with the ironing-board at his feet and the washing-machine humming with a new load behind his head.

Later, lying with Alice half naked and replete, the towels and sheets rumpled around them, the smell of clean damp clothes intoxicating them with love, Harlan feels that at last his travels are over, that he has come home safe, though scarred, from his adventures. He is Odysseus returned to Penelope; he is Tristan reunited with Isolde; he is Romeo waking to find Juliet, not dead, but very much alive beside him.

Alice, feeling the weight of Harlan's thighs on hers, so light and slim and hard compared to Jordan's soft massive legs, is having serious regrets over what she has just done. It isn't guilt, though this is the first time she has done this sort of thing since her marriage; it is more like self-preservation, these doubts that are suddenly assailing her. The act of love with Harlan, so sublime and sweet and lovelier than anything she has known for years, maybe ever, has, instead of freeing her, like her painting has, bound her in some way, imprisoned her. She recognizes that this is because she has opened herself up to the possibility of hurt, of pain, of suffering. This act of love with Harlan, rather than liberating her, has somehow inextricably made her vulnerable.

It is because she is beginning to truly love him now, instead of the insouciant infatuation she felt on that day – only a few days ago? – he had admired her portrait and she had felt grateful. Just now, in this squalid little room, the washing-machine still ridiculously spinning round and round, Harlan had made love to her with such tenderness, such maturity, such a selfless desire for her own pleasure, that she feels quite shaky and weepy about it all.

This isn't what infidelity is supposed to be about, she thinks warily. It is supposed to be a lark, or a dangerous thrill, or liberation, or even a vengeance. It's not supposed to be soppy and deep and scary, like all the things she is feeling now.

But it is too late to turn back. Alice, suddenly wise, knows now, after one stab at it, that infidelity, like love, is as varied as the people involved in it, and that there is no telling, until you have begun, just where on the chart you will end up.

Frightened, she turns to Harlan, runs her hand down his strong flat belly, and as he responds her fear bursts into elation, like a butterfly emerging from a chrysalis. For the moment there is only this: Harlan's hand on her breast, his mouth on hers, and the low sweet hum of the washing-machine commenting like a Greek chorus on the scene unfolding in front of it.

Chapter Eleven

Hugo decides to tell Cara first, then he will face Esme and Richard. It is Easter weekend and Hugo and Cara are sitting outside the Sloop Inn drinking cold lagers, along with several of their friends and a great milling crowd of visitors, for the weekend has been fine and sunny. The young people are spread out on the ground on the cobbled walkway in front of the Sloop, about twenty or thirty of them, many of them in shorts and bare feet and totally at ease in the summery day. In front of them the harbour buzzes with weekenders meandering between the boats, for the tide is on its way out and the sand shines like the shards of a billion stars. It is a perfect day, idyllic and happy. Hugo hates having to ruin it for both of them.

Cara forces him to speak by taking him aside from their friends and going on about Plymouth again, making plans for the two of them to go up there soon and start having a look around, see what area they'd like to live in, get to know the place before next September. Cara is full of sensible ideas like this, Hugo thinks, and wonders if she will see any sense in what he is going to tell her. He hopes so, for he does not want to lose her. He knows he is risking it, but he also knows he must go ahead.

'Uh, Cara. About Plymouth.'

Cara, looking like a rainbow with her bright red hair, blue T-shirt and short yellow cotton skirt, puts her arm around his waist and rests her head on his shoulder. 'I can't wait,' she says. 'I wish we were off right now.'

'I can't do it,' Hugo blurts. 'That is, I don't want to.'

Cara is stunned into silence. Hugo, stumbling on, says, 'It's not that I don't want to be with you. I do, but I can't just follow you around like some stupid dog.'

'I'm not asking you to follow me around,' Cara says stiffly. 'I thought you wanted to come to Plymouth, go to university—'

'*You* wanted that for me. It's not my scene, never has been.'

'How do you know until you've tried?' Cara lashes out at him.

Hugo looks away from her angry face, out towards the sea, hoping by some miracle it will help him to explain. Beyond the harbour, a fishing boat sails serenely out towards Carbis Bay, and near the pier a seal lifts its brown inquisitive head out of the shallow water for a few seconds. '*You* haven't tried going to college, moving from here, but you know you want to, know it's for you,' he says finally. 'Well, it's the same for me. I know I belong *here*, at least for a while.'

'Oh, brilliant,' Cara says sarcastically. 'Don't you have any sense of adventure?'

Hugo wants to say that his life is full of adventure, that the sea is vast and mysterious and changing and he explores it nearly every day on his surfboard, which is all the excitement he needs right now. But he doesn't know how to put these things into words, and anyway he doubts if Cara would understand them if he could.

'So what do you intend to do with your life?' Cara asks. Her voice is scornful and hard, but only because she is upset and doesn't want to cry in front of everyone.

226

'I'd like to own a restaurant one day. Become a chef, maybe.'

'What?'

'Look, I was talking to Oona, that old lady artist I work for sometimes. She asked me if there was anything I liked doing other than surfing, and I started to tell her about the restaurant, how I really dig working there. She said the solution was simple: I should train to be a chef.'

Cara is looking at him sceptically, and Hugo doesn't dare tell her all the other things Oona said. He didn't understand it very clearly himself, but at the time it made sense. All about something called Zen, and concentrating your mind wholly on what you are doing, whether it is painting or surfing or preparing a meal. It was all, according to Oona, connected with the light in the painting on her wall, that strange luminous light that touches everyone, once in a while. Then she went on to reminisce about some time she spent in Japan learning these things, which Hugo found fascinating, if a bit obscure at times, and finally brought herself firmly back into the present. 'My ex-husband used to own a restaurant,' she said to Hugo. 'So I know a little bit about it.' She then went on to give him some practical advice.

'Oona says that if I'm working at a decent restaurant where I'm allowed to experiment, take responsibility, then it's an ace place to be. Like being an apprentice, she said. I've got that now, so there's no point moving on. Later, Oona says maybe I'll want to get more formal training—'

'Plymouth?' Cara says, suddenly happy again.

'Yeah, maybe, I don't know. But, like, I'm not ready to go yet, you know?'

Cara is paralysed by an uncharacteristic indecision. She had vowed to herself that she would split with Hugo if he didn't come with her to Plymouth and get a degree eventually. But in truth, she realizes now that perhaps it would be counter-productive: she loves him, loves to be with him. Besides, she rather likes the fact that he is making some decisions about his life, even though they are not what she wanted for him.

So she says, with the slightest beginning of a smile, 'How do you know we'll last, being apart like that? How do you know I won't find someone else?'

'I don't,' Hugo says, and the pain is like the one he had experienced once when he fell off his surfboard and it cracked him soundly in the ribcage. 'But we'll just have to take it a day at a time, OK?'

'And see what happens.' Cara nods as she says this, suddenly feeling much older, much wiser. She has just learned a valuable lesson in life, taking one day at a time, and though it won't be easy for someone as obsessed with planning ahead as she is, Cara decides to give it a go.

The relief Hugo feels when he realizes that Cara is not giving him up as a bad job is like the explosion of joy and relief when he has safely executed, not just a difficult, but a potentially dangerous, wave. He puts his arm around her, and together they sit watching the old familiar sea, the sea they grew up with, would be leaving one day, but would probably always come back to.

'It's pretty good, eh?' Hugo says, meaning the sea, life, Cara, the world.

'Ace.' They snuggle together in the hot sun, drinking cold beer, glad to be part of it all.

Molly, dawdling because she loves the sun on her face, the strong smell of the warming sea, finally meanders to Oona's studio, which is above a kind of courtyard and cellar with an old row-boat, fishing nets and lines, stashed away in it. Molly likes this proximity of the fishing community to the artistic one, which has existed in St Ives for the past hundred years. Sadly, the fishing community has dwindled and dispersed, though she feels very much a part of what is still left.

Molly doesn't usually visit Oona in her studio, not wanting to interrupt her work,but she had had a note from her grandmother saying she wanted to see her as soon as possible. Oona opens the door quickly and draws Molly inside. 'See this painting?' she says, without preamble. It is the one Oona has done of Hugo surfing, though all that is recognizable is a great swirl of blue and green and grey, and cloudy foamy whites, with a black streak across the centre. The colours are stark, powerful, the texture and form compelling. Molly stares at it for a long time, loving it.

'It's for Hugo Cochran, when I die,' Oona says. 'I don't have time to go putting it in my will, though I'll do so when I get round to it. In the meantime, I've written a note stating clearly my intentions — here, you can witness it. And when I pop off, you just come right round here and take the damn thing, so the family doesn't fuss.'

Molly nods, bewildered, but doesn't ask questions, so Oona rewards her by explaining. 'I hope I have a few years left ahead of me, by which time Hugo should be trained, experienced, and perhaps ready to take on a restaurant on his own.'

'Restaurant? Whatever would Hugo want with a restaurant? He's going to do marine biology, like Cara.'

Oona smiles enigmatically. 'As a wise old Buddhist monk said to me once, "The way is clear when we close our eyes and look into ourselves." Or as Gauguin said, "I shut my eyes in order to see." Perhaps Hugo shut his eyes.'

Molly shakes her head fondly and impulsively kisses her grandmother. Oona is wearing baggy cotton trousers which sag at the knees, and the loose black smock that Molly remembers from her childhood. Her hair, which began the morning tied back with a large brass clip, is standing all over her head, white and wild and fractious. Her only jewellery today are her amber earrings, hanging like tear-drops in a silver setting. The sun streaming into the window from Porthmeor Beach outlines every line on her face, and Molly realizes, with a pang, just how very many there are. But then Oona smiles, and her eyes, so like Molly's, are clear, her mouth strong. The slight ripple of fear, like a warm breeze on the sea, that went through Molly, evaporates. She needs her grandmother, she realizes, and doesn't want to be reminded of her mortality.

Oona is looking out the window now, and Molly follows her gaze. Hugo and Cara, arms around each other, are walking across the sand and as they pass the window, Hugo waves. 'I'm fond of that boy,' Oona says softly. 'He reminds me of a young man I knew in Argentina, many years ago.'

Argentina? Molly looks questioningly at Oona, aching to know more, but Oona is not saying, and Molly knows not to ask. So she says, instead, 'I like Hugo too. He's so unlike Crispin, yet the two get on very well together.'

'Ah, Crispin. I suppose I should congratulate you? What does one do when young couples decide to cohabit? Send a card? Give a gift? Would you like one of my paintings?'

'I have your most beautiful painting, hanging up in Crispin's house now. Or our house, I should say.'

'I do wish you'd sell it, you know. Then you could give up all those ludicrous part-time jobs you always seem to find and paint full-time. Or is Crispin going to support you?'

Molly bristles at this. 'I wouldn't dream of letting him, though I know he would, he's generous enough.'

'I suppose you'll want babies?'

Molly smiles at the interrogation. '*You* had one,

230

Grandmother,' she says affectionately. 'You're not sorry you did, are you?' she teases. 'You wouldn't have had me.'

Oona looks at her, and is filled with such a rush of love that she has to sit down on the wooden stool she uses when she is painting. Pulling herself together she says briskly, 'I didn't let my child interfere with my painting.'

Molly laughs, spontaneously and happily, and Oona is compelled to smile back at her. 'Crispin is doing an attic room up for a studio for me,' Molly says. 'It was entirely his idea.'

The relief Oona feels on hearing this piece of news is overwhelming. She had been filled with trepidation when Molly had told her on the phone that she was moving in with Crispin, frightened that her grand-daughter would give up her painting, or that Crispin would try to distract her from it if she continued. Some kind of purist in her would have liked to see Molly remain single, dedicated only to her work, for Oona has high hopes for her granddaughter. But then she thinks of the young man in the Argentine, and of the lover she had for years right here in St Ives, and knows she would not have missed any of it. She even thinks of her long-dead husband with a kind of fondness, for he gave her Molly, in the end.

She would not wish Molly a life devoid of what she herself enjoyed, such sumptuous riches. She can only hope that Molly, like her, will hold her work, her painting, like a beacon in front of her, like the light on the ship in the painting Hugo so admired, like the light that shines on anyone with a vision.

Molly, reading Oona's thoughts, says, 'I won't stop painting, Grammy. I promise you.'

Oona doesn't know if it is the use of the old childhood nickname that brings tears to her eyes, or her grand-

231

daughter's promise. She hides them by looking out to sea again, and is almost blinded by the strong radiant light reflecting on the water and on the shining sands. Molly, joining her at the window, says, 'Look how calm everything is. No wind, the sea quiet, and even the people on the beach aren't moving, are impaled by the sun. It's like a still life, isn't it.'

Except that it is on sand, Oona thinks. And soon the tide will turn and it will all be gone, like us, like our lives and desires and passions and ambitions. If we are very very lucky, maybe something will remain: a memory in someone's head, a tree we've planted, a good deed we've done, a painting.

A painting. Oona turns to Molly, not bothering to try to hide her wet eyes this time, and says, 'We should be working, you and I. We are wasting time.'

Molly, moved, understands what her grandmother is saying. Nodding her head she embraces Oona lovingly, kisses her on both cheeks and is gone.

Oona stands by the window for several moments, composing herself. The sun continues to shine and to dazzle; the sea remains azure, still, innocent. She takes several very deep breaths and then turns to her canvas and begins to paint.

The days remain warm and tranquil as April continues. On Wednesday evening Lizzie doesn't even wear a jacket over her pink track suit as she heads up the hill to Jordan's studio. Cutting across the train station she meets Sid Hocking who is taking a stroll on the road above Porthminster Beach. 'Where are you off to in such a rush, my handsome?' Sid calls.

'Oh, uh, I've got my yoga class.' She blushes furiously as she remembers that she had already blurted out the truth to Sid: that Jordan is painting her. She winks broadly, to show Sid that she knows that he knows and

232

that it is all some harmless joke, which it is, of course, to Lizzie. The trouble is, she feels uncomfortable about it. She was flattered at first, then coerced by Jordan's sensible persuasion. She doesn't like lying to Tom, but it's too late to do anything about it now. Anyway, he'd kill her if he ever saw the painting; her with not a stitch on. Lizzie has already decided that when her sittings are finished, she won't mention it to either Tom or her mother. She hasn't any fears that they'll ever see it, or that anyone she knows will see it, except maybe Molly because she's a painter too. But nobody else she knows would dream of setting foot inside an art gallery, especially the kind they have these days, with all those paintings of red circles on black backgrounds, or yellow squares like she used to do at school, or just masses of squiggles with no sense to it at all.

Sid Hocking is a bit taken aback by Lizzie's wink, but then he remembers the secret she confided in him, about being painted as a surprise for Tom, and he winks back merrily. He is rewarded with a dimply smile, as Lizzie waves goodbye and trots on up the hill. He watches her buttocks roll and ripple like long grass on mountainsides as she walks away, and it revitalizes him, makes him sparky and jaunty as he heads past the railway station and towards Smeaton's Pier.

Outside the Sloop Inn he meets Alice Culpepper, and that American lodger, Harlan something or other with the funny name, who came in February for a holiday and shows no sign of leaving. Alice and Harlan are sitting on the bench outside the Sloop drinking beer and enjoying the last of the evening sun, feeling free and rather reckless as Alice's children are all at another birthday party and Jordan is locked in his studio.

'Evening, Captain,' the American says, which so delights Sid that he decides to join them on the bench, especially when Alice smiles particularly sweetly at

233

him. She is doing that to everyone these days, though Sid doesn't know that.

Harlan and Alice make room for him on the bench, and they talk of the weather, the fishing, the visitors. Harlan is intrigued by Sid Hocking, by his captain's hat and enormous sideburns and moustaches and his hearty chuckle. He goes inside to buy Sid a pint and to refill their own glasses. 'Ah, what a life, eh?' Sid beams on Alice. 'I'm happy as a gull on a trawler, sitting here in the sun, a pint of bitter on the way.'

'Hmm,' Alice replies languidly. 'So am I.' She thinks of Harlan, of their morning in the laundry-room, when Jordan was off in Truro delivering some paintings.

'Seems a crying shame, to be in doing yoga on a night like this,' Sid continues. He likes having a secret, likes the fact that pretty plump Lizzie entrusted him with one. He's not a man for betraying a maid, so he'll go along with the pretence of a yoga or keep-fit class or whatever it was. 'For your Jordan, I mean, shame he can't be out here joining us in a pint,' Sid goes on. 'I just met Tom's wife, Lizzie, and she said she was on her way to his studio.'

'Oh, they don't do yoga, not while Molly's arm is still in a cast,' Alice says tersely. 'She's modelling for Jordan.'

Sid is keenly disappointed, having a secret which everyone seems to know. He is quiet for a moment, and Alice stares out at the harbour. The tide is in and the boats bob gently in the water, the seagulls screaming around them looking for bits of fish they might have missed. On Smeaton's Pier Tom and a couple of other fishermen are sorting out tangle nets, oblivious to the holiday-makers strolling up and down the pier and sometimes tripping on the nets.

'Ah,' says Sid Hocking with a short chuckle. 'As a matter of fact, I did know about the painting.'

Alice, assuming by this remark that everyone knows

234

what Jordan is up to with Lizzie, is slightly cross for a few moments, especially as Sid's chuckle sounds to her like a snorting leer. She had asked Jordan at the very beginning to be discreet about his affairs, maintaining that if *she* didn't want to know, she certainly didn't want the whole town to either. Now, she feels she has been made a fool of, and cannot help snapping, 'I'm surprised Lizzie's husband doesn't mind, her posing in the nude like that for someone like Jordan.'

Sid's mind, like his mouth, snaps open and shut dumbly. Nude? he thinks numbly. No wonder that rogue Jordan looked so furious at Lizzie when she let it slip that he was painting her. No wonder he wants it all a secret.

Sid drinks his pint quickly, thanks Harlan with a hollow chuckle, and walks purposefully towards the pier, feeling grim and determined. It's one thing keeping a maid's secret, it's another conniving with her, getting her into trouble, deep trouble. Besides, Tom is his mate, a fisherman, like himself, and what are mates for if not to alert each other when a storm's brewing.

Full of righteous indignation, Captain Sid Hocking steers his rotund frame up the pier to confront Tom.

Jordan Culpepper, staring at an empty canvas, knows that the time has come to make a move. He has done some vague sketches in charcoal of Lizzie, but they are only a sop, to soak up any suspicions she might have. Jordan does not want to paint Lizzie, he wants to fuck her, and she is being incredibly obtuse about it. She must surely know that he fancies her, but she is playing it exceedingly cool. He rather admires her for this. He didn't think she had it in her.

Though not rejecting him, Lizzie has certainly not responded to his advances. He has let his fingertips brush her nipples like tiny feathers, pretending he wants to move her this way or that, and he has placed his hand firmly high up on the inside of her naked thigh, ostensibly to show her how he wants her to pose. Any self-respecting model would have thumped him by now, but Lizzie just closes her eyes and doesn't even flinch, as if pretending it hasn't happened. Jordan has decided that she is playing hard to get, and it's time he took a firmer line with her.

'Relax, Elizabeth,' he says, leaving his easel and coming towards her. Gently he parts her legs, which have been pressed tightly together, and says, 'There now, that looks much more natural.'

Lizzie gets that awful heaving sinking feeling in her chest, like she does every time he touches her. But she is as powerless to tell him to stop as she was to tell her stepfather, when she was twelve, not to put his hands down her knickers. Lizzie is paralysed by authority, when it is big, male, powerful. She has let domineering teachers smack her knuckles for offences she has not committed; she has, before she married Tom, let herself be seduced by older men that repulsed and hurt her.

When Tom came along, crazy with love for her, she knew what it was like, for the first time, to want what the men wanted. When she got pregnant, Tom was delighted and insisted on marrying her at once, not even just living together like a lot of their friends were. Tom, like all the men in her life, was bossy sometimes and tried to tell her what to do – like going on at her to lose some weight – but at least it was equal, for she got on at him sometimes too, to quit smoking, or take her out to the pictures more often.

Lizzie hates modelling for Jordan, and wishes the painting would hurry up and get finished. She hates it when he touches her, like he is now, but she assumes it is what all artists do when a model is posing for them.

236

She would like to put on her clothes and run out of there as fast as she can, but it would be like running out on her form teacher, Mr Anderson, when he was telling her off for smoking in the loos. She is afraid of disobeying. She remembers hiding once when her stepfather called her, and being beaten when she was found for not doing as he said. When she disobeyed Mr Anderson and he found her smoking again in the loo, he put her in detention for weeks, which was like prison must be. But far worse was his disapproval, that special male sulkiness he treated her with, like she was some kind of a scumbag.

Jordan would be the same, she just knows it, if she ups and leaves before the portrait is finished. She knows too that she would be made to look ridiculous if she went all funny on him now, after she agreed to model for him. So she grits her teeth and keeps her eyes tightly shut as Jordan fusses with her, moves her arm away from where it was partially covering her breast, moves her legs wider apart. With her eyes closed she cannot see Jordan pull down his dark track-suit bottoms and hitch the elasticated waist down over his hips. For a moment he surveys the scene, not with an artist's eye, but with a look of pure lechery. Lizzie's arms are outstretched, one draped along the back of the velvet settee, lifting her milky breast high and exposed, and the other arm swinging loose to the floor in a gesture of abandonment. Her legs are spread lewdly apart, one hanging tantalizingly down off the seat. *She's ready for this*, Jordan thinks crudely, forgetting that it was he who arranged Lizzie in such a suggestive manner.

He is about to pounce on her when two things happen almost simultaneously. First, Lizzie opens her eyes, sees Jordan half naked and towering above her like a great hairy satyr, and starts screaming her head off.

Within seconds the door of the studio is torn open,

the small bolt which Jordan has recently installed ripped right out of the wood. Tom, racing into the room, knocks over easel and paints and a wooden chair as he rushes to Jordan, grabs him by the shoulders, turns him around, and knocks him out flat.

'I'll kill him when he comes to,' Tom says, squatting down in front of Jordan as if waiting for the first sign of life, to pummel it out of him again.

'Oh Tom, I've never been so glad to see someone in all my life!' Lizzie cries, scrambling around for the discarded dressing-gown.

'What're you up to, Lizzie, posing for that poser?'

'Well, I, uh . . .' Lizzie, for the life of her, can't think how she got into this situation.

'Sid Hocking told me, that this painting thing was supposed to be a present for me. A surprise for my birthday, I suppose.'

'Uh, yes, yes.' Just in time Lizzie remembers that Tom's twenty-fifth is next week.

Tom stops watching Jordan's breathing long enough to look at Lizzie and say, kindly, 'It was a nice idea, Lizzie, but daft, love. You know you can't trust these artists, especially this berk here. Old Sid was that worried that you might be taken advantage of, he came to me. Bloody good job too.'

Lizzie, awash with gratitude and relief, throws herself on Tom and clings to him as if he were a hero, shedding a few grateful tears as she does so. Her dressing-gown falls open, leaving everything hanging out in all its glory for Tom to admire.

Which he does, suddenly with new eyes. 'Can't blame that poser for fancying you, I suppose. I've heard tell them artists don't like the skinny ones much, judging from the old paintings you see around.'

Lizzie lowers her eyes modestly. 'He did say I had a . . . what did he call it? – a voluptuous body.'

238

Tom growls low in his throat, thinking of the bastard saying such things to his beautiful Lizzie, of nearly forcing his way with his darling maid. 'I heard you screaming, Lizzie,' he says. 'I knew you were in bad trouble when I heard that scream. Luckily one of the guests let me into the house, and I was just on my way upstairs when I heard you shouting.'

Jordan stirs, moans a few times. Tom takes up his post at Jordan's head as Lizzie quickly gets on her pink track suit. 'Come on, Tom,' she says. 'Let's not have trouble. You've shown him what you can do; he won't dare come near me again.'

With gentle persuasion she manages to get Tom out of the studio before Jordan is fully revived. 'You come near anything belonging to me again – Lizzie, my son, my boat – and I'll kill you. Understand?'

Jordan understands. Painfully he nods his head, thinking he'll go down to Newlyn or Penzance to paint from now on. It'll be a long time before he goes near the harbour at St Ives again.

To console Lizzie, who looks suitably washed out, chastened and meek, Tom takes her to the Sloop where he plies her with shandy and two packets of salt and vinegar crisps.

'I'll never lose weight,' Lizzie moans as she eats both packets and orders another shandy.

'You're fine just the way you are,' Tom says, remembering her body under the dressing-gown, seeing it through Jordan's eyes, liking what he sees. He can't wait to get her home and into his bed.

'Look at them two, cuddling like doves in a dovecote,' Sid Hocking, standing at the bar, says to everyone around him. 'You'd never know they was married.' He abandons his usual chuckle to roar with deep genuine laughter.

'Have a pint on me,' he says to the bartender

magnanimously. Someday it will be a fine story to tell, how he kept a maid's secret and did proud by his mate as well, but for now he'll keep it all to himself. He likes having secrets, does Sid.

Thinking with pleasure of all the days ahead when Lizzie will be smiling gratefully at him with that lovely dimpled smile, calling him Cap'n and sitting lazily with him in the sun as the two of them watch Tom bringing in the catch, Sid lifts his glass and says, to the world at large, 'Well then. Cheers.'

Soon it will be summer, and he'll be out with the punters every day, after the mackerel. Captain Sid Hocking, thankful for life, for secrets, for the sun and for mackerel, drinks his pint and decides to go home to his wife. He's thankful for her too, but that is another secret.

A full moon hangs orange and heavy over the sea as he slowly, happily, makes his way home.

Lance Giddens is also in the Sloop Inn, sitting alone in the corner and drinking double whiskies. Ever since last weekend, when he had dinner with Esme and Richard, and Harriet and that London critic were there, Lance has been drinking far more than is good for him. It is not, he knows, either wise or helpful, but he is finding the secret he has from Esme almost impossible to keep, yet he knows he must. Today he ran into Richard and Harriet having a drink in a pub in Penzance. It was at lunchtime, and Lance had spent the morning at the art-auction rooms. Coming in from the rain, needing a stiff drink before catching the train back to St Ives, Lance walked into the pub and spotted Richard and Harriet immediately. They weren't eating, just drinking and smoking and laughing at something, and Lance saw Harriet reach over and stroke Richard's hand in a familiar intimate gesture. Lance, distraught, walked out again, not knowing or caring whether Richard saw him or not. He supposes that Esme knows that Richard sees Harriet occasionally in Penzance; after all, they both work there. But he knows she does not know the extent of their relationship.

Lance drinks his whisky, oblivious to the buzz of conversation around him, not noticing one or two acquaintances who greet him casually as they come into the pub. He is in an angry mood, upset for Esme. But in the core of his anger, like a tiny little worm, nibbles the thought that if Esme knew about this, she would turn to him, Lance, for comfort and consolation; for love, perhaps.

He knows he will not tell her. He cannot hurt her, even though there is a chance that he could profit by her hurt. He supposes this proves how very much he loves her, but the thought only makes him more miserable. Ordering another double Scotch Lance sighs, thinking, not for the first time, that life's a bitch and then you die. He'll drink to that, he decides. And does so with alacrity.

Samuel Tolling is also in his home in London this evening, thinking of Esme, and of Richard and Harriet. He is writing his light-hearted article about St Ives, concentrating not on the Tate this time, but on what else is happening in the art scene there. He is pleased with it so far; it is full of gentle witticisms, perceptive insights and astringent humour.

Samuel stops in his writing, pondering a dilemma. He has mentioned Esme, of course – she is very fashionable now, and no article on St Ives would be comprehensive without at least a mention of her. What is tempting, is to give the merest tiniest hint of what he witnessed at dinner that night, the very obvious signals that Esme's husband and that other objectionable female were putting out. Samuel cannot understand why Esme suspects nothing, but then the ways of heterosexual couples are often baffling to him. He knew within minutes when his last partner was cheating on him, merely by the way the man shut the door when he came in one night. Perhaps women are not so perceptive, Samuel muses. Or could it be that they are just more trusting?

It wouldn't be difficult to put in just the slightest allusion, he thinks, going back to his article. He could describe the little dinner party – commenting favourably about Esme's cooking (his readers will be sick with envy to learn that she is not only a brilliant sculptor but can cook as well) and mention the solicitous husband, the arty guests. But then, before Esme could be disliked for being so perfect, for having it all – doting partner, family, friends, fame – Samuel could write something about Richard paying particular attention to one of the guests, just a line or two, nothing libellous, merely intriguing. His readers would love it, and it would give him such great delight to imagine Richard squirming.

In the end, he does not mention the dinner party, does not mention Harriet at all, and Richard only curtly, as Esme's husband. He writes about Esme, of course, and the town, and mentions one or two of the younger artists that Esme introduced him to, including Alice Culpepper, whose self-portrait he saw and thought was most promising. Lance Giddens and the Sandpiper gallery are mentioned, as is the seafood restaurant where he took Esme to lunch before he left, which had some decent drawings by local artists hanging in strategic places.

Samuel regrets not being able to use his intuitive knowledge of what Esme's husband is up to in St Ives, but he has decided he likes her far too much to compromise her in any way. There are not many artists he would have the same scruples about, but Esme is a trusted friend, and God knows there are not many of those in a person's lifetime.

Feeling infinitely virtuous, Samuel finishes his article, to be sent off in the morning. As he mixes himself a Campari and soda in his stark minimalist kitchen which contains nothing but white marble counter tops, a painted white wooden table, and one tubular stainless-steel chair, Samuel feels pleased with his evening's work. The article sits on his desk, ready to be faxed to his editor in the morning, for next Sunday's paper. He thinks it is innocent, innocuous, harmless; he would be appalled if he knew what damage it is about to create.

But like Esme, what he doesn't know cannot bother him. Guileless, blameless, he drinks his Campari and soda, reading the article one more time with justified admiration.

Chapter Twelve

Richard reads Samuel's article on Sunday morning in Harriet's kitchen, sharing a clandestine pot of coffee with her. Esme is busy in her garden shed which has, predictably, made Richard cross, causing him to make the usual acid comments about her work. His resentment is more manifest now; Richard knows it and doesn't care any more. Stomping out of the house, barely acknowledging Esme's protests that she had planned to stop work at noon and was going to suggest they go for a walk on the coastal path, Richard had gone to the newsagent and called in to see Harriet on his way home.

Harriet loves Richard popping in on her like this, unbidden, impulsively. She feels married as she pours him coffee, shares the Sunday newspaper he has brought. Harriet would like to be married, or at least live with a man. She's had several short bouts of live-in lovers, but they've never lasted long. Harriet is sure that she and Richard could live together compatibly for years; indeed Richard has said this, has hinted that she would indeed be not only his soul mate but his living-in mate, if it weren't for his duty, his obligation, to Esme.

Harriet sighs, tightening the belt of her red kimono which is pulled chastely around her waist. Richard has made it very clear that they dare not risk being caught

244

in any kind of compromising situation, not on a Sunday morning when someone, a friend, a mutual acquaintance, could easily drop in to see Harriet. If that should happen, Richard will tell Esme that he called in for coffee; but if no-one sees Richard in Harriet's house, there is no need to mention it.

'What is Samuel's article like?' Harriet asks. She's aching to read it, Richard had grabbed that part of the newspaper first.

'Oh, the usual stuff,' Richard says, taking off his glasses and laying them on the kitchen table. 'Goes on about Esme, as everyone seems to be doing these days.' He is, as a matter of fact, quite miffed over the way that Samuel mentions him so tersely, an aside: Esme's husband, one of her minor accessories, in the same category as the wallpaper in her living-room, the silver earrings she is partial to. Indeed, Samuel spent more time describing these latter two things than he did describing Esme's husband.

Harriet grabs the paper and sits down opposite Richard at the kitchen table. Richard puts his glasses back on and notices how much less oriental she looks without her make-up, which she hasn't put on because Richard surprised her when she was not long out of bed.

Harriet begins the article with pleasurable anticipation. She is sure that Samuel Tolling will mention her, for he did say he liked her sculpture that day at the Sandpiper gallery. And Esme helped, Harriet has to admit, by praising her work and then inviting her to dinner with him that night. She is sure she made an impression on Samuel, and cannot wait to see her name mentioned in his article. Harriet's work has never been mentioned in a national newspaper before.

It isn't, of course, mentioned now. Harriet, hurt and angry, says, with as much control as she can muster, for she doesn't want to appear jealous of Esme, 'What do you think of this, then?'

'A bit trite,' Richard says noncommittally.

Harriet, cheered, says, 'I thought it was rather predictable. The same old stuff, no new insights.'

They smile at each other with lifted spirits, both slightly mollified, though, in truth, Harriet is still seething about the article. None the less she tries to remain calm and smiling because she knows it would be churlish to start banging her fists on the table as she longs to do, and indeed would if Richard were not here. But she knows that married men get enough aggravation at home, understands that to keep him sweet and in love with her she must always be his darling, malleable and accommodating and sugar-tempered.

So instead she determinedly puts her career out of her head and turns to love instead, the area in which she has proved so superior to Esme, and says to Richard urgently, 'Let's go up to bed now. Come on.' She takes his hand and starts to gently pull him up from the table.

Richard is tempted, though it was not his intention when he came here: this was just a spur of the moment visit. But he feels slighted after reading Samuel's article, and the old hurts come back. He feels like a solitary ball left on the beach, forgotten, or even discarded. Pursuing this image he imagines the incoming tide sweeping up on the sand, claiming the ball, losing it for ever in the deep swollen sea. I am that ball, Richard thinks sadly; Esme has discarded me, and if it were not for Harriet, the deep sea or the void would swallow me completely.

'Richard? Come on!'

Richard shakes his head to clear the image away and looks reluctantly at his watch. 'There's no time. Esme's expecting me at noon; she said she was stopping work then and wanted to go for a walk or something.'

Harriet goes to him, wraps her arms around his waist.

'I need you much more than Esme does,' she murmurs.

Richard knows this to be true. Harriet is the one lone traveller who remembers that discarded ball on the beach and comes back for it. Gratefully he kisses her, but says, 'I'd love to, you know that. But we must be careful or Esme will get suspicious. I don't want her to come looking for me.'

Harriet acquiesces, for she has no choice. But she doesn't like it, not one bit. She seems to have no say in this relationship, no power, no equality. Richard comes and goes when it is convenient for him, and she is supposed to put up with it.

Those are the rules, of course. Harriet knows this, knows she accepted this when she began the relationship. But she also knows rules can be flexible, or even broken.

When Richard goes, Harriet reads Samuel Tolling's article a second time. It makes her angrier than ever, so she opens a bottle of Frascati that has been chilling in the fridge in case Richard had arrived unexpectedly last night. She pours herself a glass so that she doesn't start throwing books and shoes and maybe even cups around. She drinks the first glass quickly, medicinally, and pours herself a second which she sips more slowly. Lighting a cigarette, Harriet stares at the Sunday newspaper, at the offensive article, and simmers and stews like a hot fish soup very near to boiling point.

Richard and Esme have, surprisingly after such a bad start, a good day. When Richard gets home Esme is waiting for him, having had a quick shower to get the stone dust from her hair and the crevices in her fingers and hands. Richard's earlier sulkiness has disappeared after his surreptitious visit with Harriet, and he agrees with Esme that lunch at the Sloop would be pleasant, followed by a walk along the coastal path which is punctuated this time of year by the white flowers of the wild garlic now in bloom. The fine weather has remained, though there is a slight breeze now, and the sea is choppy. On the way they stop above Porthmeor Beach and watch the surfers, wondering if Hugo is amongst them.

'I'm glad he's finally decided what to do with his life,' Esme says as they walk on towards the town.

'He's not decided anything,' Richard grumbles. 'He has some fool notion of being a chef, owning a restaurant one day, but he hasn't a clue how hard it is or what it entails. Or how much it would cost.'

'He'll learn.'

'It's probably a whim. In the meantime he's hanging around here, surfing all day—'

'And learning something about the restaurant business every night. It sounds like the best life possible for him, for now.'

Richard, enjoying the day, decides not to argue. Perhaps Esme is right, who knows. He doesn't want to talk about Hugo any more so he puts his arm around Esme's shoulders and she wraps her own around his waist. Entwined, they walk slowly home.

Harriet, going out to buy cigarettes, sees them, though they do not see her. She is stunned to see Richard and Esme with their arms wrapped so affectionately around each other. It makes her face the fact that if they do this, they could very well be sleeping together, making love together.

Rationally, Harriet knows that Richard and Esme must make love, but she has not let herself think of this. Richard has never said that that part of his life with Esme was over, nor indeed has he ever said that he no longer loves her. Harriet somehow assumed that the passion between them had died or was at least moribund when she entered Richard's life, and this open display of affection in the streets hits her like a physical blow.

By the time Harriet has returned home, she has convinced herself that Richard's arms were around Esme purely to placate her, so that she doesn't suspect his infidelity. None the less she decides she needs another drink, and makes herself a strong gin and tonic which leaves her cold and angry. It is late afternoon and she is lonely, bored, missing Richard. She wonders if he is sitting in the living-room with Esme, watching the news perhaps, and thinking of her.

As a matter of fact Richard, though at home, is upstairs in bed with his wife, making love to her. They have not made love in the afternoon for years, what with their two sons in and out of the house, and various friends occasionally dropping in. But Hugo had come in as they were having a cup of tea and told them that as soon as he got out of his wet suit, he was going to Plymouth with Cara, staying the night and the next day with friends as he had the evening off. Crispin was out on the boat, Hugo said; he had seen him earlier.

When Hugo had gone, Esme had gone over to Richard, sat on his lap, and one thing had led to another. Now they are in bed, the curtains drawn, the room dim and peaceful, only the sound of the gulls coming in through the open window.

Later, when they have dressed again and gone downstairs, had a bite to eat, Esme says, 'I'm going back down to my workroom for an hour or so, just to sort out something in my head. I need to sit and look at my latest effort, it's not coming right.'

Richard, knowing he shouldn't, knowing he mustn't spoil what has been a good day, says caustically, 'Oh, of course. You only spent all morning down in that shed, you couldn't possibly leave it until tomorrow.'

Esme looks at him and despairs. After their lovely

249

lunch and walk, then the love-making and the lingering happy supper, he still begrudges her an hour on her own, in her studio.

'Richard,' she says. 'Please. Please don't do this to me.'

Richard would like to relent, to go to her, hug her, say it's all right, he was only joking. But years of resentment, of bitterness, are hard to erase in one loving afternoon. Looking at her with a wounded, acrimonious, accusing expression which she will remember later, he turns away without a word, goes into the living-room and turns on the telly.

Esme, in her studio, weeps. She cries for herself and Richard, for the damage done to their marriage. She does not know who is to blame; perhaps she should not have been a sculptor, or, conversely, maybe she should never have married. Perhaps she is not capable of being so divided, of serving two masters. And yet she had not seen marriage as being in opposition to her work. Rather, each was an essential part of herself, two horses pulling the same plough. They were both necessary to her life; one would not have been enough.

Esme weeps, and Richard watches television, silently, stonily. It is a beautiful April evening, lost to them both irrevocably.

In her own home, Harriet smokes another cigarette and reads once again the article by Samuel Tolling. It strikes her as being horribly unfair. After all, the man had liked her work, had seemed to like *her* when they first gathered in Esme's living-room. And then he mentions three or four other artists working in the area – that Culpepper woman, Alice, amongst them, as well as Molly North, which irritates the hell out of Harriet because she is sure it is only because she is Oona North's granddaughter – and not a mention of her. Brooding, she wonders what went wrong, wonders whether Lance, or even Esme, put Samuel off by telling him of that dreadful scene in the Sandpiper when she had lost her cool and shouted at Lance. It must be something like that, she is sure. The article is so pathetic, really, she thinks, reading it yet again, so fawning about Esme, who has had so much bloody publicity lately; surely she could have stepped down a bit to let Harriet have her day.

She will yet, Harriet thinks. She will yet.

Getting out her black raincoat, for the evening feels damper – a mist is gathering out at sea – Harriet gets ready to go out. On the way to the door she sees the newspaper again and picks it up, looks at it once more with contempt, and hurls it as hard as she can into the dustbin.

As Harriet walks out of her house, Percy Prynne wanders out of his and heads for the Island. The mist which Harriet sensed was approaching is beginning to slide inland from the sea, damp and chilling after the fine early evening. Percy shivers. He is coughing a great deal now, but his arthritis has eased slightly. Yesterday he had lunch in the Union with Crispin, who seemed troubled when he began talking to Maggie over the bacon rolls. Percy thought that perhaps it was because Crispin felt it rude, talking to his wife like that instead of to Crispin, so for the rest of the lunch Percy tried to ignore Maggie's singing and concentrate on what Crispin was saying. Nevertheless, as they parted outside the pub, Crispin said, 'You know, Percy, your cough is still lingering. I think you need to see the doctor again, for a thorough check-up.'

Percy muttered something vague and Crispin knew he had no intention of seeing anybody. Percy knows that Crispin will ring the doctor himself first thing Monday morning, and between them they will try to get him up to the surgery. Percy knows he doesn't need a doctor.

After his lunch with Crispin he went to Crispin's house and there, looking out towards sea, was the young Percy Prynne again, confident, strong, assured, waiting for the tide to fill the harbour so that he could take the *Fair Celt* out once more, miles out to where the fish were.

He's just waiting for the sign, that's all. Sitting on the bench in front of the old stone chapel, watching the mist crawl over the sea and around the rocks below him, Percy sits, waiting for the lady with the lantern, come to look for her baby, come to signal endings and deaths and disasters for any who see her light. Percy longs for the ending now, for he knows it will be a beginning, knows he will then be with Maggie always, back in their house in Downlong, before rising prices forced them to sell and move Uplong, too far from the harbour, from his boat. And he'll be back too with his young brothers, watching their father and older brother and the other fishermen sail out of the harbour in the herring season, dozens and dozens of boats proudly going for the catch. A shiver runs through Percy, and he is there, feeling the thrill and excitement as the fishermen return, singing, boats laden with herring and the women and girls washing the fish in barrels, preparing them for kippering.

There's no more herring now, nor pilchards, but this doesn't trouble Percy Prynne as it did years ago, because he knows now that they *are* out there; his father and brother have whispered to him, are whispering to him now, to get into his boat, steam out to where the fish used to be, shoot his herring nets. His father has promised that the fish will be there, and Maggie is telling him now how she will soak the herring in strong pickle before taking them to the smoke house, like she did as a girl all those years ago.

Percy, though longing to go, stubbornly resists. In his fuddled brain he knows he cannot find peace until he has seen the woman with the lantern, knows he must be patient, stoic, until then. Getting up from his bench he paces restlessly up and down around the chapel, the fog clinging to him like limpets on rocks, echoing the voices of Maggie and his father and now all his brothers, as they sing and sing and sing.

Harriet knocks on the door of Richard's and Esme's house and waits patiently for someone to answer it. Richard, surprised but not displeased to see her, invites her inside.

'I haven't seen either of you for ages,' Harriet lies blithely, looking Richard straight in the face. 'So I thought I'd pop in and say hello. Where's Esme?'

'In her shed,' Richard replies dismissively, risking an illicit fondle as he gives her the usual comradely kiss chastely and briefly on both cheeks. 'Come into the living-room, there's a fire. It's a bit cool tonight, though it was such a lovely warm day.'

'And Esme is not tempted to join you? She *is* keen on her work, isn't she.'

'She won't be long,' Richard warns, noting the gleam in Harriet's eyes. 'She said she was only going down there for an hour or so, and it's more than that now.'

'So I must be on my best behaviour,' Harriet murmurs softly with a sly smile. 'I understand.' She reaches in her bag for her cigarettes and offers Richard one.

'Don't do that,' he says.

'Oh, darling, does she still think you're trying to give it up? All right, I won't let on. You don't mind if I smoke though?'

'Go ahead.' Richard pokes the fire, then smiles at Harriet. 'I can breathe in your smoke. Can I make you a drink? Gin and tonic? Or would you like some white wine?'

'A gin and tonic would be grand.'

Richard pours them each a drink and they sit in silence for a few moments, aware that Esme could be in the kitchen and walking towards the living-room at any moment. So they content themselves with polite chatter, happy to be circumspect in the sure knowledge that they will be alone together as soon as it can be arranged.

Finally, after some time, Richard says reluctantly, 'Perhaps you should wander down to the garden shed, see Esme.'

'But she's working, you said.'

'Not seriously. She only went down to look at what she's been doing, ponder on how to continue or some such thing. She'd probably welcome the comments of another artist.'

Harriet smiles. 'I'm rather enjoying it here, sitting with you, talking about inconsequential things. It makes me feel—'

Richard interrupts her hastily. He knows what she is about to say, that it makes her feel that they are married, or living together, or whatever. He doesn't mind that kind of talk, but not here, not in his house with Esme about to walk in any moment.

He permits himself a slight touch, the brushing of fingers against her slim calf as he leans towards her. She is looking good tonight, dressed in a loose grey trouser suit with a soft creamy jumper underneath. The only colours are in her bright red lips and nails, and the two round discs of pink on her cheeks. Her eyes seem black in the lamplight and firelight, as black as her hair. He will go over to see her tomorrow night, whatever happens, and permits himself to whisper this to her, at first making sure that Esme has not entered the room.

'But in the meantime, I think you ought to go down to see Esme,' he says in his normal voice. 'She's not seen you since the weekend Samuel Tolling was here. I'm sure you two will have a great deal to talk about.'

Harriet sighs, rolls her eyes, but doesn't move. She has been friends with Esme a long time, and it would seem odd if she left without calling in to see what she was up to, what she was working on. But she is so enjoying sharing a drink with Richard by the fire, so receptive to his obvious admiration, that she wants to bask in it all evening, wants to be soothed and petted and oiled with love to make up for the slight she received from Samuel Tolling, in that wretched and disappointing article in the Sunday supplement this morning.

'Oh all right, I'll go,' she says petulantly. Richard smiles encouragingly, gratefully. They both know that her longstanding friendship with Esme is beneficial to their relationship, for Harriet is free to call in at the Cochran home any time, and if Richard is found at hers, it would not be suspect.

Harriet walks down to Esme's workshop reluctantly. Although in her head (and to Richard) Harriet still professes to be fond of Esme, this is no longer possible. Esme has what she hasn't, what she wants – both Richard and success – and the unfairness of it all has eaten into Harriet's old affection for her friend like a tiny furry caterpillar eating a pale-green leaf.

'Harriet! How nice to see you.' Esme greets her warmly, hugs her with genuine enthusiasm. She has not seen her since Samuel Tolling was here, and her relief that Harriet is not hanging about quite so often is tempered with guilt that she should feel this way. 'What have you been up to?'

Harriet has been up to sleeping with Esme's husband, and indeed this is why she hasn't dropped in on the Cochran household. It hasn't been necessary; she saw Richard several times last week. 'Not much,' Harriet hedges. 'What about you?'

Esme points to the piece of sandstone standing on the floor next to her workbench. It is larger than Esme's other work; indeed, it is almost life-size. On one side, as if trying to break out of the stone, is an elongated thigh; strong, eloquent, passionate. Harriet looks closer. She is sure it is a thigh, the beginning of a leg, but it could also be pure shape, pure abstraction, for it is whole and true and perfect as it is, without being allocated a name, a label.

Harriet looks at the embryonic sculpture and knows that it is, simply, a work of pure art, pure creation. A flash of malevolence goes through her, compounding envy, jealousy, a sense of injustice and anger. Turning her eyes from the stone, which has acquired majesty from that one sweep of thigh, or line or shape, Harriet looks obliquely at Esme. She is staring at her sculpture with the same look that Harriet, being an artist herself, should have recognized: a mixture of fear and despair and exultation, knowing that the promise is there, but unsure whether the potential can ever be fulfilled. But Harriet, too wrapped up in wanting Esme's husband, wanting for her own work what she sees in Esme's, misinterprets what is in Esme's face. Because it is calm, she sees smugness; because it is intense, Harriet believes she sees triumph.

She faces Esme and waits patiently, even calculatingly, for her to turn and look at her. When she does, Harriet says, quietly but very, very clearly, 'Richard and I are having an affair.'

There is a moment, just a moment, when everything seems to Esme exceptionally bright, defined, static. Then it evanesces: Harriet, her sculpture, her tools scattered around the stone, the windows of her workroom, seem to fade, disappear, like tiny fishing boats swallowed up by fog and mist.

Harriet waits. She doesn't have a clue what will happen now, but she knows she has won, knows that her day has come at last.

Esme is staring at her, her face no longer in repose but working frantically, lips rubbery as she opens and closes her mouth soundlessly, eyes screwed up into tiny odd shapes, jaw trembling like a jellyfish. 'No,' she whispers at last, the word sounding odd, strident, dry, as if wrested out of wind on a sand dune.

Harriet does not look down, does not flinch as Esme searches her eyes to see if it is true, and then begins slowly shaking her head from side to side. 'No,' she whimpers again. 'No, no, no.'

Harriet says nothing, and Esme, after staring at her in horror and disbelief for a few moments, starts to moan, first softly, like a feral animal in pain, then louder and louder, until the moans become disjointed sobs, cries, gasps.

'What the hell is going on?' Richard, missing Harriet and deciding to stroll nonchalantly down to the garden shed, looks at Esme with concern. 'What's the matter, what's happened? Are you hurt? Esme, please, love, say something, answer me.'

Esme, who has slumped on the floor in a foetal position, tries to speak, but the only thing that comes out is a thin eerie cry, like a sea-bird in distress. Tears are running down her face and she is clutching herself tightly, as if she is in terrible pain. Richard, frantic, shouts, 'For God's sake, someone tell me what is happening! Are you ill? Has there been an accident? Shall I call a doctor?'

Esme is trying to catch her breath and is making deep rasping sounds, like the tide ebbing on shingle. Richard, holding her, rocking her, looks at Harriet for the first time since he heard Esme's cry. 'For God's sake, what is it? What's wrong with Esme?'

Harriet looks at him coolly. In truth, Esme's reaction has startled her by its intensity, but she refuses to believe it is genuine, refuses to acknowledge that a bit of adultery, which is going on constantly all around them, should put Esme into such a state. She says to Richard, 'I just told her about us.'

Richard, stunned, stares at Harriet for a moment as if seeing her for the first time. 'Oh Jesus,' he whispers, his voice as cracked as Esme's. He is still crouched on the floor, holding her, and now his head drops down in despair, his face buried in her hair. For one bizarre moment Harriet thinks what a wonderful sculpture Esme could make of that scene, and the thought so infuriates her that she says, brusquely, 'Oh for fuck's sake, get up, Esme, and stop being so dramatic.'

Esme gets up. She pulls herself from Richard and tears away from him as he tries to stop her. She is making for the door of her workroom but Harriet is there, blocking her. 'We have to talk,' Harriet says calmly. 'Pull yourself together so that we can discuss this like adults.'

Esme looks at her as if Harriet were insane. Tears are still streaming down her face which is distorted, ugly, swollen. She is emitting little cries and sobs that seem to be torn out of her involuntarily, and her breathing is loud, raucous, precarious. With choking gasps she says, 'Let me go, let me be by myself, let me go.' She tries to struggle past Harriet but Harriet holds her ground, repeating, 'We have to talk about this.' Esme tries to pull herself away from Richard who is holding her again, trying to soothe her, and cries, 'Please, just let me go, I can't bear it. Let me go, please, please.' With a sudden burst of strength she wrests herself out of Richard's arms, pushes Harriet aside, and runs out of the studio, up the garden and out the gate into the street. Richard tries to follow her, but Harriet blocks his way, causing him to fall over. 'Get out of my way,' he says.

'Leave her, Richard. Let her have time to cool off. She'll be back, and then we can all three talk about it in a sensible manner.'

Now Richard looks at her as if she were mad. 'Talk?' he says, as if he cannot believe what she is saying. Then he pushes her aside and runs out to follow Esme.

Esme doesn't know where she is going, what she is doing. She is not thinking, only feeling, and what she is feeling is like some animal wounded and about to die, wanting to crawl off somewhere to be alone, to suffer in peace. Instinctively turning away from town she heads towards Porthmeor, but even at this hour there are still people ambling around outside the Tate and strolling in the sand, despite the thickening mist.

Esme cuts across the beach and makes for the Island, going up the incline and heading for the path leading around the headland. She passes a woman with white hair clinging to the arm of a bald stooped man as their black Labrador scampers beside them. The couple look at her strangely, for copious tears are still pouring down her face. The woman steps forward with an inaudible cry, as if to help, but the man pulls her back and whispers, 'None of our business, dear.'

There is no-one on the narrow cliff track. Esme goes a short distance and then veers off the path, heading up the grassy incline towards St Nicholas' Chapel, collapsing on the grass by a rocky outcrop under the ancient stone church. Facing her is the sea, fuzzy and deceptively quiet underneath its soft duvet of fog. Esme, slumped on the damp grassy verge, is in shock, as after a serious accident. She feels weak, displaced, numb, stunned, disoriented. She is also in considerable pain, though she could not, if asked, pinpoint it. It feels physical; it runs from the top of her head to her belly, her heart seems to be bursting with it, her lungs crying both for air and for relief. She loved Richard – loves him – and his betrayal is like a burning shaft of iron plunged into her softest, most vulnerable, places. In a few brief

259

moments her life, such as she has known it, has been burned off her like straw stubble burned off a field of barley.

Esme, unable to bear it, begins to sob again, softly, desolately. Though her crying is quieter now, more muffled, the despair in it is deeper, somehow more poignant.

Several yards above, sitting on his bench in front of the chapel, Percy Prynne hears weeping. At first he thinks it is the sound of the mist rubbing itself on the rocks, then he thinks it is his father calling to him from the sea. But as the sound persists, he recognizes the music of desolation, of grieving, of deep impenetrable sadness.

Slowly, Percy stands up and stiffly hobbles towards the sound, peering over the low stone wall surrounding the little church. There right below him, hunched next to some rocks, he can just make out, through the mist, the shape of a woman, weeping and sobbing. In her sorrow she doesn't see him as he squints intently through the dark.

It is *her*, of course. The lady from the shipwreck, looking for her baby. Grieving, crying, because her baby is dead, drowned, claimed by the sea. As Percy looks at the woman he can see a great light shining from her, radiating everything around her, coming towards him, *touching* him. She has come with her lantern, her beacon, to shine on him, to dazzle him, to tell him that it is time at last.

Percy's eyes no longer see the fog, the huddled form of the woman on the path, but only the light which he has been waiting for all winter. Like a lighthouse, it beams powerfully on him, pierces through the thick mist, points with luminous clarity towards the harbour, and from the harbour towards the sea. Percy, his heart filled with joy, turns and follows it.

*   *   *

Richard, hoping to follow Esme, has lost her. When he broke away from Harriet and ran out of the garden gate, she was nowhere in sight. She could have gone down any one of a number of streets, and he could weep with frustration for he doesn't know which way to go. Like a wild rabbit caught in the sudden glare of bright white headlights, he stops, frozen, and then plunges in quite the wrong way, towards the other beach, Porthminster, thinking he will find her there on the shoreline.

Harriet, left alone in Esme's studio, suddenly, erratically, bursts into tears, but they are tears of rage and impotence. She cannot believe how badly Esme behaved, and Richard too, for that matter, running off and not sitting down and talking about it in a civilized manner. Richard, at least, could have stayed with her; he must know that she'd be upset after Esme's theatrics.

Harriet has a good cry. When she finishes she finds a box of tissues on a shelf in the studio and blows her nose, looking at Esme's unfinished sculpture as she does so. For a moment rage fills her again, and she picks up Esme's mallet and chisel to grind that strange emerging elongated shape into unrecognizable shards.

But for once, Harriet holds her temper, stops suddenly as she is about to attack, realizing what a stupid mistake it would be, what a predictable, banal cliché, to maul Esme's sculpture. Even if Esme won't, she herself will remain civilized, will conduct herself as an adult. She doesn't want to cause Esme any damage; after all they *are* friends, and Harriet, feeling suddenly optimistic after her cry, doesn't see why they can't be again, one day, after they have sorted all this out.

Putting down the chisel and mallet, Harriet, rather satisfied with herself, decides to go home, where she will wait for Richard. She is sure that he will eventually come to her, though she understands that this might not be until the small hours of the morning, that Richard will have to both placate Esme and to admit to her that he loves someone else.

No matter, she will wait. At least everything is out in the open now; at least Harriet is acknowledged and will have to be dealt with. She does not know how all this will be resolved – perhaps Richard will choose to stay with his wife and continue to see Harriet, but in the open this time; or (and Harriet hardly dares hope) he may even move in with her. She will be magnanimous if that happens; she will make sure that all three of them remain friends; she will be kind to Esme. But whatever happens, Esme will never be able to look at Harriet again with that serene smug complacency.

Harriet goes into the kitchen to collect her raincoat, puts it on and leaves the house. She is glad that she did not damage Esme's sculpture; it would have been a petty and churlish act, beneath her. On the whole, she thinks she handled the situation fairly well, and knows that Richard, once he has got over the shock, once he has calmed Esme down, will see that what she did was right and necessary.

Going into her house, Harriet, restless, cannot settle. She knows this is going to be a long night, but she doesn't mind; she feels excited, stimulated. She is at her best in a crisis; she loves the drama of it, the feeling that all her nerve endings are plugged into high voltage.

Flopping into the big flowered armchair by the television, Harriet stares into space, ready and waiting for whatever is to come.

Chapter Thirteen

Percy Prynne, following his light, runs to the harbour. It is late by now, the tide well in, the boats secure. The *Fair Celt* is moored alongside the pier, near the stone steps leading to the water. The mist rolls and drifts like seaweed floating on the waves and the beam of Godrevy lighthouse is hazy, opaque. But the beacon that Percy sees is brighter and whiter and more radiant than ever, and gives him far more strength and energy than he has had for months.

Clumsily, Percy climbs down the stone steps leading down to the *Fair Celt*. He still has a key to the engine; he has kept it in his wallet since selling the boat to Crispin. The boat starts quickly, obediently. Percy lets the engine idle for five, ten minutes until he sees a lone male figure walking slowly down the pier, a holiday-maker taking one last stroll before turning in for the night. Percy calls out to him from the *Fair Celt* as the man stops to look down at the boat, the only one in the harbour with its lights on and its engine running; Percy asks him to undo the ropes that tie the boat to the pier. The holiday-maker, delighted to be part of the real life of the town, does as Percy asks, and watches as the *Fair Celt* slowly chugs out of the harbour and out to sea.

Percy, at the wheel, feels his old heart filled with an

indescribable rapture as he sees the harbour lights fade from view. As the *Fair Celt* is swallowed by the fog, Percy finds that the light that compelled him here is so blinding that he can hardly see the wheel, but he knows the boat like he knows the voice of his wife Maggie who has started to sing again, a song of lilting exultation, for Percy Prynne is coming home.

Home. Steering the boat further and further out to sea, to the mist and the mysteries out there in the deep waters, Percy laughs out loud, with joy filling his lungs like the spray from the sea fills every crevice and hollow in his poor worn body. He is after the herring now, like his father and grandfather before him; they are pointing the way, calling to him, singing to him, laughing with him as he roars with delight and ecstasy and reckless anticipation.

'I'm on m'way, my darling maid!' Percy shouts to Maggie.

'I'm getting there as fast as I can, my lovers,' he cries to his brothers, pushing out the throttle so that soon the *Fair Celt* is racing, racing, racing through the fog, following the bright phosphorescent light to home.

Richard finally finds Esme over an hour later. He has stopped by Crispin's house, asking with forced non-chalance whether they had seen her that evening, but Crispin and Molly have friends over and have not seen Esme. It is Molly who suggests the Island, saying that Esme often walks that way when she is stuck on a piece of work and needs to think. Richard curses himself that he doesn't know this fact about her. He wonders how many more there are to find out, wonders with despair whether it is too late for him to do so now.

He finds Esme sitting as if in a trance on the grass by the path, staring out towards the sea. 'Thank God,' he cries, holding her, lifting her up. She is wet and cold and shivering, but he has found her, she is all right.

Esme lets herself be led back to the house, Richard holding her up as if she were convalescing from a long serious illness. 'I'm sorry,' Richard says as they stumble off the Island and head towards home. 'Oh God, I'm so sorry, I was such a fool. Oh Esme, Esme!'

In the house Esme holds him and comforts him like a child while he cries and cries. 'It's all right,' she soothes. But she knows it is not.

They try to talk, but they both are too shocked and shaken by the events of the night, and tears keep interfering with the odd disjointed things they attempt to say. 'I love you,' Richard repeats over and over again. 'I never stopped. Please forgive me, forgive me; I don't want to leave you, I don't want you to leave me.'

'I love you,' Esme says, and tears roll down her cheeks as she realizes it is not enough.

'I was infatuated with Harriet. I turned to her when I thought you were turning away from me.'

'I know.'

'You weren't to know. About Harriet. I didn't want to hurt you.'

'Oh, God!'

'She *promised*. She swore she would never tell. If she hadn't, it would have all blown over eventually, I'm sure of it.'

'Oh God,' Esme repeats. Then, 'She's not important.'

Richard realizes that Esme is right. 'It was *you* I wanted, always – I still do – but I felt I never had you, not fully. It was as bad as if you had another lover; you *did* have a lover: your work, your sculpture.'

Esme closes her eyes. They are in the living-room and the fire is in ashes, the room is cold, but neither of them notice it.

'Please give me another chance,' Richard says. 'Please.'

265

A great weariness comes over Esme. 'I can't talk any more,' she says brokenly. 'Let's go to bed.'

Richard, heartened by the fact that she is letting him back into their bed, agrees with alacrity. 'We'll talk in the morning. It's nearly morning now anyway. I won't go into work, I'll call in sick. I *am* sick, sick in heart and soul. Oh Esme, we'll be all right, won't we?'

But Esme does not reply, and turns her back to him when they are in bed, lying stiffly in his arms until his heavy breathing tells her that he has finally fallen into an exhausted sleep.

Esme silently leaves the bed, too agitated to rest, too mindful of Richard's slumbering body to relax. She creeps downstairs, but the house seems alien, unfriendly. Unable to stay in it, she goes to her workroom, turns on the light. She stares at her embryonic sculpture, but it is meaningless to her right now. Everything is meaningless.

A sudden tap at the window startles her. Peering out, she sees an ancient white face, a tumble of fractious white hair. Opening the window she says, 'Oona.'

'Are you working? I don't want to disturb you. I saw your light switch on, but the house is dark. I was afraid of prowlers, so I thought I'd better check that it was you. I've just finished for the night and needed a walk, a bit of communion with the fog.'

'I'm not working,' Esme says brokenly.

Oona looks closely at her face and hastens away from the window, through the small gate in the garden wall and into the workroom. 'What's happened, Esme? What's wrong?'

Esme gives a little moan, sinks down onto a stool. 'Richard,' she mumbles. It is all she can say.

Oona knows, of course, about Richard's growing antagonism towards Esme's work; she has noticed strain between them during the odd times she has seen them together. Now Esme looks beaten, defeated. It will not do, Oona thinks angrily, it just will not do. She says slowly, 'You'll have to choose, you know. I think it has come to that.'

Esme says, 'I never wanted to choose. I wanted both.'

'So do we all. Sometimes we are extremely lucky. But if we are not, we must decide what comes first.'

Oona does not know about Harriet, of course, and Esme knows she is not able just yet to talk about it. But somehow what is happening is beyond Harriet now.

Oona is looking at Esme's new beginning sculpture, the thigh struggling out of stone. Esme follows her look. 'That,' she says finally. 'There is no choice after all, just what has to be done.'

Oona nods, relief flooding her. 'At last you've realized it. At last.'

Richard and Esme wake early, unrested. Oona had not stayed long, wisely leaving Esme alone to sit and stare at her piece of stone for a long time. Then she had gone to bed, this time falling at once into a deep oblivious sleep. Now, in the morning, Esme's eyes are swollen, her face blotchy, she looks years older. Richard brings her coffee on a tray in bed, with six perfect red tulips in a white vase. 'From the garden,' he says. 'I thought, this is like an anniversary, you know? A new beginning. Oh Esme, I've never loved you so much, never appreciated you so much as I do now. I've been such a fool.'

Esme looks at the tulips and the tears well up again under her swollen eyelids. 'It's no good, Richard. I'm sorry, but it's no good. I can't live with you any more.'

All day they talk, and cry. They do not answer the telephone, which is just as well because Harriet is frantically trying to phone them from work, having tried Richard at his school and found to her annoyance that he hadn't come in that day. They don't answer the doorbell either, though it has rung several times. Esme and Richard sit huddled upstairs in the bedroom like invalids, occasionally going downstairs for a cup of hot lemon tea, too ill to eat, or to drink anything stronger. Fortunately Hugo is away and won't be back until it's time for him to go to work.

'I'm sorry,' Esme says at last, after they have exhausted themselves, after they have gone round and round in circles, repeating themselves, explaining themselves. 'I'm not trying to punish you, Richard.'

'I wish you would, I despise myself, I've been a fool. I don't blame you for wanting revenge, but don't leave me, Esme. Please. You know I'll never see Harriet again, don't *want* to see her again—'

'God, Richard—'

'I slept with her out of vengeance, to get even with you. I know that now, I can see it so clearly. She was *there*, always so kind, sympathetic, willing to drop her own work to listen to me, something you never did—'

'Richard, stop! Stop this. Don't you see that this is the issue here? Why we have to part? It's not Harriet; she's only the symptom. You've always hated my work, always been jealous—'

'I'll change, Esme. I swear it. Just give me a chance.'

Esme looks at his familiar face, contorted with pain, distress, fear, and begins to cry again. She loves him, but the damage they have done to each other is too intense, too deep, and the love is scarred, pitted, rotten even. There is no point in carrying on building a marriage which has such radical structural faults: one day it is bound to crack irrevocably. It has happened now, Esme thinks. Harriet was the final fault, not even a major one perhaps, but the one that was just too much for the crumbling edifice which is now tumbling around their heads in ruins.

'No-one changes,' Esme says sadly. 'We are what we are. You will always be the kind of man who needs someone to love you like I never can, for I'll never stop being passionate about my work, never stop losing myself in it for hours.' Richard, who has talked and pleaded all day, is silent. Esme goes on. 'And however much I want to change, I'll always be a woman who not only needs to work, but needs the help and support and encouragement of those closest to me. You never gave me that, Richard. I understand now that you couldn't; it's not in your nature.'

'You make me sound like such an ogre.'

Esme looks startled. 'Do I? I don't mean to. I just meant we're too different to live in harmony. I couldn't give you what you wanted either, so you had to turn to someone else.'

Richard gives an anguished moan and goes to Esme, buries his head in her lap. 'I don't want anyone else.'

Esme smiles, for the first time in what seems like years. It is a weak wry smile, and very sad, but it is a promise that perhaps she will survive this, and Richard too, though not together. 'I don't want anyone else either,' she says, 'but that's all right. Maybe it's time we tried it alone.'

Richard knows it is no use saying anything more. Esme says, gently, 'I won't tell the boys about Harriet, unless you want to. We can just say we've decided to live apart for a time, if you like.'

Richard, who feels like his life is the scene of total devastation, clings to her words 'for a time'. They give him hope, but he wisely doesn't mention this for fear Esme will retract them.

When the doorbell rings, Esme rushes into the bathroom, telling Richard he'd better answer it now, since they have been in hiding all day. It is late afternoon and Esme has not combed her hair, washed her face, since yesterday. Running a bath, she stares at her ravaged pitiful face in the mirror, and once again tears brim over and fall. She wonders if she will ever stop crying, wonders if she will ever really get over Richard.

But at least she doesn't have to fight him any longer. At least she doesn't have to do constant battle for her work, her sculpture, the thing that makes her who she is, what she is. She realizes now how tiring it has always been, trying to cajole Richard into accepting her work, trying to avoid his sulks and tempers, trying to struggle with her art while trying to keep her marriage sweet and steady.

All that will be over. As Esme gets into the bath, she hopes that one day, when the pain subsides, when the loss and betrayal are no longer so salient and the grieving is finished, she might even feel a tremor of relief. It has been hard, she concedes. It has been bloody hard.

It is not easy now. Sinking down low in the bath, Esme tastes the salt of tears as the hot water washes over her tired exhausted body.

'Harriet. For Christ's sake. Why are you here? Haven't you done enough?'

Harriet moves past Richard and is through the door, into the house. 'We have to talk, Richard. Esme, too. Where is she?'

'She's not well, Jesus, what did you expect?'

'Then you and I can talk.'

Harriet goes uninvited into the living-room where yesterday evening she sat with Richard in front of a cosy intimate fire. The ashes from that fire are still in the grate; no-one has made an attempt to either clear them or light another fire. The room feels cold, lifeless, even though the fog has lifted and the late afternoon sun is warm and bright.

'Why did you do it?' Richard asks, as Harriet sits in

an armchair and crosses her legs. She looks groomed and immaculate, and Richard can't help comparing her bright eyes, glossy lips and smooth hair with Esme's poor dear face.

Harriet's lower lip trembles slightly. She is not feeling as poised as she looks; the fact that Richard has made no attempt to contact her has disconcerted her. 'I don't know why I did it,' she says. And in truth she doesn't. Somewhere in the murky regions of her subconscious there is an answer: to force Richard and Esme to split, leaving Richard free to come to her? To show Esme that she can't have it all? To take control of the situation?

'I just don't know,' Harriet repeats, for Richard is looking at her questioningly.

'I asked you never to hurt Esme. You promised. You promised *me*. You betrayed me as surely as you betrayed Esme.'

Harriet starts to cry. Richard, weary of tears, is unmoved. 'I didn't want to lie any more,' Harriet sniffs. 'I wanted everything out in the open.'

Richard moves away from her, towards the lifeless fire. 'There's nothing any more. It's over.'

He is talking about himself and Harriet, but she misunderstands. 'Is Esme leaving you?'

'Let's just say we've agreed to a separation,' he says. 'For a time.'

Harriet's heart does an odd flip, like an erratic drum beat. 'You can move in with me, Richard,' she says. 'We dreamed of that.'

Richard looks at her impassively. He doesn't even want to be in the same room with her, let alone live with her. All his old passion, infatuation, is as dead as the fire, as lifeless as the ashes in front of him.

'It's over, Harriet,' Richard repeats, and this time Harriet knows that he is talking about them. 'It's over,' he says again, as if making sure she hears. He says it softly, gently even, because in truth he is slightly afraid of her now. He is remembering what she did to Esme, how she deliberately inflicted such cruelty on her. He will never forget last night, and Esme's animal cries, her anguish.

'Go away,' Richard says brokenly. 'Just go away, please, and leave both of us in peace.'

Harriet stares at him disbelievingly, her eyes filled with tears of rage, but Richard is unmoved and turns away from her. After a moment Harriet walks out of the room and into the garden where she stops by Esme's workroom, picks up a steel-tipped hammer and, with all her strength, smashes it down on Esme's new sculpture.

When she is finished, when the stone is no longer recognizable, Harriet leaves the studio, leaves the garden through the gate leading into the street, and doesn't look back.

Crispin doesn't realize that the *Fair Celt* is gone until early in the morning when he goes out to the harbour to sort out his nets. At first he thinks he is hallucinating, but the boat just isn't there. As the alarm is raised and the fishermen and other curious townspeople gather on the pier, Sid Hocking remembers passing Percy Prynne late last night hobbling as fast as he could towards the harbour. 'He was that rushed, he didn't see me,' Sid explains. 'I had a touch of indigestion, and the wife said I should walk it off. I was just coming away from the harbour, 'twas murkier than a mullet's gut with the fog, and Percy was headed, all in a rush, towards the pier. I didn't pay him no mind; Percy's been going about in a daze for weeks now.'

'Did he go near the *Fair Celt*?'

'Now how'd I know? I went up Fish Street, didn't I, and never looked back to the quay. Didn't see the harbour again till just now. But Percy ain't home. I called in at the house just now, no-one there, and it looks like no-one was there all night, the curtains drawn and all.'

Crispin is sick with apprehension. The boat has obviously been taken – the ropes weren't cut or frayed; it didn't drift away – and Percy probably still has a key. When Crispin took over the boat he retained his own key which Percy had had made for him. It never occurred to him to ask for the original one back.

Luckily, the holiday-maker who untied the ropes on the *Fair Celt* last night is taking his morning stroll on Smeaton's Pier and, seeing the crowd, soon finds out what has happened and is able to confirm the fact that a man looking like Percy Prynne had indeed gone off in a boat late last night.

The coastguard is alerted, and a helicopter is sent out to look for the *Fair Celt*. In the meantime, anguished and desperately afraid for Percy, Crispin goes to his house, to double-check that no-one is there. The house is indeed empty, with a strange eerie emptiness as if no-one has been living there for a very long time.

'I should have kept a closer watch on him,' Crispin groans to Molly, having returned to his own home to let her know what was happening.

Because Crispin cannot just sit still and wait, he and Molly scour the cliffs, hoping to spot something; some clue, or Percy himself, anything. But there is no sign of Percy Prynne. Nothing at all.

The helicopter finds the *Fair Celt* drifting listlessly about twelve miles out to sea, and the lifeboat, with Crispin on it, is sent out to it. It is empty, a ghost ship, unharmed and unmanned, floating aimlessly in the calm sea. The tranquil waters around it are dark and secret and still, not giving up anything. A search is mounted for Percy Prynne, whose rusty key is found in the engine of the boat, but the sea refuses to reveal his whereabouts.

'It's the way he wanted to go,' Molly consoles a bereaved Crispin who blames himself. 'He loved the sea. He told me once that not one day went by, since he retired, that he didn't long to be out there.'

'He said that?'

'Yes, once on the pier when we were watching you go off in the *Fair Celt*.'

'Poor bugger.'

'Not so, Crispin. Not at all. He lived the way he wanted to, and died the way he wanted to.'

Crispin sighs, still bereft with grief. 'He was hearing voices in the end, you know. He kept talking to Maggie, his wife.'

'Do you know something, Crispin? Do you know what else he told me? He said that not a day went by, when he was a fisherman, that his wife didn't cry when he went off to sea.'

Crispin looks at her with love. 'Like you,' he says.

'How did you know? I thought I hid it rather well.'

Crispin smiles at last, and Molly goes weak with relief. 'He's all right, Percy is,' she says to him gently. 'He's where he wants to be.'

The memorial service for Percy Prynne is in the old parish church of St Ia, just off the harbour. The church is overflowing, not only with all the fishermen and lifeboat crew, both retired and working, but also with the many people who have loved and respected Percy Prynne throughout the years and know that their lives will be less rich through his passing.

Esme and Richard are there together, for they decided it would be inappropriate to tell Crispin immediately about their decision to separate. Percy's strange haunting death is all he can cope with right now. As the tears stream down Esme's cheeks, only Richard knows she is crying not just for Percy Prynne but for herself, and for Richard as well. As Esme rises to sing a hymn, she spots Crispin standing with Molly, their heads inclined towards each other as they lean over the hymn-book. Esme gives way to her hidden fear that Crispin and Molly's relationship will suffer because of her split with Richard; she is afraid that Crispin's old wariness of marriage, of long-term commitment, will resurface, like the old seal in the harbour when a fishing boat comes in.

But there is, in the end, nothing she can do about that now. She cannot alter her life for Crispin or anyone else, and she no longer even wants to try.

Standing in the back row, on her own, Oona North salutes Percy Prynne in her heart, thinking he has died victoriously, riding that last perfect wave in splendid defiance of old age and infirmity. She hopes that when her time comes she will be as courageous.

Sid Hocking, also in the last pew with his wife, cannot stop an unbidden tear or two from flowing down his robust cheeks and into his bushy moustache. Percy was his friend, his mate, a fisherman just like himself. Though they had squabbled in the past, what did it matter in the face of all they shared, all they had known, all they had done together in the past fifty, sixty years. In spite of the mild late April weather, Sid feels cold, his hands tremble on the hymn-book. He feels his own death a step or two closer with Percy gone, without the buffer of another mate, another old seaman like himself.

Sid tries to sing, and finds he is crying instead. His rotund wife, seeing his distress, squeezes his arm kindly and lovingly, and Sid, grateful, smiles down at her through his tears.

'Goodbye then, my handsome,' Sid says silently to his dead mate Percy Prynne. 'Save some of them shoals of fish wherever you are, for Captain Sid Hocking will be there before too long, don't you worry, my lover.'

The organ finishes the hymn with a resounding chord. As Sid and his wife leave the church, Sid could swear that there is a strange yellow light hovering over the harbour, colouring the rising tide and the bobbing boats with an eerie golden light. He doesn't know what it is, but he finds it oddly comforting. Blowing his nose loudly on the clean handkerchief his wife has just handed him, Captain Sid Hocking looks out to sea, makes a final silent farewell to his old friend Percy Prynne, and slowly begins the uphill walk towards home.

Chapter Fourteen

It is a strange wedding, the oddest ever seen in St Ives. It is held at St Leonard's, the tiny medieval fishermen's chapel at the foot of the pier, which hasn't been used for anything other than a shelter for decades. An accommodating vicar agreed to marry them there, and permission was sought, copious letters were written, phone calls made, and here they are.

The chapel is so small that the ceremony is performed in the doorway, the guests lining Smeaton's Pier and mingling with the tourists standing around the harbour, gaping with curious open mouths at the festivities. Luckily the early September day is warm, sunny, pleasant.

'I knew it would be,' Molly murmurs as Crispin, her husband of a few moments, kisses her.

The bride, dressed in a long cream silk frock, her irrepressible cinnamon hair newly cut and ordered into place for the occasion, holds onto the groom's arm as they stroll down to the end of the pier, followed by a hundred or so wedding guests. The pier is scrubbed clean of salt and seaweed for maybe the first time ever, and nets have been neatly put out of the way for the occasion. Tom and the other fishermen have hung balloons from the two lighthouses, and Lizzie and her friends have garnished the pier with plants and fresh flowers.

Molly, carrying a bouquet of deep rusty chrysanthemums, walks with Crispin to the pier's edge. 'For Percy Prynne,' she says clearly, and with love, as she throws the bouquet as far as she can into the water.

As they stroll back down the pier, to walk to the restaurant where the reception is held, the guests break into clusters, smiling in the sunlight, laughing and chatting. Oona North stays slightly apart, remaining at the edge of the pier watching Molly's bouquet sink out of sight in the sparkling, dazzling water. Silently she pays a tribute to Percy Prynne, and once again hopes that when her time comes she will be as intrepid in the face of death as he was.

Someone else lingers too. Alice Culpepper and Harlan Zayevich are standing by the middle lighthouse on their own, saying goodbye. Harlan is off to America; he is catching the train in a few moments to Penzance and from there to London, where he will go to Heathrow for his flight back to Florida.

'I'll be back,' he says urgently to Alice, as he has been saying for weeks.

He won't, of course. He is off to university, having promised his parents to complete his degree, and he is twenty-one. Alice understands how long a week is, let alone a year, when you are twenty-one. She understands that Harlan will find solace with other girls, girls his own age, which is as it should be. Were she not married, perhaps, had she not three young children, the age difference might not matter, but Alice has no plans, at least not at the moment, to become unmarried. Her children love Jordan, and she would not deprive them of him. Besides, since his aborted painting of Lizzie, Jordan has, for some reason, left Alice alone, not nagged her about getting out to draw the holiday-makers; he has left her in peace to pursue her own work in her beloved laundry-room. Soon she will have her first major exhibition, and she hopes the euphoria of that will take away some of the pain of Harlan's departure.

'I don't want to go,' Harlan says in despair, clutching her hand. Jordan and the children have gone on ahead, are already at the restaurant, and Harlan and Alice are quite alone now, except for Oona who is staring at the sea and appears not to notice them. 'God, I can't go. I can't leave you.'

Alice, recklessly, allows herself to be kissed in public the way Harlan has been kissing her in private for the past few months. She does not promise him anything, not undying love, not a future together, nothing. And yet it is Alice whose heart will be broken when Harlan leaves. She remembers how afraid she was of hurting him, how worried she was that he would suffer, being in love with her. Now she knows that it is *she* who will suffer, more than Harlan who is young and has the knack of falling in love often in his short lifetime. Alice has learned that you cannot go into a love affair carelessly, that there will always be prices to pay, penalties to be exacted.

'You must go,' she says. 'Now. Right now. You'll miss your train.'

Harlan looks at his watch, picks up his rucksack and the well-wrapped self-portrait of Alice which he bought from the Sandpiper gallery, and kisses her again. 'Run,' she says.

'I'll write.'

'Go.'

'I'll be back again. Soon.'

'Go, Harlan. You'll have to run now. But don't look back, please? Promise? I couldn't bear it if you do.'

Harlan nods, and turns and sprints down the pier,

scaring the sea-birds perched on the edge and causing them to fly, squawking, over the harbour.

He doesn't look back. Alice, watching until he is out of sight, feels something shift, break into shards, inside her.

Oona, who has turned away from the sea, waits for a few moments before approaching Alice. Finally she says kindly, 'Shall we walk on? We don't want to be late for the wedding reception.'

Alice nods, unable to speak. Oona links her arm through Alice's and together they walk slowly down the pier, towards the harbour which is festooned with colourful hanging banners celebrating a fisherman's wedding.

A splash of something wet hits Oona's hand, the one linked through Alice's arm. At first Oona thinks it is salt spray, but the sea is at peace today. Then, as another drop falls, she realizes that Alice is crying.

Ah, these young girls, she thinks compassionately, reflecting on not only Alice but on Molly and Esme, who will always be young to her. Such a struggle it all was, she remembers, all that love and pain, all that striving, all that passion. And always going back to the work, to the canvas or to the stone, because only there could you make sense of it, only there could you bear it.

'You'll be all right, my dear,' she says quietly to Alice as another tear hits Oona's elegant black leather shoe. 'Your portraits are superb. The one you did of your young American friend is particularly arresting. I would have bought it, but Lance says it is not for sale.'

Alice is moved by this. It is no small thing to be praised by Oona. Still unable to speak, she squeezes her arm gratefully.

Oona goes on, 'Molly said some time ago that you wanted to do one of me. I told her nonsense, that I haven't the time to sit for a portrait. But now she has said that this is all she wants for a wedding present, so if you would still like to go ahead, I'm quite willing.'

Alice stops walking, turns to Oona, face shining with tears and excitement. 'I've always wanted to paint you, always,' she cries. 'I've never had the nerve to ask.'

Oona, thinking of the years Alice has spent doing those hasty sketches of tourists on the harbour, says craftily, 'I'll pay you what Lance charges in his gallery for your oils, of course. And you won't have his commission on that. How pleased Jordan will be when he sees that your proper work is turning out to be just as lucrative as the other.'

Alice knows, as Oona does, that though Jordan won't exactly be pleased, there is nothing much he can say about it now. As long as Alice is contributing to the family income, Jordan will acquiesce to anything. Alice hasn't done a pastel sketch all summer, but the oil paintings bought by Crispin and Harlan have earned her almost as much money as her drawings of the visitors did last year. And Lance, in his gallery, hopes to sell quite a few others at her first exhibition in a few months' time.

Oona and Alice link arms again as they approach the harbour, heading for the wedding reception. They see Molly and Crispin ahead of them, holding hands, laughing, kissing well-wishers, kissing each other. Alice has another sharp moment of grief as she thinks of Harlan, going farther and farther away from her with each passing moment.

Life and love, Oona thinks, how complex it all is. All except art, she muses. If you let it, it is the only thing that stands pure and uncomplicated. She thinks of her husband, of Molly's father, of Molly herself; she remembers her own past loves. It's been fun, she concedes with a small smile, jolly fun, mixed with not a little pain. She hopes that one day Esme and Molly and

Alice will be able to say that too, hopes also that they, like her, will have, in the end, no regrets.

Esme and Richard, sitting on a bench facing the harbour, are trying to compose themselves before going into the restaurant which is just behind them. Esme is crying, as mothers do when their children get married.

Lance Giddens, passing them, wants to pick Richard up and throw him into the sea, but he goes into the restaurant instead. Esme has turned to him often since she and Richard separated; he has held her during the bad times – early in the morning or in the middle of the night, when a quick phone call was all he needed to rush to her house – and he has been her companion during the rare good days, accompanying her to an exhibition, a gallery opening, once or twice to the cinema. He is under no illusions that she is beginning to love him, or will ever love him, but somehow this doesn't seem to matter any more. What is more important is that he has her company, is important in her life, and is able to cherish her in some way at least.

'You are allowed to cry,' Richard is saying now to Esme. 'Mother of the groom and all that.'

Richard is living alone in Carbis Bay, just out of St Ives, in a rented cottage. Esme is still in the house – her studio is there, of course, and Hugo is living at home – but she has offered to put it on the market so that she and Richard can both buy smaller places of their own. Richard refuses to do this, saying he is happy where he is. He is not, of course, but he does not want to sell the house in St Ives. He clings to it like a talisman; as long as it is there, with Esme living in it, he can cling to the rather fragile hope that he will be allowed back in one day.

Harriet has moved to Penzance, to be nearer to Bernard. He was the logical one to turn to when Richard proved to be such a bastard. Bernard, at a loose end, rather liked having Harriet crying on his shoulder over another man. It was far less cloying than her crying tediously over him. They now see each other regularly, and Harriet thinks that she has never stopped loving him. She has great plans for their future, which Bernard knows nothing about yet, but they keep Harriet so preoccupied that she has abandoned, for a time, her sculptures and constructions. She has no need of them in these heady days of love. She has not seen Richard or Esme since the day she walked out of Esme's work-room, and she rarely thinks of either of them now.

Esme, staring across the harbour, thinking of the wedding, of Crispin and Molly so hopeful, so vulnerable, says to Richard, 'I can't believe they are actually married. I was afraid Crispin would have second thoughts after you and I separated, but it seems they both have enough faith in their relationship to make it permanent.'

'You still believe in marriage?' Richard asks with a rueful smile. 'After all that has happened?'

Esme has to think for a bit before she can answer this. There were times when she did not believe she would survive the break-up of her own marriage, but so far she has; so far she is whole and intact. She is at a good place now, the rawness of grief, bitterness, loss, steamed over by time and work, the support of family and friends. It will still be a long haul, she is aware of this, but her marriage was a long haul too, and she survived it just as she will survive the break-up.

'Well?' Richard is asking her.

'I believe in Crispin and Molly's marriage,' she says at last. 'One has to, don't you think? One has to at least begin in hope.'

Someone from the restaurant calls to them, to say that

Molly and Crispin are waiting for them. 'You go,' Esme says. 'Tell them I'll be there in a minute; tell them that the groom's mother needs another moment to dry her eyes.'

Richard leaves, and Esme sits alone looking out at the harbour. The tide is ebbing, leaving the boats stranded and looking lost and bereft on the wet shining sand. But Esme knows this is just an illusion, that the boats will come to life again when the tide, as it always does, turns and lifts them buoyantly, jubilantly, out into the sea.

THE END

TALK BEFORE SLEEP
Elizabeth Berg

'A RICH COMING-OF-AGE NOVEL . . . A
LUMINOUS WORK'
New York Times Book Review

'*Until that moment, I hadn't realized how much I'd been
needing to meet someone I might be able to say
everything to . . .*'

Ann and Ruth have always talked as only great friends
can – honestly, and about everything: husbands and
marriages, sex lives and children, their work, their
hopes, their disappointments, and their dreams. For
Ann, cautious and conventional, her closeness to the
outspoken and eccentric Ruth brings about discovery, a
chance to say whatever she wants, and, most important,
under the insistent tutelage of Ruth, to become herself.
Over the years, the women have shared recipes, child
care, delicate and dangerous secrets and each rests
secure in the knowledge that they will be friends forever.
But then, everything changes; faced with a crisis that
redefines the meaning of friendship, they begin to share
something more profound than either of them might have
predicted.

Written with an unerring ear for how women talk, laugh,
and cry together, and with a gift for capturing the
magical uniqueness of personality, *Talk Before Sleep* is
sure to find a place in readers' hearts.

'A SEARING STORY OF FRIENDSHIP AND DEATH
AMONG FORTY-SOMETHING FEMALES . . . A
TRIUMPH OF CREATIVITY'
Time Out

0 552 99725 0

BLACK SWAN

A MAP OF THE WORLD
Jane Hamilton

Because Alice and Howard Goodwin run a small dairy farm in the midst of encroaching suburbia, and because their eccentric ways betray their city origins, they are shunned as 'that hippie couple', outsiders in the small Midwestern town of Prairie Center. Nevertheless, they feel that they and their two small daughters are living in a self-made paradise.

But Alice has always believed that all it would take to fall from grace is 'one stupendous error, or else an unfortunate accident'. And one morning, while Alice is babysitting her neighbour's children, a tragic accident does occur on the farm. This sets into motion a devastating and irrevocable string of events that will change the Goodwins' lives for ever as they find themselves trapped in a nightmare from which they cannot escape.

A Map of the World is a harrowing tale about guilt, betrayal and the loss of innocence. Spellbinding, lyrical, and universal in its themes, this powerful, emotional page turner shows that Jane Hamilton is a writer of exceptional talent.

0 552 99681 5

BLACK SWAN

A WING AND A PRAYER
Mary Selby

In the quiet village of Great Barking, strange doings are afoot. Up at the Hall the squire, Sir George, seems to have exhausted his wife Angela – leaving her quite unable to contemplate the rigours of hosting the annual village fête in the Hall grounds. Caroline, the doctor's wife, has her time taken up with her three tiny children, but feels that as a newcomer to the village she should offer her own rather more modest garden as the venue for this important local affair. But who is to open it? Will Sir George's elderly mother, now somewhat unpredictable, be asked, as tradition dictates? Or should Sarah Struther, the voluptuous lady potter who prefers to work unencumbered by clothing and who has just been featured in a smart Sunday newspaper, be invited?

The village fête committee decides that a commission to Sarah to fashion a special pot for the fête, to be entitled The Organ (suggesting the need for funds to combat dry rot in the organ loft) may be a better idea, little suspecting that the title may be open to misconstruction. And in the churchyard the tall privet bush has been lovingly fashioned by old Jacob Bean into a shape so curious that coachloads of sightseers start arriving to view it . . .

0 552 99672 6

BLACK SWAN

A SELECTED LIST OF FINE WRITING
AVAILABLE FROM BLACK SWAN

THE PRICES SHOWN BELOW WERE CORRECT AT THE TIME OF GOING TO PRESS. HOWEVER TRANSWORLD PUBLISHERS RESERVE THE RIGHT TO SHOW NEW RETAIL PRICES ON COVERS WHICH MAY DIFFER FROM THOSE PREVIOUSLY ADVERTISED IN THE TEXT OR ELSEWHERE.

99629	7	**SEVEN FOR A SECRET**	*Judy Astley*	£5.99
99618	1	**BEHIND THE SCENES AT THE MUSEUM**		
			Kate Atkinson	£6.99
99725	0	**TALK BEFORE SLEEP**	*Elizabeth Berg*	£6.99
99648	3	**TOUCH AND GO**	*Elizabeth Berridge*	£5.99
99593	2	**A RIVAL CREATION**	*Marika Cobbold*	£5.99
99587	8	**LIKE WATER FOR CHOCOLATE**	*Laura Esquivel*	£6.99
99602	5	**THE LAST GIRL**	*Penelope Evans*	£5.99
99622	X	**THE GOLDEN YEAR**	*Elizabeth Falconer*	£5.99
99589	4	**RIVER OF HIDDEN DREAMS**	*Connie May Fowler*	£5.99
99656	4	**THE TEN O'CLOCK HORSES**	*Laurie Graham*	£5.99
99610	6	**THE SINGING HOUSE**	*Janette Griffiths*	£5.99
99681	5	**A MAP OF THE WORLD**	*Jane Hamilton*	£6.99
99392	1	**THE GREAT DIVORCE**	*Valerie Martin*	£6.99
99688	2	**HOLY ASPIC**	*Joan Marysmith*	£5.99
99649	1	**WAITING TO EXHALE**	*Terry McMillan*	£5.99
99693	9	**IMPOSSIBLE THINGS**	*Penny Perrick*	£6.99
99696	3	**THE VISITATION**	*Sue Reidy*	£5.99
99608	4	**LAURIE AND CLAIRE**	*Kathleen Rowntree*	£6.99
99672	6	**A WING AND A PRAYER**	*Mary Selby*	£6.99
99650	5	**A FRIEND OF THE FAMILY**	*Titia Sutherland*	£5.99
99056	6	**BROTHER OF THE MORE FAMOUS JACK**		
			Barbara Trapido	£6.99
99643	2	**THE BEST OF FRIENDS**	*Joanna Trollope*	£6.99
99646	7	**A SCHOOL FOR LOVERS**	*Jill Paton Walsh*	£6.99
99673	4	**DINA'S BOOK**	*Herbjørg Wassmo*	£6.99
99592	4	**AN IMAGINATIVE EXPERIENCE**	*Mary Wesley*	£5.99
99641	6	**A DESIRABLE RESIDENCE**	*Madeleine Wickham*	£6.99
99591	6	**A MISLAID MAGIC**	*Joyce Windsor*	£4.99

All Transworld titles are available by post from:
Book Service By Post, P.O. Box 29, Douglas, Isle of Man IM99 1BQ
Credit cards accepted. Please telephone 01624 675137, fax 01624
670923 or Internet http://www.bookpost.co.uk or
e-mail: bookshop@enterprise.net for details.
Free postage and packing in the UK. Overseas customers allow
£1 per book (paperbacks) and £3 per book (hardbacks).